M000306857

REALM

OF THE

BANISHED

JULY HOUSE
publishing

July House Publishing

This is a work of fiction. All of the characters, places, and events portrayed in this book are are entirely fictional and products of the author's imagination. Any resemblance to actual persons living or dead is entirely coincidental.

REALM OF THE BANISHED
Copyright © 2021 by Jennifer M. Waldrop
All rights reserved. Neither this book, nor any parts within it may be sold or reproduced in any form without permission.

Cover Design and Interior Formating: Damonza.com
Editing: Alison Rolf

www.jennifermwaldrop.com

July House Publishing | Your story, your way

www.julyhousepublishing.com

REALM
OF THE
BANISHED

SKYBORNE SERIES BOOK ONE

JENNIFER M. WALDROP

JULY HOUSE PUBLISHING

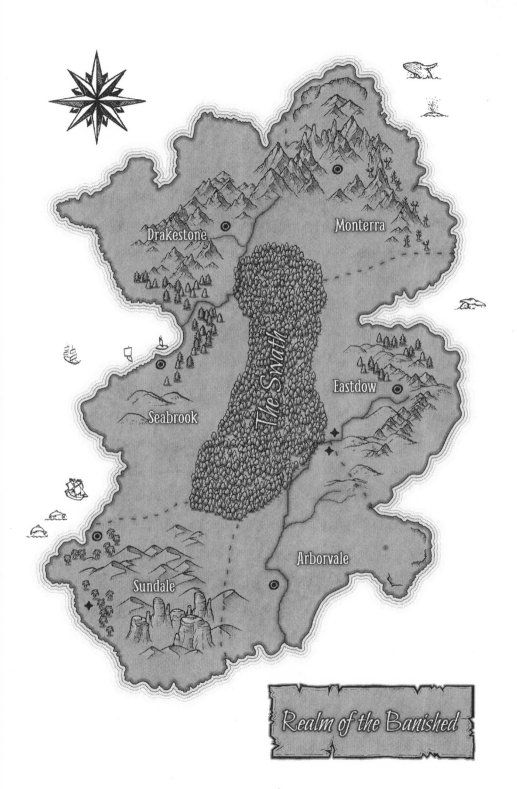

Realm of the Banished

PROLOGUE

S HE WAS WITH him again. That Eastdow girl wasn't even supposed to be here. None of the rest of the territories ever deigned to show up. Roslin leaned a little past the hedge to get a better look. Another perfect bullseye. He looked back at Vera and shrugged his shoulders, laughing coyly. Why did Darius care to show off for this foreigner?

It was staged space, the Regent's formal training yard. Clean and manicured, unlike the real training yards the military used. Tall hedges and flowering plants that could handle the crisp winters here in Drakestone surrounded the lawn with staged targets and the tidy racks of decorated practice weapons. The Regent's residence sat at the end of a long open-air promenade past the training grounds. The grey stone it was built from felt sharp and regal, and its peaks and spires reached up toward the jagged mountains surrounding it. It was spring now, and the foliage was in bloom. Roslin took a deep inhale of the sweet air. *It would be romantic if it had been me*, she mused.

Vera was nearly as tall as Darius, with sun-kissed skin and cornflower hair, which normally flowed down to her shoulder blades, and was pinned up to one side with a simple gold comb. It softened her athletic build and gave her the perfect combination of femininity and strength. Today she wore it in a long braid which fell over her right shoulder. Her hair combined with her sea-blue eyes made her stick out like a sore thumb here in Drakestone, where most Skyborne had a darker olive complexion and deep brown and black locks. Darius gravitated toward her immediately. *Away* from Roslin.

Darius laughed at something Vera said. Roslin didn't know which of his traits made her fall for him first. He was tall and muscled with a military stature about him. No one had such perfect posture, except maybe his older brother, Malik, who was the flip side of the same coin. Darius, unlike his brother, the territory's heir, had kind and warm eyes, and his face was just less than chiseled, so he still appeared approachable. Utterly masculine but gentler.

Darius undid the leather tie that held his shoulder-length black hair back and ran his hands through it before he re-tied it.

Vera made another joke, and he reached up and yanked on her braid. Their flirting was nauseating.

He handed the crossbow to her. Even as strong as Vera appeared, she struggled to hold it steady. Roslin's stomach plummeted as he wrapped his arms around Vera to help her hold the weapon. He leaned into her ear and whispered something. *Shoot* maybe, because the cross-bolt went flying and hit the target some forty yards away. She *must* have hit it because he gave her a proud tug on her waist, pulling her closer against him. He took the weapon with a single hand, making it look light, and tossed it on the ground. They were bantering back and forth as she spun around in his arms to face him.

Not happening, Roslin thought. She stepped a few feet into the pathway, walking toward them casually as if she hadn't just been spying on them. "Well done, Vera," she called out.

Darius startled, but Vera took her presence in stride as they stepped apart. "I didn't realize we had an audience," he responded. "Roslin, you look well."

She couldn't help beaming at his remark.

"Maybe sometime you can give me lessons?" She asked coyly, playing with the dark curls that grazed her exposed collar bone, trying to show him what he was missing. She was not about to let him forget her.

"Yeah, maybe," he said.

Vera looked at her and cocked her head, "I expect we'll see you at the festivities tonight, Roslin?"

'*We'll,*' *she said. She shouldn't even be here*, Roslin thought resentfully. She tried not to let it show on her face. "I will, and I hope to see you both there." *Separately.* She pressed her lips into a forced smile at Vera, curtsying deeply to him. Her smile warmed when she met Darius's eyes.

Ever since Roslin was little, Regent Karish would invite the other five territories' Regents and their families to their Half-Light Ceremony, which celebrated the Light Star's annual eclipse and the largest three satellites that orbited this planet. It was a magical celebration where the eclipse created darkness in the daytime. There was the ceremony, of course, then music and dancing. None of the other territories would accept his invitation. Everyone knew why, though no one talked about it. Drakestone had kept the ember long past their time, and no one had mustered enough force to get it back.

And now, out of the blue, Vera Tiernach, the Eastdow Regent's daughter, was flaunting around the city, flirting relentlessly with Darius. *Her* Darius. She just had to bear it one more night. Then Vera would leave, and things would go back to normal. And it was his duty after all to make the stay of their guest more pleasant, she reminded herself. Roslin could be patient if it meant winning Darius and marrying into *that* family.

She looked in the mirror. The dress was a little lower cut than what Roslin would have traditionally worn to the Half-Light Ceremony, but she had a message to send. It was a deep burgundy satin that snugged in at the waist, displaying her best feminine attributes. She selected a softer shade of rose to warm her cheeks and a warm gold on her lids. No dark kohl liner today. Just a little on the lashes. She didn't feel the need to overstate her intention. *Yet.*

One last look before she stepped out of her generously appointed guest room, which the position her father held in the Regent's cabinet afforded her, and into the hallway.

This year the ceremony started a little later in the day than the last one. It shifted by a few hours every year following the Light Star's pattern and the three moons of this planet. This year they predicted the first would align early and cover the Light Star, and the others would follow, creating darkness in the daytime for several hours.

It felt decadent because it was like having a nighttime party during the day, which would continue well into the evening. Other territories had parties, but none were like the event put on by the Regent and his family in Drakestone. Up at this elevation, high at the foothills of the mountain range, the air stood still. The priest said his prayer in total darkness. Regent Karish or one of his sons would light the first candle, then guests would light theirs. Once the room was aglow with warm candlelight, the party would begin.

Other guests were filing out of their compartments and arriving in carriages, heading to the great hall. Roslin got swept up in the flow of excited bodies.

"Looking for someone?" Malik sneered; a dark eyebrow arched in her direction. She looked at him, failing to hold back a flinch. He'd appeared out of nowhere. He looked similar to Darius, just several shades harsher. He unsettled her—and that facial hair—it made his features sharper. Not for her at all. Roslin was glad she'd caught the attention of the younger of the two brothers, even if it meant she'd never be a Regent's wife.

"They'll be up on the stage with my father. He's having Darius light the first candle this year," he continued, pity dripping from his voice as he watched her from the corner of his eye. Her scanning of the large room must not have been as discreet as she'd thought. Malik looked her up and down. "Trying a little hard, aren't you, Roslin?" Malik chuckled. "You should be careful," he warned before he slipped away.

The ceremony started, and Roslin saw Darius walk onto the stage, followed by *her. Unbelievable, Karish is allowing this*, she thought. They carried the procedure out as expected. When darkness hit, even though they all knew what would happen, the crowd gasped. They did it every year.

She smiled because she knew Darius was about to use his power to light the first candle—power that he loved. Mainly because it seemed a little stronger than everyone else's. Another reason she knew he was the superior choice between the brothers.

The wick caught beneath his hand, and the crowd applauded. He looked to Vera, almost seeking her approval.

Roslin cringed.

Vera grinned and nodded before Darius was motioning to her, offering her the second candle.

Much to Roslin's dismay, Karish nodded. "Excellent idea, son. As our guest, Vera Tiernach, daughter of our sister territory of Eastdow, it would be our honor that you light the second Half-Light candle."

The bitch had the audacity to look shy and act as if it wasn't her place. *It wasn't.* But Roslin could see it was an act nonetheless.

"Please, Vera," the priest said and motioned for her to go on.

Vera stepped up to the candle, and Darius put a reassuring hand on the small of her back. She held her hand up over the candle, surveying the barely lit room before she glanced back at him.

"Go ahead," he encouraged, grinning like a fool.

A small flame. Then the candle glowed and swayed, falling into the rhythm of the candle Darius lit. The crowd erupted. Karish lit his next, beckoning the crowd to follow suit. When the room was aglow with candlelight, Karish initiated the festivities to commence.

Skyborne moved about, and Roslin pushed her way through the crowd toward the stage where Karish was standing talking with Vera and Darius. He put an approving hand on her shoulder.

Roslin stopped short. Even as she'd expected Regent Karish to be her future father-in-law, the Skyborne she knew was still cold and strict. She'd never seen him show warmth to anyone, save his family. And even that was a rarity. He finally walked away, and she approached them.

Darius, still on stage and blissfully unaware, grabbed Vera's wrist and spun her into his arms. She laughed before he kissed her deeply in front of the Makers and everyone else under the now blacked-out Light Star. Roslin's vision departed for a moment, and her legs became so weak she stumbled, grabbing ahold of a startled female next to her.

Noooooooo.

She couldn't tell if it was in her head or she'd screamed out loud. A few Skyborne looked her way, but fortunately, the room was noisy from the revelry. Vera would leave tomorrow or the next day. She just had to keep calm until then.

Roslin threaded through the crowd toward the banquet tables with the refreshments. She poured herself a full glass of the strongest smelling wine she could find. She planned to get good and drunk tonight.

"Roslin was looking for you, brother," Malik chided Darius as soon as he caught him alone.

"Funny, I hadn't seen her," Darius replied, scanning the room.

"I don't think you've seen anything but Vera since she's shown up."

Darius chuckled at Malik's comment, straightening the dark red jacket he wore. "Is there something you wanted, Malik?"

"Do any of them know about each other? I mean besides Roslin now, obviously."

"Since when are you so concerned about the delicate hearts of females?" Darius asked, eyes trailing after a low-cut dress that breezed through his line of sight.

Malik shook his head. "Way to prove me wrong about your wandering eyes. Well, between Emerson, Roslin, and now Vera, I don't know how you keep it up."

"There's nothing wrong with enjoying the scenery. Don't worry; I'll eventually settle down. Continue on the family line on your behalf. Make our father proud." Darius caught sight of Vera and gave a predatory smile. "Maybe sooner than you think." He popped a piece of cherry fruit that he'd plucked off a waiter's passing tray into his mouth and wiggled his eyes at Malik before taking off after her.

Roslin stumbled back to her room late in the evening. She had about every available Skyborne male in the place approach her, except *him*. She wanted to get her stupid dress off and end the misery of tonight, but she couldn't remember which direction her room was.

Then she heard his voice. The hallway was pitch black, but she still tucked into an alcove. She didn't want him to see her like this.

"Darius, you can wait five more minutes," Vera giggled, and Roslin heard the slap of a hand on flesh.

"Feisty today, are you?" He asked Vera as they passed her. "How about in here?" Roslin heard him say. He must have pulled them into an alcove a little down the hallway because voices became quieter.

"Darius," Vera moaned his name in protest.

"Vera, since I've met you, I know it's not been long, but it's like an entire realm has opened up to me. I need to say," he hesitated. "I mean, I want to tell you, you see... I think—"

"Wait, Darius," she cut him off. "Not here, okay. Come on."

Roslin waited until she no longer heard footsteps. She heard a door shut, then it was quiet. She dreaded the thought of what was happening next. Her head spun. She felt her way out of the alcove, back into the dark hallway, and vomited her guts up.

⁓

Pain rang in her head the next morning. Roslin had no idea how she'd made it back to her room. She laid there all morning and afternoon. There was no reason to get out of bed the next day either.

She replayed everything that had happened in the last six months between Darius and her. Finally, she settled on a thought. Obviously, she'd not given him what he had wanted, and Vera had without so much of a promise of a future. *Fine*, she thought as a plan stirred in her mind. Vera would be gone by now. And he would get lonely, and she would be there.

Roslin decided a few days after the Half-Light ceremony would be perfect, so she extended her stay through the following week. Darius would have enough time to get Vera out of his system, and the absence would make him long for company. She could wait a few more days to make her move.

⁓

It was a little past midnight. Roslin pinched her cheeks to give them a little color and slung her silk robe around the delicate, irresistible items she wore underneath. She snuck down the hallway and up the stairs that led to the wing where his suite of rooms was. Almost there. She'd never been with a male before, but she figured this wasn't so bad since Darius was her future husband. She worried her hands as she walked, her emotions a mix of excitement and trepidation.

She looked up as she heard a creak. Roslin narrowed her eyes, focusing. The few dim lights in the hallway in her vicinity went out. She flattened herself against the wall, easing her way toward his door. Whoever was leaving wouldn't see her, but she could see them as they quietly shut the door. She was good at being unseen when needed. *If I'd been a male, I'd have made an excellent spy*, she thought smugly.

Roslin stifled a gasp. It was *her*. Vera was still here. Sneaking out of his room. Odd though, she was fully dressed in some sort of traveling gear. She crept down the hallway in the opposite direction, her boots silent on the stones. Roslin followed even quieter as Vera tracked a memorized maze of hallways and stairs deep into the keep to the complex's military side. She watched how Vera slipped past the guards when they looked the other direction.

Waiting, mimicking, Roslin kept up. She felt ridiculous sneaking around in only a nightgown, but she was desperate when she saw the chance before her. The Eastdow girl was up to something, and she was going to find out what it was. She smiled, bathing herself in the imagined gratitude the Regent, and more importantly Darius, would no doubt feel toward her. So, she followed.

After a long while, Vera and her shadow came to a guard station. It was a basic wooden shack, serving only to protect the patrol from the harsh climate they experienced during the winter months. The hallway was the same cold, smooth stone that the rest of the keep was constructed with. One side followed the building's curvature, and the other side had large openings that revealed a military training yard below connected by a set of wooden stairs. The large posts holding globes of flickering fire created the perfect shadows to slip between.

Several males were patrolling below, but only one Skyborne stood outside the door of the empty guard shack. He turned. Vera sprung from the shadows. She was so quick coming up behind him. She caught his dead weight as he fell. Roslin blinked, and Vera pulled the guard into the shack.

Roslin froze, trembling at what she had just witnessed.

A few moments later, the guard peered out the cracked door, glancing down the hall, before he slipped out the doorway as if nothing had happened. Roslin put a hand on the wall to steady herself. The guard left his post and walked further down the path and into a door that required several keys to access.

The guard must have incapacitated Vera, or at least Roslin hoped he did, and now he was going to alert someone. A wave of relief hit her, but she needed to see the proof with her own eyes before she went to Darius. She would like to have been the one to take Vera out herself after how she seduced him. But conveniently, Vera got herself out of the way. The guard left the door to the shack cracked. Roslin made sure no one was looking before she skipped from a shadow and passed through it.

She dropped to her knees. The guard was lying lifeless at her feet, a light stream of blood trickling from the split skin at his temple. She was going mad. She'd just seen him walk out of this shack and down the hallway.

With a master ring of keys. It couldn't be. Roslin covered her gaping mouth.

Heart stuttering, Roslin worked out the entire story of why that manipulative, deceitful bitch was here. Her breathing came in shallow sips. She had to tell Darius. Vera didn't want *him*. Vera was here to steal the—Her thoughts cut short when the door snap closed behind her.

CHAPTER ONE

As sensation crept back into my overtaxed limbs, the fog clouding my mind began to clear. I gasped, taking in the change in my surroundings. A heavy mist clung to the lush foliage surrounding me. *No... steam,* I thought. My eyes were adjusting to the gloom as I realized whatever power that hit me must have sent me, not just to the edge of the Swath, but well into it. The thick, squat trees created a dense and shallow canopy where I could see moss draping over the branches. Droplets of moisture clung to the moss, making the few tiny rays of sunlight creeping through the canopy strike them and refract and glow with the light. I thought they would have glittered with any movement if the air wasn't so still and stagnant.

The last thing I remembered was fleeing with all my remaining speed toward the border of Eastdow. If I could have made it across, the Covenant would, *or should* have protected me from Darius and his gang from Drakestone. I fled, all the while wondering if retrieving the ember was worth the cost. For almost ten years, every moment of my existence was devoted to my training, all designed to sneak through Drakestone and retrieve this relic I now carried. I'd spent years learning the regional dialects and perfecting my shifts so they would come so effortlessly I'd slide unnoticed through the maze of the mysterious northern territory.

I tried to determine where exactly in the Swath I landed. Time was not on my side, I knew, but I couldn't help but wonder where it had all gone wrong.

My advisors and instructors had almost convinced me I was the one who would bring the ember home. They dubbed me their very own *Chosen One*. It was ridiculous. I bristled at the thought. They began training me when they detected the extra inklings of power I developed during my adolescence, which, in the past, would have bloomed at adulthood—unheard of in my lifetime. The seers claimed I was the one from the prophesies who would end the banishment and bring us home to Idia. It was a pleasant idea at first, the idea of being a fated hero, but when my power never grew into anything more, distrust blossomed. Now that I was kneeling in a steaming marsh deep in the Swath, I knew they had been wrong about me and the alleged prophecy. Yet, I had done it. I could hardly believe it.

I surveyed my body. Though I'd traveled what had to be miles, I did not have a scratch on me. Only what felt like would bloom into some fine purple and black bruises on my thighs and rear from where I had landed and tumbled. I had no explanation for what had happened to me. One minute earlier, while running, I glanced back to see Darius—my former lover—'s loaded crossbow perfectly aimed at my back, then blackness. Thinking of him now made me wince.

The forest was warm and moist, and the air clung to me, making it hard to breathe. The fall knocked the wind out of me, but I was recovering quickly. I knew they would keep searching for me. If my internal compass held true, it was unlikely they'd be eager to join me on this side of the Swath's barrier. The pools in this forest ranged in temperature from scalding to bathwater warm. Fortunately, my fall hadn't landed me in one of the deeper, hotter pools.

Scanning, I noticed the angle of one of the few streaks of sunlight permeating the canopy had moved past forty-five degrees, suggesting daylight was running out. After everything I'd been through, the last thing I wanted to do was die in this Makers-forsaken forest, knowing full well the bloody treat I'd make for the creatures who lived here.

With that thought, I identified east and began making my way. I chose a path that would put me in the Swath longer than I preferred but would not land me at the feet of Darius and his gang. It was a risk, and according to my knowledge, no one had ever escaped the barrier, so the odds were good I'd die here. Still, it was useless to be idle. As I walked, keeping so quiet as to not attract the attention of one of the many horrors that lived in this forest, I couldn't shake the feeling that the pervading quiet that hung in the air was wrong.

Wrong. Even for this place.

It made no sense. I knew that Skyborne, who crossed the invisible boundary of the forest's edge, never escaped it, which meant some silent, hungry creatures were lurking alongside me under the canopy. There were stories and legends of death sentences carried out by executioners who pushed the condemned at spear point across the invisible boundary. I thought of the chilling illustrations I'd seen in books of the hooded men with lengthy poles prodding the ill-fated past the Swath's barrier, depicted as a shimmering wall. The condemned would spend hours frantically running hands along the interior, searching for a way to escape, becoming increasingly desperate as the hours drag on and the forest sounds near. Sometimes, they would last days. Lingering at the edge of the forest must have been terrifying, knowing what awaited them inside. While a clever deterrent, it was still a cruel punishment. I shuddered, imagining being eaten alive.

The strip of forested area called the Swath lay in the center of the large continent. The Swath did not belong to any of the six territories surrounding it. On the other three sides, each territory had two neighbors and a sea border.

I admired the fore-mothers' architecture and the seemingly equitable system the matriarchs birthed for their new realm and the Skyborne who crossed over with them. Since then, however, half of the territories shifted to a patriarchal system. The fore-mothers intended that each of the six territories would alternate its guardianship, so no one territory would ever hold power over the others. They considered using a single central location, but considering the central location of the Swath, they decided on an alternating watch. The agreement continued effortlessly until it was time for Drakestone, who was fifth in the rotation, to pass it on to Eastdow. Some dead Dsiban Regent refused to relinquish it.

There was a rustling near but not within my range of vision. I heightened my senses and pinpointed the direction of the sounds. They were coming from the direction I was heading. Next to me, the moss stirred as if in the wind created from something passing.

A foot squelched in the mud. Something was right there. I flicked my gaze toward the sound and met a pair of eyes glowing with intensity. Green, the color of sour fruit.

Shit, shit, shit.

I'd sensed my death was imminent before, though maybe that had been my pessimism and not a premonition. But now? Was this it? When I was so close to delivering the ember and this assignment's end. With my freedom in sight, I could either run now like I had never run in my life— on already drained legs and a stomach that hadn't seen food for days—or fight. Whoever or whatever those eyes belonged to would likely enjoy one of my bruised thighs before long.

Regret flooded in. I wouldn't be in this situation if the full powers of the so-called prophecy had befallen me. I still accomplished the task, regardless, which gave me more than a little pride.

Fight.

I stood, gathering my reserves as the creature approached.

"Give me the ember," an otherworldly voice echoed in the forest.

The voice came not from the creature directly but from all around me. My arm hairs stood on end from the eeriness of it.

"Not going to happen," I said defiantly, reaching for my breast pocket. The ember hummed under my touch as if in agreement.

"Then you will die, and I will have it anyway," its slippery voice echoed.

I knew my life was forfeit, but I stared toward the eyes, seeing it sensed I carried the ember and that lying was futile. I refused to let it sense my fear. "I find it hard to believe you'll let me live either way." I drew the long knives I had managed not to lose in my fall, motioning to it invitingly, "Shall we?"

As the creature came nearer, I could see long, narrow black pupils in the center of its iridescent eyes glaring down at me from a bulbous head that towered over me. The yellow-green skin on its gangly limbs was molting and limply wrapped around a plump, vaguely humanoid body like an aged, sagging canvas. Recognizing my surprise at its girth, it cackled, "Yeesssss, girl, our diet improved when your kind showed up in this realm, our realm of the banished." It rubbed its fleshy belly, taunting and sloughing skin off as it did. A slimy grey tongue flicked over its cracked lips as it watched me. I could tell it was enjoying making its live prey squirm.

"What—*who* are you?" I asked, eyes wide.

It sneered and gave a light laugh, its flesh jiggling.

"Answer me," I demanded, becoming increasingly nervous. I pushed the hairs that had slipped from my braid out of my face.

"I am no more than an ancient cousin of yours and the master of this forest you call the Swath. I was here before your kind arrived. I assumed we'd be stuck here forever." It was hesitating now, staring at my pocket. Watching the maze of emotions on its sagging face, I guessed it was contemplating a fantasy of sorts. Settling in on a thought, it continued, "I have no names or titles like your kind. We don't find them useful. But you can think of me as Uden, what we call the Realm we came from, for your few remaining breaths, if it pleases you. I have been waiting a long time for someone to awaken it. It appears you have. And I see you are ignorant to this fact. Ah, what a feat for such a diminutive Skyborne. Too bad it will also be your last. Now, release the ember to me, *cousin*."

It paused, the talons on its webbed feet curling into the mud as it gazed at me—no, at my pocket—with urgency. But it did not approach.

I now had a better understanding of the legends of species which time and distance had turned into unholy creatures. Even after everything I'd seen so far in this life, I couldn't paint a realm that evolved the creature standing before me. Not that the Skyborne, my own kind, were necessarily any better if I was honest with myself. Unlike Uden, we still physically resembled our human ancestors. It was what was on the inside that was different, enhanced from our deal with the Makers.

"It seems I've struck a chord. Well, considering the history of your kind, it's hard to believe you'd find our close relation appalling. Our mutual ancestors were so malleable and evolved quickly—no doubt how they won the Makers' favor. And now we have you, the Skyborne, unnatural in all of your inherited mystery. Even my blood is less tainted than yours." Uden sneered, exposing several rows of small but vicious-looking rotten teeth.

I didn't exactly love the story of how the Skyborne came to be, and Uden was reveling in my discomfort.

"How superior of you. No doubt how you ended up here." I huffed as other eyes of differing sizes came into view, all glowing green, like Uden's. An audience gathered while I focused on the larger creature, creating an impenetrable ring around us. Each creature bore a strong resemblance to Uden but had its own unique characteristics, like spots or spines. Some even desperately flapped flimsy bat-like wings to keep their rotund little bodies hovering at my eye-level.

Run, damn it, I should have run when I had the chance.

The blood in my chest and neck hummed as my body readied itself for an attack that was moments away. Fear lost its control over my body in the months I'd been working my way through Drakestone. I'd almost been caught so many times my heart eventually stopped stopping. It was as if my nerves didn't have the energy to stay that wired and would no longer subject my tired body to the starts.

With steady limbs, I took a step forward. I stood facing my enemy as I had numerous times in recent memory, ready to meet my fate. Another step.

The creature paused. Its head tilted inquisitively to the side. A deathly quiet descended upon us as if the collective onlookers surrounding me had paused not only their breaths but their hearts.

"Interesting," the creature considered as it reached a webbed claw out and stroked an invisible wall between us. As it ran its webbed digits along the barrier, it started humming and gurgling, making painful, frustrated sounds. The onlooking creatures began mimicking its sound, creating a terrifying symphony of monsters. My senses were reaching the point of overload when I felt something crawling up my right ankle.

You must hold the barrier, Realm Walker, an ethereal voice slipped into my mind, anchoring me to the present. I resisted the urge to swat the insignificant being the voice must have come from and stole a glance down at it. A small figure, clouded in darkness, which I could barely make out in the fading light, clung to my pant leg.

Go quickly. While the shield holds. Not all of us in this wood want your flesh. Now go, the high-pitched feminine voice added urgently, answering my forming thoughts.

I took a hesitant step. Another step. As I moved, the gathering of creatures, including Uden, gave way. I passed, turning to see if they followed. They held their place, seething.

"I have your scent now, female. I see you can't feel the power pulsing through you now, and I doubt you'll be able to keep that shield up for long. I'll be back to check on you soon enough." It snarled, eyes flaring with promise.

I needed no further encouragement. I sheathed my weapons, pausing to reach a hand down for the being at my feet. *I think you'll fit in my pocket. It will be an easier ride there.* I had to enhance my vision to make out the little bug-like being that was the length of my outstretched palm. Its body was a dim yellow and in the general layout of my own, except with two insect-like pairs of wings protruding from its back, which it had tucked in tight. I set it on my chest, and it crawled into my breast pocket opposite the ember.

If this is a trick to get to the ember, you'll be really easy to squash, so don't try me, I threatened the little being.

I glared at Uden one last time before I took off running. I didn't want to be in the Swath any longer than necessary. There had to be a way out of the barrier. Hours passed. My legs moved on sheer adrenaline alone.

You're a godfly? I asked insistently. I had only heard tales of beings like the one in my pocket. I never really believed them.

You recognize my kind. I'm called Meethra. Rest assured, I don't intend to steal what's yours. You are?

Vera, I thought. *I can't believe you're real. And there's an entire realm of your kind? Where are the others that came with you?* I shook my head, peppering the godfly with my questions.

I was flying with a host of godflies in my home realm to investigate a disturbance when we flew into a field of dark power. We plummeted into this realm. Some of us landed here in this forest, stuck well over a millennium. She hesitated before continuing.

Most of us in this realm were extinguished. Some must have landed here outside this forest, but it's been a great time since I last sensed my kind. Sorrow laced her voice. *I gave up hope long ago, but the fear of the final darkness kept me hiding. When I sensed your presence, I could feel the object you call the ember's power too. So, I made my way to you.*

I thought godflies were beings of light? I asked her.

It is true; the forest drains my light. I miss it. As it faded, I could feel a deep ache growing within me. I lost many of my kind, exhausted by the darkness or consumed by the creatures that dwell here. She paused contemplatively. *We must stay a distance inside the forest border as long as your shield is holding strong.*

You think it will fail? I thought nervously, thinking of the creature Uden.

That is what I would suspect. Eventually. The power in the realms is limitless but not without cost. And considering you didn't even know you were making it... or how... I doubt you'll be able to control it for too long. Can't you feel it, the tapestry of power around us?

I... I stopped to gather my bearings and catch my breath, taking in the details of my surroundings. Not only the flora and fauna of the Swath but also the essence of things. Meethra made it seem so easy. There was something different I could barely recognize. Everything had a vague but unique vibration I'd never noticed before. *I think so.*

I feel other essences outside. Your enemies? The godfly asked.

Something like that.

It would be wise to get closer to your land before we attempt to leave the canopy. I suspect the shield you've created around us may counteract the Swath's barrier and let us pass through. Let's keep going.

I lurched forward. Fatigued and hungry, I couldn't keep the previous pace, but I continued at a constant steady speed. I fell into an exhausted melody of movement. Keep going and think. We had to be only a few hours now from the border. Maybe less. If my shield held, we'd make it.

At first, I thought the shield was yours. My opposite pocket hummed as if there was a third party to this conversation, contradicting me no less.

The trace of energy comes from you, Realm Walker, Meethra countered.

I scanned my energy. I felt a slow drain I hadn't noticed in the intensity of earlier. The web of power shivered under my scrutiny.

Why do you keep calling me Realm Walker? I asked, irritated as I tried to figure out how to control the impenetrable field of energy I'd unknowingly surrounded us with.

Steady, Meethra urged.

I had to reel in my tendency to overthink and allow my instincts to keep working as the shield re-solidified. The buzzing in my pocket continued as if the ember itself was encouraging my body's natural protective instincts along. Did it want to flee the Swath as badly as Meethra and I did?

Good, the godfly thought. *The name? Did they not tell you what you carry?*

I was glad for the conversation. It was keeping me from focusing on my fatigue. *Our High Priest thinks it opens portals between realms. He's convinced the elders its power is awakening again from some type of dormant period after it went haywire when it was used to banish the wrong sect of Skyborne. High Priest Lathrais wants to use the ember to open a portal so we can return to Idia, our kind's home realm. That is the gist anyway,* I told her.

Your high priest sounds like a fool. He can never use its power.

How can you be so sure? I asked her, surprised at her certainty.

I think you can feel the answer to that question. The object you carry is something very ancient; I can feel it. Its essence feels like the Ephemera themselves. You know them as the Makers—the only ones who can truly walk between the realms. You have much yet to discover. And you should be wary of giving it to your High Priest.

If I knew, it was certainly subconscious, though I felt a distinct energy growing inside me since it'd stolen it. And I would never admit it, except maybe to Conall, but it drew my curiosity until I caught myself unclasping the little latch to the ornate metal box and peered inside to see its contents. Despite its lure, I convinced myself I didn't care. I wanted to be rid of it.

Tell me your age, Meethra requested.

I'm six months to the day away from my twenty-ninth birthday, I thought for her. My power was what the godfly was trying to understand. How had I not seen this was my shield that produced around us?

As we moved through the forest, I explained as concisely as I could about how I'd come to this certain impasse. *It was legend that in Idia, our home realm, my kind, the Skyborne, could control the energy tapestry that always surrounds us in a much deeper way than we can in this realm. Our High Priest Lathrais thought the fact that I had such strong abilities at such a young age indicated my control would continue developing more substantially after my adulthood ceremony. But it had stalled. I could do all the stuff most of the other Skyborne could do, known as the Common Power; light healing, create a small flame, warm a room, create wards that would alarm of intruders, and other similar useful tasks. Some of us Skyborne in this realm can even enhance our senses and speed. And I still could do what I think of as my little party tricks I developed in childhood which the priesthood had sought me out for. Those tricks are what make me a hair more impressive than anyone else. The priesthood had continued on with their fervor, though, and sent me on this mission, anyway. Worst case, they'd have seen me as a failure.*

Meanwhile, they'd appear to have kept up their end of the bargain, fulfilling what they'd prophesied. Still, in Eastdow and several other allied territories, we're gathering forces and spending valuable resources for our glorious return to Idia—the realm taken from us. Or at least that's the story they teach.

Thinking about my power always made my thoughts spiral downward. I went there—the pit where the darkness lay. Where the secrets lay.

My power faltered, I thought. *I'm not chosen. That's the truth of it. And now we're both going to die in this Makers-forsaken forest.*

It was the unspoken truth that threatened to suffocate me, that no one would acknowledge out loud. Yet I thought I could see in their faces. The Regent, elders, and priests. They knew who I was supposed to be. Who they'd wanted me to be—the ones who knew the secretive mission I had been set up to go on. I didn't know if it was disappointment I had seen. Perhaps a truth that existed, that a religiosity of denial surrounded. Strangled. And extinguished. They knew but did not want to believe. Their chosen one was a lie. And for some strange reason, I confessed it all to Meethra.

Chosen One, Meethra said, at last, huffing a laugh. *I have lived for over a thousand years, and I still cannot get over this childish idea of a chosen one. Still, there could be some evidence you're overlooking. The little remnant of power in that box seems to connect with you. I even think it may have saved you,* the godfly said, and left it at that.

I didn't know what she'd meant, and I wasn't mentally prepared to delve any deeper. As far as I was concerned, when I turned the ember in, I was done with it, and I would be free to figure out what to do with the rest of my life.

Night fell quickly, and the sounds of the forest came alive. I walked until my momentum staggered, catching my boots on rocks and gnarled tree roots. *I have to rest. Just for a moment,* I said, stopping to take a seat on the thick trunk of a fallen tree. A breeze blew my loose hair into my face. I reached for the end to re-braid it, but my favorite gold ribbon I used to tied it with was gone.

This is not wise, Meethra urged; *we should keep going.*

I heard sounds getting closer, but I didn't care. I had my shields.

When I got comfortable, I heard Meethra practically screaming inside my head, *WAKE UP, WAKE UP, YOUR SHIELD!*

I must have drifted off, for how long I didn't know. The shield was down, and the sounds of the forest were rushing toward us. I panicked, reaching for my weapons.

You can't fight your way out of this. Concentrate.

It was no use. Before I could come up with another plan, I was face to face with the Uden. Two swipes with his webbed hands, and he disarmed me. He moved impossibly fast. He had a wicked *I told you so* grin plastered across his face exposing his jagged rotten teeth. I could feel the other creatures moving in behind me. I shivered as he reached toward me, wrapping his clammy digits around my throat. I swore I saw a flash of uncertainty across his features before he squeezed. I clawed at his grip as my airway closed when he lifted me off my feet.

I could feel unfamiliar energy slowly coming to life inside me and intensifying my desire to get this creature away from me. *He hadn't ended me,* I thought, confused. His one hand was surely powerful enough.

He jerked me toward him quickly, so I was within inches of his maw. Instinctively, I shot my hands out to push him away from me. The moment they contacted his flesh, a flash of purple sucked the surrounding darkness into its depth, and he jolted a few steps away from me. It was enough to send my focus down the pathway I'd felt the power draining from before. Some of the smaller aerial creatures began zipping around us, skittering off my newly restored shields. I fell to my knees, gasping down air as I rubbed my throat. I looked up at Uden, who was swimming in my vision. He focused on two dark handprints on his chest. Red marks spidered out from their angry centers. He ran a finger over one and winced.

"Interesting," he said, stroking them.

"Why didn't you kill me?" I asked him, still recovering.

"I couldn't," he echoed quietly, studying his new hand-shaped marks. "You're not like the others who have ended up here."

From a distance, I could hear shouting. My pursuers from Drakestone must have felt the flash of power and identified the direction it had come from.

Let's go, Meethra commanded.

I took advantage of the fresh burst of energy and took off running. When I glanced back to see if we were being followed, the creatures were gone. At last, the edge of the forest and the border to Eastdow came into view.

As we neared, I looked toward the forest border to the left and saw Darius, my lover, in front. I grinned. He was so handsome. I don't know if it was caused by seeing him, but I was starting to feel lightheaded. I knew it was wrong, but I enjoyed how being with him made me feel. But even from a distance, I could see that he was seething. I didn't know why. I glanced at the men with him. They, too, men whom I'd shared a toast with before, now looked at me with bloodlust. I walked into their range, swaying a bit. They shot arrows in my direction. I didn't understand. Spears and knives flew, but the few that got near enough I dodged, or they ricochet off my shield. I tripped and stumbled to a knee. I blinked several times, trying to clear my swimming vision.

Get up, Vera. I could hear Meethra insisting in the background. *Your power has you in a haze. You've used too much. Focus!*

Next to a steaming pool a few feet ahead lay a cross-bolt. I tilted my head to the side, examining it as if it was a piece of art. The feather fletchings were Darius's colors. Red for blood and black for the ember. I only understood after I saw it.

I was supposed to be focusing on something.

Reality slammed back into me. I shook off my haze. I almost laughed as I snapped my eyes up to look at them. *What were they going to do if they killed me? Enter the Swath to collect the ember?* I remembered now.

I picked up the arrow and walked close enough to see their eyes, and they mine. Darius watched me hold the arrow up for him to see. I sensuously ran the tips of my fingers up its shaft and across the red and black feather fletchings. I considered it and shrugged, discarding it over my shoulder as I continued in the direction of Eastdow. *That* was for attempting to shoot me in the back. I savored the betrayal and vengeance shown on their faces. I had bested them with only a hair's breadth more power than the common power. And they knew it.

It served them right, keeping the ember for themselves for that long.

I approached the Swath's boundary into the Eastdow, catching sight of a group of sentries attracted by the commotion on the other side. Torin had them waiting on me, searching the border. To do this by the covenant, they had to stay on our side. Otherwise, it would be war.

I gave one last burst of energy as I made my way toward the soldier and the edge of the forest. I put all my focus on my shields so they would not falter and walked through the wavering boundary of the Swath. The second after I knew I made it to freedom, I slowly turned to Darius and gave a giddy yet boastful wave, reveling in the shock in his eyes. I turned toward home, feeling the rising sunlight on my face. My boot caught on a tree root, and I was in a free fall right toward the ground, the sentry blazing my way. *So much for an impressive return.*

Before I hit the ground, I felt a movement in my pocket. *Meethra.* A bright, almost blinding light slammed into my eyes. Meethra, darkness shed, hovered in my line of sight. *I'll see you again, Chosen One. I am in your debt.*

There was a light striking out across the morning sky, and the godfly was gone.

CHAPTER TWO

WHEN I CAME around, I was attended to by the female sentry I first saw when I crossed out of the Swath.

It was two days' travel from the border to the capital city of our territory. I spent the time we traveled eating, resting, and trying to reconcile the report I was to give upon my return.

Drakestone Proper's stronghold was strategically nestled upriver in a protected valley in the mountain range that reached across much of their land. The only way in was across the mountains or up the river, which flowed through a heavily guarded pass, a position which made retrieving the ember with an armed force challenging if not impossible. In fact, after many early failed attempts, I wasn't aware of a territory that'd attempted it in my lifetime. When Regent Karish sent the annual invitation to their Half-Light Ceremony, a gesture of peace by all outside appearances, we decided it was the perfect ruse to gain access to their keep.

I knew my acceptance of the invitation would cause quite a stir, because to my knowledge, none of the other territories ever attended in some sort of unspoken show of solidarity. Symbolically it seemed like a reasonable event to make a coming together gesture with. It was clear that Drakestone was trying to gauge the rest of the continent's temperature toward them as the turn of the millennia was fast approaching.

On the first hundred, then five-hundred years since the powerful event the Skyborne of this new realm came to call the Crossover, they expected the banishment that sent our kind here would end. When those dates came and went, the seers reinterpreted the story to have meant a thousand years after the crossover. Generations waited eagerly on the next anniversary, hoping it would reignite our power, raising it to the magnitude it was back on Idia. When it never came to fruition, they would eventually move on, grow old, and die. Time would pass, and a new generation would carry on their legacy. As children, they even made us memorize that history to know what to do when the way home to Idia opened for us, through the ember presumably. The stories became religion for Skyborne, and lore only built upon itself, fanning the fervor the nearer that we came to another significant anniversary.

I knelt over a little stream outside not far from the city and splashed cool water on my face. When I arrived at the gates, which opened to the seat of Eastdow's power, I was determined to not appear as bedraggled as I felt.

"Here, you can borrow these," the female sentry, whose name I learned was Kora, said as she tossed me a supply pack carrying a fresh set of clothes, similar to what I would typically wear.

"Kora, you are Makers sent," I told her, switching out my all-black ensemble for the almost unisex yellow-tan tunic and high-waisted, grey trousers. "Socks too!" I exclaimed as I tugged them on and slipped back into my utilitarian black leather boots, lacing them up to my knees.

I bound my cornflower braid with a coordinating ribbon, also borrowed. It was so thick that it was the only practical way to deal with it aside from cutting it all off. And I learned it had even become a tell because I tended to play with it when I was nervous. I felt so much more comfortable in this practical attire with my signature braid compared to the elaborate updos and feminine costumes I wore, playing the role of the dutiful and diplomatic daughter of Eastdow while visiting our new *allies* in Drakestone.

I kept my face clear and hopeful as our horses strolled through the arching alabaster gates of Eastdow's cherished capitol. I knew I was recognizable. Excited whispers and the occasional wave followed me as we passed through the city. The simple cream buildings that lined the main corridor leading to the keep were in contrast to the cold grey rock used in construction in Drakestone. We passed a baker's shop, yeasty baked goodness wafted through the air, making me glad to be home. Kora eyed me as if she knew what I was thinking, and I sighed, nudging my horse along.

Ahead the keep came into view. It was a heavy, imposing structure with varying levels like rectangular blocks had been stacked upon each other. Intentionally practical, except for the ornate images of swirling planets and stars carved into the alabaster stone that framed the main public entry. Guards, recognizing our party, whistled a command, and stable hands rushed to take our horses.

It was a welcomed sight, especially after what I had been through the last two months. Ancient cities in our home realm of Idia were told to be similar but more magnificent in their splendor. And that was almost a thousand years ago. Eastdow started from nothing and became one of the two wealthiest territories in this new realm. With only untouched raw land and hidden resources, they created buildings they claimed rivaled the legendary edifices of the realm where we were banished from.

Most would not dare to speculate, but some, like me, dreamed of what those cities would be like now if we hadn't been banished. What novelties and conveniences would we have if we could have advanced from where we were then? From where we are *now*.

Those thoughts were usually not productive, so I shoved them aside.

"Good luck," Kora said, nodding to the large wooden doors the guard was holding open for me. I thought I should have felt more as I made my way into the fortress. The sentries sent word of my arrival and confirmation that I possessed the ember. I felt a buzzing numbness in my soul, though. The act, however, was intact. I was the ever-gracious champion. I plastered the mask of pride I should have felt on my face—Eastdow's *chosen one*.

My personality's practical side appreciated the progress we achieved here in the new realm and couldn't help but speculate what exact homecoming waited for us in that other realm. *The grass is always greener,* I thought of the old human saying.

"They're waiting for you, assembled in the secondary meeting chamber," a guard said, stepping forward leading me through the fortress directly to a small familiar chamber off of the great hall of the main building. The heaviness of the room's thick stone walls and the lack of windows created a suffocating feeling. It also served to prevent any spying on the classified conversations that took place there.

"Hello," I said, unsure, scanning between my father, Torin, the Regent, and a collection of priests, including Lathrais, Eastdow's High Priest, who were already seated at the heavy stone table in the center of the room. They eyed me suspiciously as if after two months, I finally apparated out of the blue. After no word for months, I was extruded out of the Swath, fully intact and in possession of the ember. The item whose retrieval and existence I felt I had become bound to.

"You're all looking at me as if you didn't believe it possible," I said, irritated. I shook my head at their lack of faith in me. I didn't know what I would do once this task was completed. I had a couple of hundreds of years of life to figure that out, though; time was ironically a gift of the Makers.

"Sit, Vera," Lathrais commanded, his voice gravelly. I obeyed. "You were away for quite a while. Twice as long as we expected. We were becoming concerned." The High Priest tapped his finger on the table impatiently. He looked tired, his white hair even thinner than it had been before I'd left, frame even narrow as if he'd lost muscle mass. Worry lined Lathrais's aging face; his watery blue eyes did show concern, though I doubted it was for me.

I slowly took the insignificant box out of my pocket and set it on the table between us. I felt it give an uncertain shiver.

The men shifted their greedy glances to the box.

"Open it," the Regent hissed and focused his dark, almost black eyes on me, impressing his command.

"Hello, Father. Good to see you too," I murmured back, widening my stare at him.

Torin Tiernach, Regent of Eastdow, the easternmost territory, had been a decent father. He was not a particularly loving or kind man to us but saw that my brother Conall and I were well taken care of and received the best education and training he could provide. His temperament darkened after his wife, Lady Elain, died suddenly—shortly after I began my training. Lady Elain, a rare and beautiful woman, stood in contrast to her husband's coolness with golden blonde hair and warm fresh skin, her eyes a knowing deep brown. And the Regent loved her deeply. Still did, it seemed.

I remember standing next to her on my adulthood ceremony, admiring her squared shoulders and the steady strength she embodied as she watched my youth ceremoniously ended and my adulthood blessed. That is why it was such a shock when they found her. I was practically her mirror, which I assumed was the cause of our father's avoidance toward me. The sight of me must gouge at that darkening hole Lady Elain once filled.

"Your safe return is a prayer answered, daughter," he obliged, running his hand down his dark well-groomed beard still staring at the box. Lathrais, who seemed content to ignore that Torin hadn't even made eye contact with me, nodded affirmingly.

I pressed my lips together in a slight frown and reached for the box. As I touched the lid, the soft humming became a vibration visible to the others. I untied the leather band I used to keep the cracked lid secured and opened it, tilting the lid fully open, so all saw its contents were on view.

The box itself wasn't anything to see and could have been one of any ornately made boxes to hold a piece of jewelry and other small baubles. It was steel with impressions of orbs representing planets pressed into the surface. The inside was lined in a deep silver velvet, now with a deep crack running the lid's length. I watched as their eyes flicked between each other, me, and the box.

There was a hammering on the door. I knew that persistent knock. Conall would not be pleased they began their interrogation without him. I glanced at my father, who lifted his hand, motioning for the priest nearest the door to let him in.

A joyous embrace would have to wait considering the somberness of the present company, though as Conall's warm chestnut eyes met mine, I could see the relief and joy at my presence in them.

I gave him the warmth he sent me right back in a smile that said, *I'll be glad to get this over with.* At that, he glanced down at the table and the open box.

"She's been back in this keep for less than ten minutes, and you vultures are already interrogating her? Unbelievable," he fumed, looking directly at our father. Conall was almost three years younger than me, and sometime shortly after his adulthood ceremony, he quit being afraid of our father. He took an adversarial stance with him, and to his credit, the Regent let his heir get away with much more than I imagined possible.

"I'm okay," I said, looking at the box vibrating on the table, and Conall tracked my gaze.

The ember was a pulsing, depthless almond of darkness that I secretly became familiar with. A deep black opaque center radiated out, becoming translucent toward its edges until it ended. It was hard to think of it as an object because it didn't look like it could be felt tangibly, like reaching fingers would move through it instead of finding something solid. It was only known as the ember because it was the last remaining bit of power that sent us here.

Conall surveyed me before he looked to the box. "Okay." He turned to my father. "What's next?"

The Regent shifted in his chair, deliberating, "Well, *daughter*, it would seem you have a story to tell."

Everyone focused on me, and Conall begrudgingly took a seat next to me. I cleared my throat and began. As I spoke, the leaders sat in rapt silence, absorbing every word. I went through every relevant detail. It wasn't until I paused toward the end that they asked the few questions they had. Namely, the glaringly obvious. *Why was the lid cracked?* I made up a lie about falling down a set of stairs as I had quickly tried to flee. It seemed to satisfy them. By the time we had finished, utter exhaustion was overwhelming me. I knew they wouldn't let me rest until I gave them what they wanted, so I had. Finally, the last part of my obligation was complete, and I sat in a chair in that claustrophobic room waiting for my dismissal.

Torin stared at me, stunned. "It was impossible. How did you do it?" he asked, distrust dripping from his voice. I looked to Lathrais, then to Conall. I met Torin's stare with emphasis, "You *know* how I did it. I *just* told you."

Conall must have sensed me reaching the end of my patience because he said, "If you all are done here, I'll walk Vera to her rooms. It sounds like the last two months were no picnic, and some rest has been earned."

He looked at the Regent with authority, who snapped out of whatever trance he was under, and replied, "Very well," and motioned me out the door.

"Take care, child." Lathrais chimed in.

As we left, I saw the Lathrais reach for the box and flip the lid closed. It responded by latching itself and went dormant with his touch. *What hypocrites*, I thought as I left.

CHAPTER THREE

"THANK YOU," I uttered as we walked down the hall of the keep toward the wing where my rooms were. I knew my fatigue was evident in my voice.

"I can carry you if you like, *Chosen One*," and he gave a mock bow, rotating his wrist at his temple as he lowered.

I punched his side right below his ribs and snickered, "You act like you're still twelve, you know…"

"If you damage my kidneys, I won't be able to split a bottle of wine with you anymore. And I know how devastating that would be for you," he warned me.

I laughed, letting a full smile show. "Good point. I relent." I said, poking him in the side. "When I'm fully rested, you and I are going to have a much-needed night out. And I want to hear everything that you've been up to while I've been gone. I'm tempted to take you up on that now if a hot bath and bed weren't calling my name."

"Well, *you do* kind of stink," he said, raising his eyebrows in my direction as we reached my door, and he turned to leave. "Don't fall asleep in the tub and drown. It sure would be a shame," he called.

"Ha. Ha." I coughed.

My door was open as I entered. I saw the few items, including my weapons, I hung onto neatly arranged on the table. A tub being filled on my behalf drew me in as I closed the door. *Felicia!* I was beginning to wonder if it would be a safer choice to sleep first.

Felicia smiled brightly as I entered the bathroom. She was a female of average build, with warm pink skin and strawberry blond hair done up in a no-fuss bun. She'd been assigned to my care not long after she moved here from Sundale.

"Thank you, Felicia! And you even kept my babies alive!" I said, noticing the vining plants in my room were green and perky. "You are Makers sent!" I attempted to throw my arms around her as she stepped away.

"Come here, miss and let's get those grimy clothes off you and get you cleaned up before we get on with any of that," she said, surveying me.

She nudged me toward a mirror. I had not realized how rough I looked. I understood her reaction. I cleaned up as best as to be expected while traveling at the intense pace we kept. I didn't blame her.

I undressed and climbed into the bath and allowed the shudder of relief I had been holding in to escape. I looked around and saw Felicia set out all of my favorite bathing items and a fresh set of clothes. The scent of salts, amber, and orange, my favorite scents, permeated the air. She laid out a soft sweater, sleeping bottoms, and slippers to protect my feet from the cold stone of the floor on a bench.

"You can cry if you need to, honey," Felicia sympathized. "There is no shame in that after what you've been through." And after a minute, she said, "And I promise I won't let you drown."

I murmured a laugh and my thanks.

I appreciated Felicia's sentiment but was never much of a crier. I watched the girls who would weep at a play or a funeral or at the terrible judgments that often got rendered by the priest and elders. I would watch. Envying their softness. Watch and even feel deeply, but never cry. Right now, all I felt was relief to have made it, and all I wanted was oblivion. I'd sort out the rest of my feelings later.

My thoughts were all over the place as I cleaned myself, but they kept going back to those red handprints I'd left on the creature Uden's chest. The more I thought about it, the more exhausted I became. Everything had become an effort. I finished and toweled off. Felicia heard and came to help me dress and comb out my mess of hair, which was outside of her job duties, and I appreciated the extra care.

"What you need is a good long sleep, love," Felicia said with a comforting mother hen tone. "Don't you worry. Sleep as long as you need, and I'll make sure you are uninterrupted."

I trusted Felicia to look after my well-being. She and Conall were the two Skybone in this territory who I knew fully had my best interest at heart. I staggered toward the bed, and without saying more, hit the soft comfort of the mattress and was out.

I dreamt fitfully, waking on and off through the remaining daylight and on throughout the night. I woke panting and in a cold sweat, only to be swiftly pulled back under. Something was chasing me in every dream. I would run and run, and right when they would catch me, I would wake up. I had never really dreamed much before, but the three nights since I found myself in the forest, I'd had these unrelenting dreams.

I knew if I told Felicia about my dreams, even as I considered how practical she was, a trait she and I shared, she'd tell me to go visit a seer. I trusted her with my secrets completely, but I could hear her say this was out of her wheelhouse and I should seek the counsel of a priest who could receive sight. Several men claimed to be seers in Eastdow that I could have spoken with, most notably, High Priest Lathrais, who had been one of my key advisors over the years, but I lacked whatever thread was required that compelled belief. The thoughts faded, and I was out again.

I must have finally gotten a few hours of restful sleep because when I opened my eyes, I could feel the early morning sun creeping its way through the openings in the curtains. I heard footsteps and tableware being placed on the sitting-room table outside my bedroom.

Two knocks and Felicia was entering my room telling me I had a visitor. I pleaded with her for thirty minutes more, but she told me she didn't think she'd be able to keep Conall at bay a moment longer. I huffed and pulled myself out of bed. I looked in the mirror. Not nearly as bad as I expected. The bit of dreamless sleep in my own bed over the last few hours had done a load of good.

Conall was unfazed that I was still in my bedclothes as I walked into the sitting room.

"Good morning, sunshine," he said, noting the effect the rest had on my unpainted face. "Makers, you look just like her." He shook his head, wiping his eyes. "May I join you?" he asked.

"Would you leave if I told you to go away?" I teased.

He laughed and pulled out a chair for me, and I sat. He took the one next to me and served us breakfast. Felicia must have told the cooks to make every dish I'd ever said I enjoyed and all the remaining options that were in the kitchens.

He surveyed the spread, "See, I've always said you were the spoiled one."

"So, what are their plans for me?" I ignored his taunt and still offered him half of the only chocolate raspberry pastry twist in the spread.

"Good news is they have called a council to decide that… next week." The tension I was holding lessened.

He continued, "I believe they aim to hold an impressive ceremony on this year's anniversary since it will have been a thousand years since the crossover, and during the ceremony, somehow activate the ember."

That was three weeks away. I'd narrowly made it back in time. "But we are not ready to cross. What are they thinking? What if they *stir* something on the other side? They should send a spy or something to see what Idia is like now."

Conall raised both eyebrows at that. "Volunteering for another mission, are you?"

"Jealous? Hoping they pick you this time?" I taunted. He threw a cream puff at me, which bounced off my nose and fell into my coffee. I picked it up and tapped it on the edge of my cup before stuffing the whole thing into my mouth. "Mmmm… good idea."

"They think the portal will be able to be opened and closed at will." He paused, knowing what I was thinking. "Not by you, though. I think you just have to show up, say a few words, and smile. Then you can spend the rest of your days drinking wine and gardening."

A huge grin broke across my face, and I eased back in my chair. *Finally,* it's over.

A thought occurred to me. "Did you know Drakestone's High Priest had a vision similar to Lathrais' about how someone from the Dsiban line would be the one to use the ember? One of the brothers, I think. Do you think all the territories think their priest or a member of their ruling house will do it?"

"Probably. And lucky for you, the High Priest plans to wield the ember to activate the portal. That *would* be what he would prophesize."

He laughed as I rolled my eyes, thinking of how Meethra mocked the silly idea of a chosen one. Well, that was a relief. Perhaps my part in this charade was done.

"So.... do you have any plans later, oh mighty heir of Eastdow?" I asked.

Juice almost came out his nose as he laughed. "As if I did clear my schedule? I've missed you and will be commandeering your time for the interim. At least until Father comes up with another outlandish plan to occupy us."

I rolled my eyes.

"Besides, I'm your only friend," he said and winked.

I looked at him with a familial appreciation. His kind brown eyes were somewhere between the dark of the Regent's and warmth that had been from his beautiful mother, which complemented his mid-length ash brown hair and tan skin. If he wasn't my brother and dearest friend, I might have found the strong open lines of his face desperately handsome. Despite the fully matured Skyborne I now saw sitting beside me, he still had a youthful quality about him. He probably always would. Even this many years after his adulthood ceremony, the playfulness in our sibling relationship remained. He had always been more serious and restricted with the territory leaders and the citizens, however. In the last few years, though, as I neared the completion of my training, I noticed something different in him, especially when we sparred. Coming from somewhere buried deep. Maybe he was becoming comfortable in his adult body or his confidence in himself, but the change was palatable for me.

"What?" he asked, seeing himself in my thoughts.

"You're still twelve," I teased.

Chapter Four

Conall and I spent the day hiking one of our favorite trails at the mountain range's foothills that rose above the city. Unlike the sharp and brutal younger ranges of Drakestone I had experienced these last few months, the range was old and refined. These were a heavily forested group of highlands and plateaus extending from North to South across the center of the territory.

The mountains were rich with resources of precious metals, quarries, and timber. Runoff from the foothills provided fertile soil, and good crop yields had come to be relied upon. We supplied much in the way of agricultural products to the other territories.

The fore-bearers had positioned the city at the western base of the range at the watershed, which created a cozy band of protection around the city. Conflicts between the territories were rare now, though skirmishes and minor disputes had broken out every so often over the thousand years since our arrival in this realm. Usually, it was a territory that felt slighted and underserved by the resources it had received when the territories were divided or after a bad production year and coveted those of another. When yields were high, trade between the territories was strong, but as thorough as the architects of this new realm had been, the resources blessed to some lands were more valued. It was precisely this that had allowed Eastdow and Drakestone to be the wealthiest and most coveted territories on the continent. Especially now, since the effects of the cycle drought affected much of the continent, which had set in during my teenage years, seemed to be never-ending.

The trail we chose today was one of my favorites because of the sparkling streams and waterfalls scattered throughout. The air was cool and crisp but comfortable as we walked, and the clean scent of hickory and pine permeated the air. The trail was covered in a soft bed of pine needles, and we crossed bubbling springs as we went. Caves and overhangs could be found in the towering rock faces along the way. Conall and I had escaped many surprise rainstorms in those caverns and had camped in them often. We both sought refuge up here, free from the expectations that plagued us below. The hills were mostly safe, especially in times of peace. There were the occasional prints of an enormous cat which we never saw or a pack of wild dog-like beasts, but they did not impose a threat. Our kind didn't encroach on their dense food supply that lived in the nearly unexploited mountains.

It had taken an hour on horseback from the city to reach the base of the trail. We had been walking for two-and-a-half hours and had reached an especially lovely piece of scenery. Large smooth boulders had fallen over time and rested strewn across a clearing up in the hills. Conall and I climbed up to the flat surface of one of the larger stones, and I laid out a blanket from my pack and began sorting through the supplies Felecia had ordered for us. Various fruits, fresh and dried, cured meats and cheeses, along with the crusty loaf of bread and a bottle of pink wine, perfectly chilled from riding in our packs.

I drank deep out of my water skin. *Normal. This could be normal.*

As if reading my thoughts, Conall said, "I would be fine if our life stayed like this. By and large, we have all we need." He paused thoughtfully and looked at me. "I don't understand what could possibly be so great in Idia that everyone is so eager to wage war again. I know I have only experienced a few minor conflicts, but the death and gore were awful enough to ruin my taste for it."

We both knew if the Priests figured out how to activate the ember and send armies back, Torin would expect Conall to lead the Eastdow forces against whatever real or imaginary foe awaited us. And I would join him. I wouldn't be able to stomach letting him go face that alone.

The spying and covert maneuvering I did would have had a greater cost if I had company. He practically demanded to join me, but our Father and I gave a rare united front about why he should not.

We finished our lunch in silence, both deep in thought.

"Conall," I hesitated, and he looked at me with concern in his eyes. "Something happened to me while I was away," I told him about how I landed in the forest and the handprints on Uden and the shields I could create. "And the thing was, the longer I used them, my perception of the way things were would get hazy. Especially after I made the handprints. I almost walked out to Darius, Conall. It's scary. But I know without it, I would be dead right now."

"That's what happened to the lid of the ember. Not what you told the council."

"Yes, when I got my bearings in the forest, my first instinct was to make sure I still had it. I pulled it out, and I saw the lid was split."

"Vera, that lid is steel. It shouldn't have been able to crack like that. Do you think it was the ember's power that transported you into the forest?"

"I don't know how else to explain it," I said and shook my head. "And I think somehow it woke something up inside me, and I can't ignore it."

"How do you feel now?" He asked.

"Raw. Empty."

"Are you going to tell Lathrais?" he asked.

I had come to be wary of Lathrais over the ten years of my training. He was a Skyborne withered with age, yet when he had blessed me during my adulthood ceremony, I recalled the unsuspecting strength in his hands as he gripped my shoulders and recited the sacred words. He was influential in my assessment and selection as the bearer of this prophecy, and I wanted to trust him. Even then, I knew he and I would walk parallel through this path; he receiving visions and guiding me. But every time I met his stare, his translucent blue eyes were so cold, as if they were about to crack. He seemed to look through me. Not seeing me, but the fruition of some plan he had hatched. An expendable tool was what I was to him. To all of them, really. All but Conall.

"I figure it is probably best to keep it between us. For now, at least. Until we can figure out exactly what is happening."

"Agreed. They'll find it another excuse to keep using you anyway, and you'll never be free." Sometimes Conall and I had these moments where I could swear he perceived more than he let on.

⤚❦⤙

Over the next week, we met every day to train like we used to, weapons combat, grappling, and self-defense maneuvers. It felt good to be active again, and the Lathrais had little use for me now that they had what they wanted.

Conall still kicked my ass. He trained under the tutelage of the greatest fighters in the realm since he was a boy. No doubt, because of Conall, I was a force to be reckoned with.

Conall was bending over, catching his breath, and I glanced around to make sure no one was near enough to hear. "I need to practice with my shields."

He jerked his head up and studied me for a moment.

"What, afraid they might give me the edge against you?" I teased.

Conall grabbed the nearest towel and mopped up the sweat beading on his brow. "We'll want to find somewhere discrete, so father and Lathrais don't get any ideas," he said. I gave him a grateful smile. It was always so easy with Conall. Nothing was a big deal. It is what I loved about him.

⤚❦⤙

The boarded-up arena he chose was ancient. Crumbling. We climbed the dusty stone stairs and followed a raised ledge that was wide enough for us to shimmy around, passing several open-air yet barricaded windows. In one, there was a split in the wood just large enough to slip through on the side of the building now in the afternoon's shadow. I hopped inside, following Conall's lead.

We were in a large entrance hall, where audiences would have congregated before they took their seats to whatever spectacle was being put on that day. Across the hall, there were wide-open archways that lead into a large open stadium with seats climbing in all directions. I looked at the wide-open stage. "Feels a little exposed," I commented.

"Smaller fighting pits are at the back. I thought they'd be perfect."

Thinking of the bloody competitions held in these fighting pits, usually between two convicts, made a shiver run down my spine. It was better than being prodded into the Swath, however. Fortunately, any remnants of those activities were bleached away by sun and time. I climbed down into the pit. Conall had already smuggled a few practice weapons inside.

I looked around at the tall chalky walls surrounding us. "Creepy, but perfect. I can't believe we've never come here before." I snatched up two long wooden practice knives, and Conall grabbed a pair of mismatched wood short swords. That smile on his face. "So eager. Come on with it then," he swaggered.

I chuckled, lunging. At first, I couldn't stop anything, except with my knives.

Conall wiped his forearm across his brow, "What's wrong?"

"I don't know. I felt it more strongly when I had the ember. Let me try without weapons." I tossed the knives to the dirt floor. "Just try an easy swing."

I closed my eyes.

"Are you sure about this?" he asked.

"Do it. I mean, don't actually hit me, but swing."

I honed into my energy. Once my awareness opened, I moved to the energy surrounding me. If I could just get the particles I felt to ricochet against each other, it would be like the vibrating barrier of the Swath.

"Now," I called. I felt the air parting for his swinging sword coming down over my right shoulder. I sent my energy there. When the wood hit the vibrating field, it shuddered and collapsed.

"Holy shit," Conall said. I opened my eyes, and he was staring at me, mouth agape.

I took a steady breath, "Again," I called.

It was strange at first. I'd stop one blow only to let the hardened invisible shield I created collapse under pressure and strike me. "It's not the same as when I had the ember. It's like, less. And I have to work harder for it." I was panting. "I can feel the channel still but can't get the energy to flow quite right."

"You're disappointed," he said.

"I don't know, maybe," I offered. "Let me try again."

We practiced like that every day for a week. When I could use the shield to catch his swing and thrust it back, I was satisfied.

⤎

"I think you secretly wished you'd gotten the power of the prophecy. And you hadn't realized that until whatever happened to you with the ember." He sized me up to see how I was going to respond to his guess as we walked down a quiet alley that led back to the keep.

"First, the prophecy is a hoax. You know that; I know that. And even *they* know that."

"Why? It could be true. Maybe it took the ember to wake it up. You should have it, not Lathrais. And be the heir too, not me. You're the firstborn."

"Are you actually going to subject me to a pity party?" I raised an eyebrow at him.

"You know I wanted to go with you. How do you think I've felt growing up in your shadow? Look at how everyone treats you, *Chosen One*," he mocked. "Being heir seems like a consolation prize at this point."

"Conall, it doesn't matter. You couldn't have gone anyway."

"It matters. And why?"

"You could have been killed."

"You could have been killed, Vera."

"But Conall, you're the heir. You'll be the next Regent. Don't you see how expendable I am?"

He winced when I said it.

"What, you know it's true. You see how they are with me."

I could see the pain for me on his face. The way the warmth in his brown eyes flickered between protective and hurt. "What I can't put my finger on is why."

When he said that, my heart ached for all the things I couldn't tell him. If I did, I'd lose him.

⤎

I lay in bed awake that night thinking about what Conall had said. *Was it really true? Was I feeling regret?* I had moved small things and shifted my appearance since the first inklings of power which had come early. When I first started, it would take all of my vigilance to keep up, but after almost ten years of training those skills, I did them without a second thought. That made it possible for me to get away with infiltrating Drakestone how I did. Taking the appearance of keep staff and guards, familiar but unnoticeable faces. I slipped through the passageways, learning what I needed to know unencumbered.

The common power was prevalent enough amongst the Skyborne here, but being able to move objects was more uncommon and to shift one's appearance was rare. In fact, there wasn't another from what I'd heard in my lifetime who was able to do it. Only a few Skyborne sprinkled over the early generations now passed on. This new energy my senses had awoken to was altogether unheard of. That is since the crossover. They thought the greater connection to that spark of power, that energy that connects everything, was lost during the crossover. As if the event had taken it. As a punishment. It was probably true thinking back to the fighting pits. According to the seers, a deeper connection to the power shown to us by the Makers would return in my generation. Though that recurring sight repeated itself every couple hundred years. I didn't know if they had gotten it right this time, but I knew something was different now. I felt a new emptiness that hadn't been there before.

It had been seven years since Conall's adulthood ceremony, which was like a birthday celebration, but instead of presents, you got the responsibility of adulthood. You had to commit to a profession, you were allowed to take a life partner, and there were certain duties like military service or city management activities which you were obligated to perform for the territory you were a citizen of. Still, it was tradition celebrated by all Skyborne because twenty was the age where your power blossomed from the whisper of your youth.

Conall's connection to his power likely had several more years before he could expect it to be fully matured. Ten years was typical for the development. Still, though, he couldn't do much more than the average Skyborne. Not even as much as Darius. I could do most of that before I reached maturity. And then some. The priests believed that was a sign of the deep connection to it I would have. Three years and two weeks into the training and I ran into drop-offs in the channels of my power. I felt this never-ending landscape of raw energy, but I couldn't figure out how to access it, regardless of what I tried. So eventually, I quit trying, and I worked to master the connection I had received.

So, yeah, maybe Conall was right. Maybe I did want more.

CHAPTER FIVE

A FEW DAYS LATER, I awoke to a banging on the outside door to my rooms. I looked outside. It was barely dawn. I knew it wouldn't be Felicia or Conall. I jumped up and threw on a robe.

"What is it?" I hollered. To my surprise, Torin was on the other side of the door.

"Father," I murmured and nodded respectfully. It was too early for bowing or anything more. I noticed he was still in his nightclothes, which looked as rumpled as his nervous energy. "Get yourself decent and be in the council room in ten minutes," he barked.

"Ten minutes?" I asked, startled. "Tell me what this is about." Dread crept into my belly.

"Lathrais has received the sight. He wants you there."

My stomach dropped. "But I thought my part in all this was over."

"Your mother would have had more backbone," he hissed, "Now get dressed."

"But she's not…" It was useless. He had already turned and was storming down the passageway toward Conall's rooms. Communicating with him was impossible. Especially after she died. He'd become more distant. Like he sometimes still lived somewhere that didn't exist anymore.

෴

The meeting was to go over the exact details of the ceremony to *awaken* the ember, as High Priest Lathrais described it. His vision gave him very specific instructions on who should do and say what, stand where. I didn't see why I needed to be dragged out of bed for glorified party planning. I looked across the table at Conall, who stuck out his tongue and rolled his eyes. *I know*, I mouthed.

The thousand-year anniversary of our arrival in this new realm was a few days away. He alleged the vision outlined some prayer that would bring the ember's power to life and give him control to open and close the portal to Idia at will. My skepticism was on high alert as his holiness had just so happened to be the one the prophecy proclaimed would wield the ember. In my brief time in Drakestone, I learned enough about the vanity of priests when I'd heard their similar stories of a *chosen one*, naturally born of a prominent Drakestone family, who would be blessed with the power to activate the ember, and their chosen high priest would wield it. It took little imagination to realize that each territory likely had similar territory-centric prophesies. I was surprised they didn't compare notes.

As I carried the relic, I felt the vibrations of its power singing through the box in my pocket when I escaped. I tended to agree with Meethra, though, on the efficacy of a "chosen one" theory. Especially considering my own lack of talent.

The fortunate thing to come from the meeting was they only required me to be there as a symbol and say a few words. To stand with my family, the priesthood, the territory elders, and cabinet members to support the proceedings.

Over the next six days, others carried out all the arrangements for the ceremony. Often the events in the great hall would involve food and drink, along with speeches and music. This occasion differed in that Lathrais planned for it to be an event not experienced but witnessed. Torin requested Conall's attention to take care of a few security details, so I had little to do for the few days leading up to it. That is, except stay out of the way.

⪗

Finally, the day came. I woke, stretching, trying to clear my head. It was as restful a sleep as I could have expected. I stirred, and before I even opened my eyes, I recognized his scent. Very near indeed. I snapped my eyes open and was face-to-face Malik Dsiban, our enemy from Drakestone and, by my previous assessment, an overall shifty character. The thudding of my heart quickened as he moved a single finger over his lips to signal me quiet.

How did I not feel him climb onto my bed? I scolded myself. The comfort of being home must have eased my guard too thoroughly, I reasoned.

"*You...* I don't have it, Malik," I hissed through my clenched teeth, still deciding whether it would be useful to sound an alarm. He was too close. I'd be dead before anyone heard me.

"That isn't what I'm here for. I figured you'd want to know what I have to tell you. Before you find out in front of thousands of Skyborne." The bastard *winked*.

"Why would you do that?" I asked incredulously, evaluating him. I saw him around Drakestone, of course, but had only brief interactions with him. When I saw *him*, he was always slinking around, acting smug, like he knew something everyone else didn't. When he saw *me*, he seemed to taunt me, studying me with that dark and enigmatic look he had. He caught me off-guard a few times. We made eye contact, his dark almond eyes softening enough that I might have interpreted it as an invitation. I didn't exactly accept them as trustworthy. Maybe creating that illusion was a trick of the trade, I thought from personal experience. The right look could disarm someone or set them at ease. I learned *and* used that skill to my benefit many times over the last few months. But looking into his eyes as I was facing them now this close, it was either real, or he was *that* good. There was something about the arch of his eyebrows and his distinctly kept facial hair that undermined the honesty in his eyes, no doubt enhancing the slippery persona he favored.

Sitting up on an elbow, he cocked his head to the side, "After all those months, lurking around our keep, stealing the forms of others, you think I wouldn't have figured you out?"

My breath caught in my throat as I realized this day was not going to go as planned. I learned what little I knew about Malik from the intimate relationship I shared with Darius.

Oh, Darius, I thought. Darius had been the softer, more sensitive brother between the two and had made my job easier in Drakestone in more than one way. My mind flashed to the way his calloused hands felt grazing over my bare skin. He was the first lover I'd taken who really knew what they were doing, not just fumbling around for their own pleasure. Now was not the time to go down that thought path.

Malik looked at me as if he could see my thoughts forming and being pushed away. He gave a knowing smile.

"He is still pretty bent out of shape over you, Vera."

"He told me he loved me only days before I left." I sighed. *Why was I telling him this?*

Malik shrugged his shoulders, a sly grin spread across his face.

"If it isn't for the ember, then what are you doing here—"

"So, you're admitting you stole it? That was much easier than I expected," he smirked proudly. When I stared at him blankly, he chuckled. "Do you know how many Skyborne the generations of my family have caught trying to steal that thing? Highly trained grown males, and here you waltz in and take it. Not to mention how many priests we lost to the thing. When I saw the look on my father's face when he found out… It was *quite* amusing."

I truly could feel no ill will on his part toward me, though that made entirely zero sense. He had *every* reason to want me dead. *None* that I could think of to help me.

"Darius is here, *Vera.* And I don't think he's planning on doing you any favors. You didn't just bruise his ego by playing him; you broke his heart."

It felt like a punch to the gut. I hadn't loved him. I wouldn't let myself. Things would have been too complicated, if not impossible, considering my assignment and its brevity. Still though, Darius, here in my home. "How? Why?" I was speechless.

"It didn't take him long to realize what you'd done. After the search party lost you, his demeanor *changed.* I don't know if anyone else noticed, but it's as if he decided something. One day, he disappeared from our camp. So, I tracked him down and followed him here."

"Surely he's not here only for me?" I couldn't conceive what his motive might be except to kill me for betraying him or get the ember back. He must feel responsible because of our relationship.

"Well, considering the cross-bolt he had aimed at your heart right before you *disappeared*. That was a fancy trick, by the way. No one has been able to use the ember before you."

I couldn't believe what I was hearing. "You saw what happened to me? That wasn't anything I did. I certainly didn't touch the ember. One minute I was staring down Darius's crossbow, then next, I was tumbling in the forest. I had an excellent time with the forest creatures, in case you were wondering."

Malik huffed a quiet laugh as I put the scenario together.

"I saw his aim. I didn't think he would do it, but I heard that telltale breath he lets out right before he shoots. I tried to create a disturbance in the air to throw off its path, but it wasn't strong enough."

I knew exactly the release of breath Malik referred to and what unparalleled aim Darius was known for. I watched him practice many mornings after we'd finally hauled ourselves out of his bed. He even taught me how to use the heavy weapon, though I still preferred my blades. And if Malik had been caught trying to help me get away. I could hardly believe it.

"A little gratitude would seem appropriate." Malik was now sitting casually on the side of my bed by the window as if his presence was totally normal.

"What is he here for, Malik?" I demanded.

"I've not followed his every move, but it seems he's been meeting in private with the Regent, *your* father," he raised a single sharp eyebrow at that.

"He's meeting with Torin. But why?" I put my hand to my mouth, trying to understand what this could mean.

"Unfortunately, I am unable to breach the wards on that room they meet in with my power, so I don't know what exactly they're discussing, but I have my guesses. And none of them bode well for you."

Before he could give me any additional details, Felicia was hammering on my door to make sure I was on my way to becoming the presentable symbol they expected me to be.

"That is my cue," Malik smoothly lifted himself off the bed and went to the cracked window I now noticed. "I'm sorry I haven't been able to tell you more now, but I'll do what I can, okay?" And he left without waiting for me to respond.

"I still don't understand why you want to help me," I stupidly called out after him. "Malik?" I called.

"You talking in your sleep again, dear?" Felicia called through the door.

"Just a minute," I cried and went to the window Malik had slipped out of. I looked around franticly for where he'd gone.

"Shh…" From an oddly deep shadow to my right, I heard him. His voice was a whisper. "My father has shown me their plans. The atrocities they're bringing into being aren't meant for this realm. I didn't know how to stop them. The first time I saw you was the first time I had hope."

I couldn't believe what I was hearing, but I see the sincerity in his eyes despite the shadow. It didn't make me trust him, but maybe there was more to him. I looked back at the door Felicia was banging on again. When I turned to say goodbye to Malik, he was gone.

Conall and I took our places on the dais next to Torin. Conall was in the territory's military regalia and looked very official with his chestnut hair slicked back, so it hugged near to his head. Torin scanned the incoming crowd incessantly and kept anxiously smoothing out the dark green Regent's ceremony robes he wore, which were embroidered with the East-dow crest depicting the east star hovering between the tips of two broad swords. Lathrais, a vision of the calm and consistent priest, was perched on a lavish seat ornamented with familiar impressions of realms, much like those on the ember's box, representing his position as the spiritual head of this territory. The rest of the priesthood and elders sat or stood as their various positions required. The cabinet members and emissaries from a few other territories stood toward the front to bear witness, which

I thought was bold of Torin. We stood for what felt like hours, waiting as the processions of Skyborne crammed themselves into the great hall.

The hall was a wide-open room built in the shape of a half-moon, with a terraced floor intended to accommodate sizeable crowds gathering to center all their focus on the dais and the figures it contained. Nearly every attendee sat or stood in a place that held an uninterrupted view of the speaker.

Lathrais decided it would add to the spectacle to have the heads of this territory and the priesthood stand to oversee the congregations gather; his holiness's approving eye blessing the entry and presence of each inhabitant of Eastdow and beyond. The highest-ranking members of the territory were on the lowest terraced levels, and for this occasion, they opened even the balconies and mezzanines up to fit in as much of the public as the great hall could hold. Sunlight streamed brightly in through the high slotted windows onto the crowd, echoing the priest's blessings.

The last guests had found their place, many of them standing crammed close together. None wished to miss this historic event. As Lathrais motioned for the gathered crowd to settle and for the Regent to begin the theater they had worked out beforehand, I nervously scanned the room. I hadn't had a chance this morning to talk to Conall about the warning I'd received from the most unlikely of persons. The scene kept replaying in my mind as I, too, scanned the crowd.

I must have been scanning the great hall a little too obviously because Conall caught my attention and widened his eyes at me. Everyone who was going to show up had taken their place, and I saw no sign of Malik or Darius.

The Regent finished his address and motioned to Lathrais to join him at an altar-like pedestal they had made for this precise purpose. Lathrais placed his hands hovering above a black silk cloth covering what I assumed was the box containing the ember and went into a medley of prayers and incantations. Torin was now beside him, ceremoniously removing the black cloth. The congregation leaned in at that. Again, eyes to the box, eyes to the priest and regent, then back. It had that effect.

I will give Lathrais that. He sure knows how to put on a show.

It was hard not to roll my eyes, but I knew if it was seen, it would warrant some excruciatingly mind-numbing punishment from the priesthood, so I abstained.

More chants, repeat after me, and the sheep standing before us were bleating them right back.

Ever so slowly, Lathrais reached his arm forward, unclasped the latch on the box, and flipped open the lid. The crowd gasped. The ember's signature glowing darkness was there, pulling the light around it into its depth.

I was still scanning the room when I caught a familiar silhouette in a balcony to my right. Malik was present. It was reassuring, somehow, knowing I wasn't the only one with secrets. No sign of Darius still. Malik gestured toward Lathrais. The Priest had become silent and was staring at me.

Shit. I must have been so wrapped up in my inner dialogue I missed my cue.

"Vera, blessed child?" he questioned, urging me to speak my lines in this play.

"It is with gratitude I serve the priesthood, my family and our kind, your holiness. And my honor to deliver upon the promise." I curtsied deep, trying to make up for my wandering mind. I repeated the rest of my rehearsed monologue, trying not to sound too monotone, and finished with the traditional Skyborne prayer, "It is with the Makers' truth, I seek your blessing."

The crowd responded, "And it is with the Makers' justice, you are judged."

Lathrais nodded, pleased. "And it is with the Makers' benevolence, *I* now bless you, child."

Pompous ass.

He turned to the box, preparing to... I didn't really know exactly what he was planning to do with the thing. More symbolic words and spherical hand gestures, mimicking a portal opening, I guessed, and he reached into the box, slipping his hands under the object. Right as his fingers touched the outer edges of the ember, they darkened. He was cradling the object in his palms, depthless dark crawling up both arms. He lifted the object to his head. I was astonished as Lathrais, High Priest of Eastdow, crowned himself with the ember.

Suddenly, his fingers turned from black to gray. He must have seen it too. His eyes widened, and his color drained. But it was too late. He tried to wipe the grey off of his fingers. The relentless grayness ever so slowly marched up his arms, replacing the priest's usually pale yet alive skin tone.

By now, the crowd was sensing this wasn't a part of the plan. From the corner of my vision, I saw the Regent summon the head of his guard with a subtle movement of his wrist. That must be why Darius was here. He warned Torin this would happen. He would have known since their territory had no doubt tried this same exercise before.

There was a small echo of darkness that encapsulated the priest for a few pulses. Then it was dormant. Lathrais stood motionless for a few heartbeats, hanging in the air, then abruptly dropped to the floor. *Dead?*

Conall and I rushed to him to check his vital signs. I had never warmed to the Priest, but dead? He was dead. The murmuring crowd escalated quickly, and I could see the Regent barking orders and pointing in different directions. I saw a rigid finger aimed in my direction. The hair on the back of my neck rose.

"Seize her," he demanded.

My glance darted toward Conall, who was, with rising panic in his eyes, barking orders furiously, trying to calm the situation and failing blatantly. Today, he held no sway with our father and was being ushered to the sidelines.

Guards grabbed both of my arms and had me pinned to a spot. I could feel the power inside my veins thrumming from the attack or being this close to the ember wanting to defend me. I looked to where Malik stood, calm and stoic as I had ever seen him. He inclined his head, signaling behind my left shoulder.

I followed his nod and caught sight of Darius making his way from a side door onto the dais.

He rushed over to the Regent, who was kneeling beside the deceased High Priest, making a show of his grief and shock. As Darius stood there with a feigned comforting hand on Torin's back, he levied an accusatory stare in my direction. We hadn't seen each other in weeks now. The last time, well besides the cross-bolt incident, had been after making love and slowly giving way to sleep. Well, he slept. For me, it was a final passionate encounter. I knew he would hate me for it, and when I weighed the consequences, I never pictured this. That Skyborne I shared such intimacy with looked so desperately murderous at me. That face was what revenge looked like, I realized.

I looked back to find Malik, but he was gone.

"You," Torin growled, pointing a shaking hand in my direction. "Why would you do this to your own kind? You stole the ember only to manipulate your own High Priest and mentor into getting himself killed."

"She's figured out how to make it yield only to her power. She never meant to help us, Torin. I don't think she is who she says she is," Darius seethed.

The barrage of accusations flew unchecked now. As their intensity built, I could see the viciousness and resentment that always bubbled beneath the Regent's polished surface release.

Oh shit. His eyes burned with hate as he looked at me. Me, who he would blame for the priest's death. Me, who would be the cause for shame on his territory. Me, who he'd blame for preventing our homecoming. Me, who betrayed the image of his beautiful wife and beloved child. I realized the story he'd constructed. Too late.

The Skyborne was practically foaming at the mouth. "Who or what are you?" a planned hesitation. "You are not my daughter!" he bellowed. Drool escaping his twisted and gaping mouth.

My eyes were wide. I was cornered, and he knew it. Torin stepped toward me close enough to see all of the fine lines on his face, the coldness in his eyes. Close enough to see the fragile grip on reality he held. He held his hand out to Darius and said flatly, "Give it here."

Darius almost hesitated, I thought, before he handed Torin a vial of what looked to be a fine red powder.

"Position her," he ordered. The two nearest guards held both of my arms to my side, and another grabbed the back of my neck. Torin pulled a handkerchief out of the pocket of his robe and poured some of the powder into it. I frantically looked for Conall. He couldn't let his father do this, but when I spotted him, he'd been apprehended and was being held back away from me. Still, Conall struggled against the guards, his face red, veins bulging in his neck. His eyes met mine, wide, urgent, then darted to his father. Torin had guessed that his son would fight for me. There were too many guards holding him.

Somehow, I knew what the powder was for as Torin held the cloth up to my nose and mouth. I instinctively held my breath. "Breathe," he demanded. I refused. He nodded to the guards holding me. One gave me a quick jab to the solar plexus, and the other, holding my neck, pressed my face down into the powder. I had no choice but to pull the powder into my lungs. I stood there breathing, trying to keep as calm as I could. Maybe it would slow the circulation.

I looked at Conall, who was struggling to get free. *It's too late*, I mouthed to him, and he stilled.

For long moments, nothing happened. Then the coughing started. Waves of convulsions shook through me, and I was coughing so hard the guards released me, and I crumpled to the ground. I coughed, on my hands and knees, until I spit up blood on the light stone.

"Maybe a little less, next time," I heard Darius caution the Regent.

The walls in my power began encroaching in until I could no longer feel the energy that connected all living things. It was like the air had been sucked out of the room. I gasped. It knocked the wind out of me. But worse. I shuddered, curling over my knees. My unbound hair was hiding my face. I saw my hands first. They were my own. Not hers. And I no longer saw Vera's honey-colored locks hanging down from my head.

At that moment, my only regret was Conall.

I looked toward him. His perfect eyes fixed on mine, asking me a thousand questions. I didn't care if I'd betrayed anyone in this room. He was right, I knew—my only friend, whom I loved fiercely. I cared about what he thought about me.

But the tone of the words in our unspoken communication changed.

I had my share of excitement, displacement, threats against my life, knives at my back, but *this* was threatening to kill me. He saw me. His eyes roved over me, studying me. He fixed on my eyes. Saw pain and regret there, the red powder coating my face. My real face.

I'm sorry, I mouthed to him. Despite the chaos around us, the realm was still.

He stared ahead blankly for long seconds, eyes blinking below knitted brows. It was like he was solving a puzzle. His eyes cleared, drilling into me. I sucked in a sharp breath. It was then, I knew he must have understood or pieced it together and had accepted it. Oh, he was pissed as fuck, but it was the only way, and with Conall, as always, logic prevailed. It's why we got along so well. And he had to know I didn't have a choice. *He had to know that.*

I turned my attention to the Regent, who was still parading about in his emotions. Darius stood next to him, a smug smile plastered on his face, glutting himself on the payback he believed he'd earned. Darius had known, I realized. How had he found out? Malik? *No*, why would Malik have warned me if he'd told Darius?

The crowd was chanting traitor now. I surveyed them and found the faces of strangers who'd cheered my victorious return weeks before, now so easily turned against me. I saw those who had believed in me, Vera, the prophecy, in whatever everyone believed in. They were afraid and confused. Angry.

I saw Felicia. Her eyes were brimming with knowing tears. Her eyes were kind, in contrast to the crowd surrounding her. She gave me a grim smile and nodded.

Damn them, I thought. With courage, I gave her the most loving and appreciative smile I was capable of and stood. The sound from the crowd made the gasp they made when they saw the ember seem quiet by comparison. Their *chosen one* was, in fact, a girl they had never laid eyes upon before. A girl not of their own territory, but from another place entirely. A fraud.

The guards, in their shock, failed to retake control of me. I turned toward the Regent and Darius and cocked my head to the side. It felt so good to be standing as myself after ten long years. I was back in my own body. My black hair tumbling around my delicate shoulders. Vera and I had been a study in contrasts. Her light to my dark. And I enjoyed the strength the shift of her body gave me. She was beautiful, but she had the physique of a female warrior. Or she would have if she hadn't succumbed to a mysterious life-draining illness. And the Regent, his wife, and the priesthood, led by Lathrais himself, plucked me from my own destiny to complete their prophecy.

"So, it appears I stand accused," I initiated the conversation, gesturing toward the priesthood, believing I had the upper hand. "Priests, please bear your witness of my innocence to my accusers."

Nothing.

My temperature was rising now as I wiped the red powder off my face. I looked at Torin. "Your beloved daughter, Vera, was taken to the grave far too early. You buried her yourself, Torin. You knew I was the replacement, sanctioned by Lathrais, blessed by each of you." I glared at each priest.

Silence.

All six remaining priests shifted uncomfortably. I turned toward Torin, heat crawling up my neck, "*You can't...*"

His gaze was icy. *I can*, he mouthed.

"Did you kill her? My daughter, my Vera? Is it power you seek? Is it revenge on behalf of your family out of jealousy of our prosperity?" he quipped unfeelingly. *Oh, his act was good*, I thought. All it took was a second. A single sweeping gesture to the crowd and Torin ensured the Skyborne of Eastdow stood against me.

I knew I wouldn't talk my way out of the little contingency plan pre-orchestrated by Torin and my ex-lover Darius.

Darius took that opportunity to run his eyes over this new version of me hungrily. I knew compared to the sturdy girl he had intimately known before, this me, the real me, looked utterly girlish and breakable. His voice was guttural as he leaned down and whispered, "As much as I enjoyed Vera, I wouldn't have been opposed to this either."

"How?" I demanded.

"How what?" he smiled back and twirled a piece of my hair around his finger.

I shivered, yanking my hair back. I didn't know how someone who I had been so intimate with could make my skin crawl as he now did.

"How did you know?" I asked.

"After Roslin came to after *you* knocked her out, she ran straight to me and told me everything she'd seen. I understood, but I was too late. You'd already made it out of the keep. It didn't take us long to catch up, though, as you found out."

Roslin. I vaguely remembered the raven-haired female who'd fawned over Darius at every turn. I hadn't touched her, though. *Could it have been Malik?*

"What shall we call you, my petite raven?" Darius inquired, running a thumb over my bottom lip. I wrinkled my nose at the disturbing nickname, jerking my head away.

From the back of the dais, a shuddering priest stepped forward. "If you would be so gracious, Regent, I have a confession to share."

By now, the crowd had entirely forgotten about the dead Lathrais laying before the open—wait, now covered—box containing the ember. They were in attendance at the greatest theatrical production of their lives and were focused with rapt attention.

"Proceed," Torin commanded to the young priest.

"I wasn't supposed to reveal it, but Lathrais knew Vera was deathly ill, so he searched the other territories until he found her," he said, gesturing to me. "He guided her personally and took care of her as if she was his own daughter. He never could have expected her to turn on him."

"Seems like a useful thing to have had a prophecy about," I muttered.

The meek priest glared at me and pressed on with renewed fervor. "And now he's dead because of *her.*"

"Nayla," I cut him off. "My name is Nayla, and I was heir to the Regency in Arborvale. That much is true. But my family made this sacrifice to send me, heir to our territory. Because I could shift my appearance. I did it for the greater good. For all of you," I said, motioning to the crowd who flinched collectively at my gesture. "So I could carry out Vera's mission and fulfill your prophecy about her, which I did. I knew her. Before she died. She helped me." I sucked in shallow breaths as my panic rose.

"Yes, see, she speaks the truth," the young priest cut me off. Finally, I had a corroborator. Relief didn't have its chance to settle in as he continued. "She has taken us for fools. She has betrayed us all!"

The guards holding me as if on cue hit me with a fist to the gut, which started another coughing fit. The crowd cheered.

Chosen one no longer, I thought, doubling over.

Caught off guard and reeling on my knees, I attempted to get to my feet. I swiped at the taller one's legs with a kick on my way up. I wasn't as strong as Vera, but I was quicker in my own body, and he teetered off balance and fell cursing. This premeditated back-up plan must have been the reason everyone on the dais was unarmed and heavily guarded. Nothing to do with the sanctity of this ceremony, I realized. I had executed a set of moves against the stockier of the two, and a few struck home, but unless I had access to my power, I knew they had me.

I had taken more than a few blows, and without a connection to that energy, I was spent. Everything was spinning now. I heard Torin order me taken to the prisons. I had lost track of Darius. As the guards practically hauled me out of the hall, I drew into myself. I met Conall's eyes one last time.

Sadness. I hoped that was not the last time I'd see him.

CHAPTER SIX

I DON'T KNOW HOW long it had been, but I woke up sometime mid-morning. I could see sunlight peeking in the one window high up in my cell. Out of reach, I had to check. I was in the group of cells reserved for special prisoners that I knew were beneath the keep. In my time in Eastdow, I had never been down here. The space was a typical prison cell aside from the tall ceilings. The light coming in through the windows was probably strategic, to give prisoners enough hope to stay alive.

A quick survey of the room and I saw the door to my cell with a few little slots, the lock must be exterior, and only a washbasin for my bodily functions. Otherwise, the room contained the pallet of hay I had been sleeping on and the clothing, my ceremony garb, still on my back.

I needed to pee suddenly, and I looked to the basin with disdain. As I undid the laces on my trousers, I saw the bruises on my legs and could feel the ones on my ribs and face.

Could be worse, I thought, though my power hadn't come back.

The urine hitting the bucket must have signaled a guard I was awake because moments later, I heard footsteps and saw a plate of food pushed through the rectangular slot. I jumped up to take it. Not that I planned on eating it, I didn't want the sticky mess all over the floor if he'd dropped it and the bugs it would likely attract. They couldn't keep me here that long. Word would get out, and my family would surely intervene, or Torin would decide he'd sufficiently made his point and want me to be the next experiment attempting to wield the ember.

Hours passed when I heard murmuring down the hall. I focused my hearing, amplifying the voices. I missed the first part of the conversation, but Torin was telling someone that he could flog her, presumably me, until he got what he needed.

Footsteps neared, and the lock on my cell clicked. A very wiry and miserable-looking Skyborne grabbed me by the arm, "alright girl, you can either walk, or I'll drag you."

So, I followed, steeling myself for the beating I was about to endure. Training, I told myself. This would be no worse than a bad day of training. It was working a little. He tied me to a chair; the miserable Skyborne was joined by the stocky one from the ceremony.

"The Regent has commanded me to find out the location of a certain object you stole?" his voice matched his appearance.

I was astonished. "The Regent already lost ember?" I couldn't believe it. I knew this would not be good for me.

Smack. The stocky one backhanded me across the face, and I could feel the cut from my struggle at the ceremony open. "He did not *lose* it. You and your friend have taken it."

"My *friend?*" My mind was racing, trying to think of who he could mean. It couldn't be Conall, or he would have used brother or something else. *Malik.* Shit, how did they get ahold of Malik? The Skyborne was practically a shadow when he wanted to be. That must have been where Darius had gone off to during the ceremony, I realized.

Smack. I could take a punch. It was only physical pain, I reminded myself. "I don't have it." Smack.

I looked at the stocky one, "You hauled me out of the great hall yourself. How would I have managed to get my hands on it? Especially in front of everyone in that room?"

Smack. "Were there any witnesses?" I asked.

The only person I had known who could possibly be that slippery was Malik, and he had apparently gotten caught. And now the ember was missing.

It went on like this for another hour until I felt like putty, and I had a new assortment of splits and bruises. They delivered me back to my cell, and I passed out from the endurance of bearing the abuse. When I came to, a mousy female cleaned my cuts and applied salves and cloth soaked in herbed water to my injuries. By the morning, I would be healed enough to start the interrogation again.

This pattern repeated itself for the next week until all parties seemed thoroughly bored. Finally, on the eighth day, I heard a new set of footsteps enter the interrogation chamber.

"Nice of you to join us, Torin," I smirked. That earned me a slap. He nodded for the two brutes to leave the chamber.

"Do you at least acknowledge what an awful predicament you have put me in, Nayla? A dead high-priest, an imposter. Don't you see how that looks?"

Oh, I saw it alright.

He continued, "Those of us who had spent years sacrificing our resources, guiding you on your journey, your task from the Makers, were waiting here, sick with worry, for your return home safe. All the while, you were making new friends. Through the use of my beautiful daughter's body, it seems. You put your own amusement ahead of focusing on the object that would be the homecoming for our kind." He was shaking now, darkness clouding his face.

I had no words, the manipulative son of a bitch.

"The silver lining is that your scorned ex-lover is now a powerful ally to us. And soon enough, his traitorous brother Malik will give up the location of the ember. You, I suppose, will have to hang along for the ride. This week was only a taste, dear. To get you softened up. A fitting punishment. Unless you tell me what you and the traitor's plans were..." he smirked.

I was seething, my fists clenched involuntarily, "you *know* I am not to blame... Did you ever consider your new ally Darius only came here to steal it back? If you were smart, you'd be questioning him."

"Still denying it, I see. Well, it's better you to take the fall than me," Torin sneered.

There it was. He'd all but admitted his intention to frame me for his mistakes right as he walked out of the chamber. After ten years and what I had done for them, I'd meant nothing to him. I had known, but it still stung. I understood revenge then.

The stocky guard and the interrogator entered the room with a set of wrist restraints. They must have seen confusion in my eyes because the miserable one said, "Regent wants us to mix things up a bit, get it moving along." He clasped a shackle on both of my wrists and attached them to rings bedded into the stone on the wall, so I was standing against the wall, arms spread, facing them. The larger one shrugged and pulled the front of my shirt up and over my head. I was breathing heavily now as the brutes took place on either side of me.

"Remember, no permanent damage," the wiry one said. "Palm only. He wants her alive. Like this."

His open-faced palm struck my bare abdomen, and he smiled, surveying the bright red handprint now on my bare stomach. The other Skyborne smiled and struck.

Sadists, I thought, *cruel, sick sadists.*

They decided I'd had enough when I was hanging from the shackles, wrists red and bleeding, my abdomen a raw, angry pink. Instead of undoing my restraints, they left me there. I must have lost consciousness because I woke up in my cell with the same mousy female tending to me. She had tears in her eyes today.

I should be the one crying, I thought resentfully. But tears would not come.

The interrogation carried on, alternating the abdomen strikes with days where the goons would attach my shackles to a higher single eye bolt and chain my feet to a lower one and leave me for hours on end. Attendants would come to help me drink, but otherwise, I was alone. After my body would eventually give out to fatigue, and my legs collapsed, they would let me hang there in my own refuse. Then either the stocky one or the miserable one would come to collect me and bring me to my cell.

One day, a different guard collected me, and he walked me a different route back. I hadn't heard another prisoner the entire time I'd been down here. Now I heard raspy breathing and could make out Malik's familiar scent among the blood, sweat, and piss. The guard must be walking me by Malik's cell to taunt me. The sound got nearer, and I paused right as I approached the cell's door, peering through one of its open slots. Malik must have sensed me about to pass because he was using what had to be the last of his strength to stand, leaning against the wall, arms crossed in defiance, ready for the brief second of eye contact he was expecting through the open rectangle between us.

He looked horrible. Worse than me.

We reached the door to my cell, and the guard threw my broken body into the room.

⤝

I passed out again. This time when I woke, my head was being cradled, not by the mousy female, but by someone else. I could feel those familiar callouses of his powerful hands stroking down my hair and onto the skin of my face and neck. Darius was petting me, rocking slightly. Icy dread filled me.

That day on the dais, what I had seen in his eyes, the mixture of lust, hate, and revenge had frightened me. I was handling the torture, but it still shocked me that Torin was sick enough to allow a rage-filled Darius to access me.

"Darius," I muttered, still suffering from yesterday's session. I could smell the alcohol and bile on his breath. "It's ok, I'm not your enemy," I told him soothingly, pulling myself away from him.

My stomach was in knots, bile rising in my throat as I met his eyes. But before I could move, he struck my face, leaving a searing handprint on my cheek. Tears instantly formed in my eyes, trying to creep over the threshold of my lower lids, yet stuck. I felt empty as we stared at each other.

"I don't care what form you take; I'll have all of them," he slurred and grabbed my shoulders, pulling me toward him. His hands were freely roaming now over my body, pulling up the drab prison frock's hem. I clawed and kicked, but he was stronger and shoved me down, straddling me, pinning my arms above my head. With his other hand, he grabbed my cheeks, puckering my lips and squeezing so hard I let out a wince, "Please, stop, please. I promise, it was real, Darius. Please. What was between us was real. Don't do this."

| 53 |

His face was so close to mine now. "You think I'm a fool? I told you I loved you." His voice shook as he gripped my hair and breathed into my ear. "There's something I need you to understand. You are mine. After the pleasure I gave you, after what we shared. Mine. I'm not going to let Torin kill you. I'm going to take you back to Drakestone, and you can be my whore. We'll make a game of it."

Of the mounting lists of violations I had experienced, this one he was poised to commit, I had been fortunate never to encounter. I couldn't stop shaking. His mouth was in my ear now, kissing and sucking and saying incomprehensible things as his other hand was fumbling to free my undergarments.

No. I reached for my power. *Come on, come on.* They had taken everything from me, but they wouldn't take this. If I could find enough for a shield. I was so drained, and the powder they'd dosed me with still hadn't fully worn off. I had almost nothing physical left to give. I found and clung to a brief whisper of energy. It was barely a breath, and they would likely drug me again soon.

With a final bit of rage and that whisper, I jerked both hands free, slamming my fists into his chest. I forced him back enough for me to drag myself away from him on all fours. His shirt singed, but it wasn't enough. Stupid fucking useless power. He was so much stronger than me and fueled by the alcohol. He grabbed my waist, pulling me toward him, fervor renewed. He struck at my head again twice as he grabbed a fist full of hair, drunkenly pressing himself against me, trying to find my opening.

I was trying to scream with everything in me, but I couldn't tell if I was making a sound. A knock came at the door.

Thank the Makers, I thought.

"Everything all right in there? Regent wants her alive," a gruff voice called from outside.

"She's fine," Darius grumbled. And *stopped.*

I was on the verge of hyperventilating, trying to predict what he'd do next.

Darius laid down next to me and pulled me into him, holding me like he had so many nights before. I was frozen, skin prickling uncomfortably from where he touched me. We lay there for long moments, his face crushed against my cheek, wetness meeting it. He was actually crying.

At last, I felt his grip around me loosen. He got up and put his disheveled clothes back together. I had sat up. I pulled my prison frock over my knees, which were curled into my chest, watching him. Motionless. I opened my mouth, but words wouldn't form. Darius looked at me with a strange mix of sorrow and disdain on his face.

"How could you?" he pleaded, voice dripping with emotion. Darius shook his head as if weighing some regret and stumbled out of my cell. I heard the lock click. "Leave her for a few days, just food and water. She needs to be presentable for the trial," I heard his slurred command to the Skyborne who'd be guarding the door. And silence.

CHAPTER SEVEN

I LAID THERE DRIFTING in and out of sleep, in shock, for I don't know how long. A new emptiness I hadn't experienced before was overwhelming me. He hadn't raped me, but it was close enough. He had taken something from me. The torture had made me feel powerless, but this assault, what Darius had done, made me feel less than nothing. Trial, I finally remembered. I didn't care. Hopefully, they would execute me, and this would all be over. It didn't matter. Conall hadn't even been to see me.

I had nothing, and I was nothing.

I thought back to the day my parents told me about the altered plans for my life. Sold me was more like it, though I had never found out what they got out of the deal. I knew that the Regent and High Priest from Eastdow were visiting, and I knew the importance such a meeting held. To have one of the regents of the most prosperous territories visit our humble land was an honor, and we had something to gain with their favor. Each family who held a territory seat had enough, but of the six territories, ours and the territory Sundale to the west of us that shared the southern tip of the continent were at the bottom of the ladder.

That day was the first time I'd seen Torin and Lathrais. In my mind's eye, I could see their faces clearly. My father had paraded my three sisters and me in front of them like prized horses. In our sisterly huddle afterward, we guessed that one of us was being married off to their territory heir, and they were here to inspect our fitness. Though the High Priest had taken a special notice to me, I knew they couldn't pick me. I was the oldest and poised to take the regency of the territory when my father was too old to manage it. Carina, the sister just younger than me, was the most eligible and the most beautiful, so I decided it was her who would be selected. Since I could remember, she had been socially adept. She followed our parents around and mimicked the protocols and pleasantries they demonstrated. She had natural governance about her—a calm authority. The prospect of marrying the future Regent of Eastdow was the next best thing to Carina.

I remembered how giddy Carina had been at the thought of a handsome betrothed waiting on her arrival. "It will be love at first sight," she had exclaimed, clasping her hands together at her chest.

"What makes you so certain?" I lifted an eyebrow at her. And she *was* certain. Her cheeks were colored pink now as I knew her mind was being swept away with her imagination. Our younger sisters, Balene and Judith, were giggling now. They were getting to the age where boys mattered.

"I know you're going to be a cranky old spinster, but it must be true. It's in all the stories!" Carina folded her arms across her chest, pretending to pout.

"I'll remind you I've had a few more boyfriends than you, thank you very much." Their blushing had made me blush. I hadn't normally been shy about any of that with Carina, but I was less forthcoming with the younger two.

"You aren't talking about that poor boy visiting from Sundale who you practically gutted? He was smitten, and you just tossed him aside."

"If I remember correctly, it wasn't my fault his family hadn't taught him to fight, which was his idea anyway, I remind you." That boy, the youngest son of a merchant from Sundale, had marveled at the notion of a girl Regent. A position of stewardship that provided both political, economic, and military leadership for its territory. "And he *had* to leave. There wasn't a choice." It had been a relatively brief relationship, and he'd been my first. He was handsome enough, and I had liked the idea of it being with someone I'd never have to see again. And conveniently, his stay was only temporary—cleaner that way.

"I guess that is one benefit of not being the future Regent. More dresses, less daggers," she quipped. She was becoming quite witty. We had all had our lessons, and Carina was beyond fond of hers because they complimented her so perfectly. She spent most days in the library, becoming a well-read lady. When she wasn't there, she had some visiting local traders or a merchant's wife entrancing them with her interest and conversation. At such a young age, she molded her mind into one that could keep anyone engaged for hours, regardless of their age or station.

Of course, when we were together, she dropped the conversationalist facade. It suited Carina well to be a diplomat, but in truth, we all knew she would have made a better candidate for Regent. But with the rules and traditions being what they were, that fell to me. And though I felt many other things suited me better too, I would do the job duty bound me to.

Life carried on as usual in the few days after our presentation, negotiations presumably being made. One morning, my mother found me in the gardens, my favorite place in all our territory.

I like to think I had a green thumb and would "help" the groundskeepers pruning and planting each year. I knew I was probably more of a nuisance to them, but eventually, the head gardener took a liking to me and began teaching me different aspects of plant care and showing me books of plants with foliage I couldn't have even imagined. He even helped me create a few cuttings from plants that would grow indoors I kept in my rooms.

It wasn't like our mother to show up out there, so it had caught me off guard. I assumed they had reached a decision, and they would require all four of us to be there when they made the announcement. I would miss Carina terribly, but I knew she would be happy and a future ally in her new position.

I followed my mother into a small room in our keep we used for intimate meetings. To my surprise, only my father and the guests from Eastdow were inside.

"Sit down, Nayla," my father commanded. He was an older Skyborne when he'd had us. His time-worn face looked particularly tired today. His first wife could not bear children and, when she died, had reached almost two-hundred years, which was a decent lifespan for our kind. After a brief mourning period, just enough to be publicly acceptable, my father had promptly married our mother. She produced him four girls, one right after the other.

I felt nervous and turned to my mother. She was the perfect partner for our father. Not only had she been especially fertile, she was content to be his beautiful, ever-graceful wife and silent partner. My father, to my knowledge, made all the decisions for himself, our citizens, and for her, it seemed. And she was fine with it, considering the impression I had of her own upbringing. She trusted him and must have been happy to have things taken care of. She put a hand on my shoulder and squeezed encouragingly before she left the room.

So I sat. My father was at the head of the small table, and the two guests were across from me. A few objects sat on the table in front of us, a box, a lamp, and a knife. "Nayla," he said, speaking to me as he would a child, "I would like you to show the Regent and his holiness your gifts."

So that's where this is going, I realized. They had been here to make an assessment of the threat, not take a bride for an alliance. Poor Carina would be so disappointed. But it was a show and tell was what they had come for.

My power wasn't much yet, but our high priest thought its early appearance was a sign of my future abilities. "Alright then, sirs, what should you like to see first?" I cockily intertwined my fingers, stretching out my arms in show.

My father looked to Torin and said, "now I did mention she was a little bit of a handful, Regent." I hated being apologized for. The other Skyborne, the Priest, replied on the Regent's behalf, "I assure you, we appreciate a girl with spirit. I could sense the power stirring in her the day we met your daughters. It does that to them, the power. Especially the girls." That had explained the extra attention. And the now-dead jerk had thought my delicate feminine mind more corruptible by the extra energy I could call upon. It was laughable as I thought back to the self-righteous pomp he had orchestrated at the ceremony a few weeks earlier. I had known that my territory was one of the three that still allowed girls to take the regency. *Lucky for my father*, I thought.

The priest turned to me, "move the box if you would, dear."

"Lid opened or closed?" I asked him flippantly.

I could tell the guest Regent wasn't amused, but the priest was too intrigued to be annoyed. I knew this was an opportunity to make my family look good. Show them that while we may not have been blessed with the richest lands and most prosperity, the Makers had shown favor to us through me. I had believed that back then. I laughed to myself.

Defiantly, saving the best for last, I directed my attention toward the lantern, which lit within a few moments. I reached for the knife, pointing it back and forth between the Regent and the priest, "who will do the honors?" The Priest was all too eager to oblige, reaching his arm across the table. "Here," he said, pointing at a spot on his forearm, "and not too deep."

"*As you wish,*" I said, and I lightly pulled the knife across his forearm, creating a shallow two-inch cut. A slight amount of blood welled to the surface. I felt I was in dangerous territory, cutting a High Priest. I doubted it was something another living Skyborne could claim. I steadied myself. Using this power was still new to me. All three watched with captivation as I pressed my finger into the beginning of the cut and slowly traced down its length, stitching it closed as my finger passed.

I'd shown the same level of power as the better healers in our territory who had been mastering their gifts for years. "It will probably leave a small mark," I had said. And it had. Every time I saw it during our lessons, it reminded me of that day, my family, and then later what a joke my power had become.

Ancient healers from before the crossover had much more advanced gifts, but since the crossover, the very best healers here could do only somewhat more. They would have been able to stitch him up without a scar, though.

I wiped my bloody finger on my trousers, making my father wince. I reached out, creating a mental connection with the box, and gave a little tug. It slid across the table toward me. I used my mind to compel the material of the box against the wooden table. The opposing force caused the box to lift. Something metal slid around inside it. I set it down and lifted the lid, keeping my hands flat on the smooth surface between us.

A small tiara ornamented with a few precious jewels that I had seen my mother accessorize with at events was inside. What a random item to put in the box for this demonstration. They wanted to see what I would do with it, I realized. So naturally, I used my mind to lift it from the box and raise it to my eye level. I appeared to be considering it, and though I figured it would cost me later, I drifted it across the room and placed it gently on the priest's head, and smiled.

My father and the Regent looked at me contemptuously. "Nayla!" my father reprimanded, but Lathrais bellowed a powerful laugh. Collecting himself, he turned to my father, "And the one last thing." He inclined his crowned head toward me.

The Skyborne I called father looked at me, becoming increasingly detached. "Show them how you can change the color of your eyes." I didn't understand how that could be a threat. I looked at the two Skyborne across the table, "any particular color you fancy?"

"Blue," Torin whispered with an odd sadness in his voice. So, I changed my sable eyes to blue.

"Oh, you and I are going to get on just fine, dear," Lathrais said, looking to my father. "We'll take her."

CHAPTER EIGHT

THERE WAS A noise from outside the door, and I heard the mousy female healer and a guard arguing. I didn't care to make out their conversation, but I wish I learned who won when I heard the lock being handled. Tremors immediately shook through me. I tried to stop, to be strong, but Darius had loosened the tight control I had over myself. Relief poured over me when it was the female. If it was another session in that chamber, I thought I'd lose it.

As the healer scanned my body, limply laying on my pallet of hay and my lifeless eyes, she shook her head, color rising on her neck. She took bottles and cloths and began treating my injuries, being especially gentle with the cuts on my head from Darius. She took my hands, examining my fingernails. I followed her gaze, noticing the dried blood under my nails. I must have clawed at him during our struggle, but I didn't want to think about it. Blacking out any details of last night, I decided, was the best approach. She got out tools and began cleaning my nails. "Are you hurt anywhere else?" she asked softly. I shook my head. "If you are, I can help heal you." I made an assessment of myself. It was uncomfortable, but there was no permanent damage. Another shake no. She pressed her lips into a line. She wasn't convinced as she continued patching me up. If she had ever had a female prisoner to deal with, I didn't know. Those were the first words she had spoken to me in the weeks since she mended my wounds.

She paused thoughtfully, "I can get you an herbal preventative if you have need."

"No, he didn't—do that." It was almost as bad as if he'd been able to go through with it. I gritted my teeth, thinking of him.

She looked at me sympathetically. "Okay." She gracefully rose, moving for the door. She stuck her head out and whispered something to the guard, who must have been standing outside all along. A few minutes later, she came back in with a basin full of water and more cloths.

"I am going to give you some privacy to take care of yourself," motioning to the supplies. The thought of removing my clothing to bathe had me on the verge of shaking again. "You have my absolute assurance; the guard outside this door will not allow harm to come to you while I'm gone." She paused, deciding the best way to assure me, I assumed. "I have... *sway* with him."

I wiped the blood and filth off of my skin, grateful for this delicate healer. She returned about a half-hour later with a change of clothes. They must have been from her own wardrobe, I thought, assessing her delicate frame, seeing we were about the same size. Words struggled to escape my lips as I mumbled, "thank you." She looked at me and gave me a somber smile.

Despite the odds, I felt a little better. The feeling of being clean-ish was renewing, and the desire for a hot soak in a scalding tub to remove echoes of Darius's touch on my skin was consuming. When that would happen—if ever again—I did not know. That brought my thoughts back to the trial I had overheard Darius reference.

I jumped to my feet and went to the door, pushing one of the little slots open. "Miss, please, miss, come back."

"Quiet, girl." The guard who'd been arguing with her slammed the little opening closed.

"When is the trial? When?" I yelled. If I had enough time, I might be strong enough to use my power and free myself. They hadn't drugged me again. Torin must have assumed they had broken me and wanted to save that vial's remaining contents for other reasons. I banged against the door.

I kept at it for over ten minutes. Finally, the guard opened the slot. His eyes met mine. "If I find out for you, will you stop banging?"

"Yes. Please." Desperation was clear in my voice.

"Give me a few hours."

～

Like he promised, a few hours later, the slot opened, and he pushed a plate of food through the hole. Proper food. I saw his eyes glance nervously down the hall in both directions before he said, "The day after tomorrow. It begins at sunrise." He hesitated. "Tell the healer... for my wife." And the little door slammed back.

～

During the two days leading to the trial, I had no more visits to the interrogation chamber or from Darius, thankfully. The healer had visited me several times, and I was appearing more unsullied each day. She had decent healing gifts. Better than what mine had been on the day I healed the cut on Lathrais' forearm.

Early in the morning of the trial, I was fully cleaned and dressed in a drab gray loose-fitting frock. I pulled my dark, thick hair back and knotted it at the base of my skull. I was a picture of humility as I sat waiting on my pallet of hay, rehearsing my defense.

At sunrise, the stocky guard and one I didn't recognize came to shackle me and take me to the great hall. When I arrived there, the important priests, elders, and the Regent's cabinet members were seated in organized rows facing the dais where a podium stood, and they had placed two chairs on each side. I scanned the room. No trace of Torin, Conall, or Darius yet. I heard a noise behind me and glanced back. The other sadist and the guard who had helped me were bringing Malik in, also chained. He looked rough. Dried blood stained his tunic, and his left eye was swollen shut. They hadn't cleaned him up so thoroughly. They seated us in the two empty chairs facing the gathered officials, along with the few voyeurs gathered in the standing area. They chained our arms and legs to the chairs. And we waited.

After about half an hour, the Regent, Darius, and who I presumed was the new high priest entered through the side door. The priest sat in the chair nearest the podium and Darius the next. Torin approached the podium and addressed the crowd.

"Before us sits two individuals who have conspired, not only against our territory but against the Skyborne of this entire realm. Each of you," he said, motioning to the elders and priesthood, "stand here today as witnesses and jury to what you have seen. It is our duty, the duty befallen on us from the Makers, to see justice is carried out." He paused. "The case against Nayla Kalederan of Arborvale and Malik Dsiban of Drakestone is clear. Those of us who do not possess their dark talents may never know how they accomplished the murder of High Priest Lathrais or the theft of the ember. What we know is Lathrais is dead, and the ember which was our salvation is missing. In the days leading up to the ceremony, I spent a great deal of time in the presence of Lathrais while he was receiving visions. They were clear and guiding, the final pieces given to his holiness to wield the ember. We spoke of the future and the inspiring history and sacrifices of our ancestors. I felt this trial was the appropriate time to remember our history, so we can understand what they," pointing at Malik and me, "have taken from us." He began his oration of the crossover for the earnestly listening crowd.

"Almost one-thousand years ago, the Sol Ros, the sect made up of the six united major Skyborne families, were banished. But it wasn't by the Makers. No, the Sol Ros never exploited the Makers, gift, the ability to harness the energy around us. Our *power*. The Makers set the rules, and the Sol Ros Skyborne were faithful."

"The Dar Kepler, without shame, turned to the power of the Void, breaking the agreement our kind had forged with the Makers. And they used that dark power, the power only the Makers should wield, to banish us to this inadequate realm."

"The families that made up the sect of Dar Kepler had lived in the Southern lands under a peaceful agreement with the Sol Ros in the North for generations. But instead of being content with the lands allotted to them, they built an army, intending to take the fruitful lands of North that *our* ancestors had cultivated through their labor."

"Our ancestors led great armies to defend the encroachment on our lands. But instead of fighting the final battle with honor, in a war they were losing, the Dar Kepler turned to the power of the Void. It resulted in our banishment. An act only the Makers, our creators, should have the ability or right to do. And when we arrived here, the only remnant of the power that sent us here was the ember."

The Regent inhaled deeply. "It's not hard to imagine what those first days would have been like, having arrived in a new realm with only the items carried on each person, mostly weapons. Certainly, no provisions. Our ancestors took tallies, and close to a hundred-thousand individuals made the crossover, some of which had the unfortunate luck to land in the Swath. We all know what happened to them."

The onlookers moaned at the gruesome thought.

"Imagine the pain they must have felt knowing their innocent families had been left behind, not knowing their fate. Imagine what the Dar Kepler did to those innocents without the strength of the Sol Ros to protect them and the weight of knowing they could do nothing." He shuddered convincingly. "We were banished from our home, not by the design of the Makers, but by our own kind and the power of the Void. Instead of giving way to some bloodthirsty instinct, those who did not die of starvation or exposure worked cooperatively to scout this continent, dividing it equally between the houses establishing the Covenant, an order that still thrives today. They used the power it left them with, the Common Power, to heal, create energy, protect and speed up productivity, not steal or kill or maim."

Laughing under my breath at that, I shook my head. After my last few weeks, I knew the way they envied my extra skill sets. Something I apparently had in common with the Dsiban brothers, I thought as I looked at Malik, then to Darius. He was sitting stone-faced.

Torin's droning continued, "Our ancestors even devised a strategy to share the guard of the ember, a trust which Drakestone broke when they kept the ember. They had wrongly believed they would make it back to Idia first and take the realm for themselves. Drakestone's heir Darius came in good faith to restore though by helping me expose Nayla as the fraud she is."

Torin might have been a fool to believe he wasn't here for only one reason, the most important reason. To take the ember back. I looked at Darius. Everyone did. He didn't have it. He had a fake smile plastered on his face. The face of a fake. In a way, I supposed I wasn't much better. He hadn't met my gaze since he arrived on the dais, specifically avoiding it, I knew. *Coward.* Oh, how I hated him now. I had killed men before, but it was never something I had wanted to do. It had always been a necessity. I wanted to look deeply into his eyes, as I had done many times before, and watch as the life stolen by my blade slipped away from him.

"The seers received prophesies that the ember would stir at the one-thousand-year anniversary of the crossover, and one blessed by the Makers would wield its power to open portals to bring our kind back home. We have waited long enough." A cheer from the crowd went up at that. "The time for vengeance is upon us. And we stand ready. My son, your heir, organizes the armies as we speak." Applause boomed.

I shivered at that, not wanting to believe that was where Conall was while I was being condemned. Torin motioned to me and met my stare, "Yet, this young Skyborne who stole the face of my daughter and retrieved the ember managed to escape the Swath alive and well. How did she do it, you ask. Nayla Kalederan has harnessed the power of the Void." Murmurs broke out amongst the crowd. Harnessing the Void was probably the worst accusation one could throw at a Skyborne. "She has used it to turn the power of the ember to her own purpose and kill our high priest." He turned to me and smiled. "Tell us, Nayla, was it your jealousy that the Makers chose Lathrais to wield the ember and not you? Did you grow attached to it as you carried it, feeling its power caress your own dark nature? Or was your fragile mind too weak not to succumb to the darkness? I don't have proof, but I know," he looked at the crowd, "I think we all *know*... you are responsible for Vera's death." Blood vessels were pulsing in his neck as the crowd gasped. His voice had gone eerily quiet with last bit with rage, causing the flock in front of him to lean in.

I couldn't take it anymore. I matched his fury. "This is absolutely ridiculous. You *know* none of that is true." I could go on for hours defending myself, telling the truth, and pointing out contradictions, but I knew it was pointless. Malik and I were already convicted. The moment he'd accused us of using power in the Void. This had been a witch trial, and someone needed to be burned.

"That is enough! A thief and a liar. It should not surprise us. Because you have not respected the protocols of this court and spoken out of turn, you have given up your right for confession." He looked past Malik, who was apparently receiving my punishment as well, to the new high priest, and the others seated in the front rows.

"Do you need to hear anything further before we reach our decision?" Mumbling, nodding, they shot murderous stares in our direction. I looked at Malik, who turned to look at me. He smiled a sinister grin as if enjoying himself. As he looked at me, the sounds in the room dulled. I could hear Torin continue, but I couldn't make out what he was saying. Malik was using his power to dampen out the surrounding sounds. I couldn't see his lips moving as I heard his words in my mind like Meethra had done.

You haven't lived until you've been sentenced to die. Malik's voice sounded in my head similar to how Meethra's had. His eyes were almost twinkling from the thrill of the words, and I felt the butterflies in my stomach come alive in reaction to his dark humor. *Tonight, Nayla, we escape.*

Malik removed the damper, and all the sounds in the room filled back in so I could hear Torin conclude. "I sentence you to death. You have twenty-four hours to share your confession with a priest. Your execution is tomorrow at sundown. And after you have joined Vera and Lathrais in death, we will discover what you've done with the ember." As ceremoniously as he entered the room, Torin left, followed by the priesthood. Darius looked confused at what to do next, but eventually, he stood and followed, still not looking toward Malik or me.

It was a joke of a trial, anyway. I should have known the outcome. Torin had so much as told me that day he came to the interrogation chamber. I knew it was whatever residual youth I still carried that had given me any sliver of hope it might have gone differently. Malik happened to be at the wrong place at the wrong time, and I knew that it was his brother who caught him. And now he'd moved up the food chain to heir. *Convenient.*

It surprised me that Conall hadn't made an appearance as I scanned the room one last time before they took us away, back to our cells. That look between us at the ceremony had convinced me he was on my side, even after everything he had seen. There were times I thought he knew I wasn't his sister. But maybe I'd perceived it wrong the whole time. Maybe it was what I had wanted to believe.

CHAPTER NINE

SINCE I'D BEEN put back in my cell, I'd been pacing, trying to figure out how Malik and I were going to pull off an escape. The guards didn't need to rough us up, considering our death sentence. And someone would likely be sent to dose us before the execution so we couldn't retaliate. We only had a narrow window.

With access to my power, the doors to the cells wouldn't be a barrier. I knew the challenge would be making our way out of the maze beneath the keep without drawing attention to ourselves. My pacing was increasing my anxiety, so I decided not to waste the energy and sat on the cold stone, not choosing the pallet for the risk of falling asleep. I watched the sunlight slowly recede through the small window up high in the cell until it was gone.

Fortunately, no guard had come with that vial of red powder, so I decided I'd wait a few more hours, and if I did not get a sign from Malik by then, I would try to get through the cell door as quietly as I could.

Sitting, waiting on what would likely be my own death, turned out to be a very contemplative experience. I thought of Vera and the brief time I'd been able to spend with her before she died. After Torin and Lathrais made the final arrangements to acquire me, they took me to a remote cottage in the foothills of Eastdow where a dying Vera was being cared for. About eight months prior, she had developed an uncommon illness that broke down the body slowly. The healers eventually declared her untreatable. By the time they brought me to her, she was a shell. I remember seeing her large frame lying on the bed, skin draping her bones that muscle might have filled, alluding to the powerful warrior she would have been. When I first saw her, I just stared. I couldn't stop myself. Seeing a female my own age being slowly drawn under by death's grip made me see my own place in the realm much differently.

An older female had approached me, motioning for me to come sit beside her and Vera on the bed. Tears lined her eyes, but she also had a weighted resolve. I understood the Skyborne to be Elain, the Regent's wife, and Vera's mother, though she did not introduce herself. She was an image of what Vera might have become, sharing her beauty and the same robust frame, though fit and taut where Vera wasn't.

Reluctantly, I sat on the bed with them. "Vera, this is Nayla. Lathrais and your father have found her to help carry out your legacy, dearest."

There was a mixture of fear, regret, and appreciation in the girl's eyes. Her pale skin and gaunt cheekbones were in contrast to the fire in her sunken eyes. Meeting her gaze, I felt pity and intimidation all at once. "I'm not trying to take your place," I blurted out. Another situation Carina would have handled more gracefully.

"But you must," Vera replied as a single tear rolled down her cheek. She reached a hand out and took mine. "With fate, there is no escape."

I sat in my cell thinking of her words. Was my impending execution a fate I could not escape? And if that was true, would I handle death with the dignity Vera had? It was in that moment, my hand in hers, that I decided to fight. To train with everything I had, to fulfill the promise that she was born to, that fate took from her and gave to me.

With her in my mind, the dear friend she had become to me in those short months we had together, I made her another promise. What her father was now doing was a slap in the face to Lathrais, though misguided, and his own wife, but most of all his brave daughter Vera. It enraged me. Same as my own parent's betrayal had enraged me.

I now realized I had not finished her mission when I delivered that ember of power. I didn't know what I was going to do or how, but I would see this convoluted prophecy through. I had denied it, but I *knew* I was bound to the ember that day in the forest when it saved me from Darius's arrow and prevented Uden and his friends from killing me. I wasn't the *chosen one*, but it *had* chosen me. That ancient power chose me for whatever it wanted, and I knew I would not die today.

I spared one last moment to remember the day we laid Vera in the ground of the forest at the foot of an enormous tree. It was only me, Torin, Lady Elain, and Lathrais. Since Vera had been declared untreatable, they decided to bring her there to "heal" while they found me. Everything was cloaked in secrecy. Even Conall hadn't been told the truth because they feared he was still so early in his youth that he might slip up. So, I spent those months working with Lathrais and Vera to copy every detail about her. I matched her eyes first, then hair, face, and body. I managed her voice and the movements unique to her. I flipped my hair as she did; I turned the corner of my mouth in the mischievous way she did. I matched her intense stare. Everything had to be perfect. She had even shared important childhood memories and specific moments with Conall, so I'd not miss a beat. Lathrais took notes as she spoke while I absorbed.

We all shared her care in those last months, and I used my power to help ease her suffering as much as possible. One day, when I went to change the chamber pot that was arranged beneath her on her bed, I found blood in it. It wasn't the blood from her monthly bleeding. It mixed with urine, and I tried not to let her see.

She went downhill fast after that. Vera Tiernach faced death with a bravery I hadn't seen in another since, and it made me wish we had more time together. Her death was expected, but it still twisted my gut when Elain woke us up in the middle of the night, saying she had passed. We stood in the room with her gaunt body silently for hours after. The next day Lathrais treated her body, and we had a small ceremony placing her in the ground. An unmarked stone sat at the top of her gravesite so no one but the four of us would ever know.

Her parents returned to the keep after taking with them the story that Vera had made a turn toward recovery, and Lathrais was keeping her to be safe. I was still perfecting being able to use all the aesthetic shifts at the same time. I would get everything perfect and forget her blue eyes.

Lathrais would be exhausted, but I would press him to keep watching and guiding me. Eventually, we decided Vera was ready to return home.

⤚⤙

Clicking from the direction of the door roused me from my thoughts. Metal on metal, but soft and precise. Someone was picking the lock on the outside of my cell. My adrenaline was pumping now, and I couldn't prevent myself from pushing open the slots to see if I could determine who was outside my door. I couldn't see anything but the glow of a lantern near the lock, the figure hidden by the shadows.

Seconds crept on. Finally, a click. But they didn't open the door. I placed my trembling hand on the wood and gave a slight push. It moved. Quietly, I opened the door enough that I could squeeze out. The lantern came into view and was blinding my night vision.

"Malik?" I whispered, still unable to see a figure. The light floated on its own accord, no figure following. My eyes were adjusting. "Meethra?" I could now make out the delicate figure of the godfly in the light. "How?"

My promise. But no time. Quiet. She was speaking inside my mind again, and I could tell she was tired from working the pick in the lock. It must have been heavy for a being her size. I took it from her and followed her out the door.

The guards?

Sleeping. Her one-word reply was good enough.

We have to get Malik, I thought. She nodded her tiny head.

I wasn't exactly sure how after only two of the briefest conversations, he'd become my ally, but I sensed our paths were joined, and I wasn't about to let Torin and Darius get away with his murder. Besides, it was a good strategy to have a life debt in my favor with someone with the talents Malik possessed.

We crept down the dark hallway, passing a repeating pattern of closed cell doors until I picked up the light sound of pacing footsteps. I pinned my focus on scent, following the sound, detecting Malik's scent coming from the same direction.

I froze as footsteps approached from the direction we were headed.

Fancy seeing you here, a new voice sounded in my head.

| 73 |

Malik came into view, and his dark eyes hit me with their deep intensity.

Took you long enough. I grinned, suspecting he could still see in the shadowed corridor.

Looks like you beat me to it. I'm impressed. What do you say we get the hell out of here? His eyes twinkled as he smirked. How he could find humor while we were in such danger was beyond me, but it was contagious. He gave an imperceptible look at Meethra as if seeing a godfly was an everyday occurrence. She looked back and forth between us, not understanding.

Malik, I thought for her. He stared ahead as if he hadn't heard. I realized I couldn't speak silently to both of them at the same time. I guess it didn't work like that.

"Come on," Malik urged and led the way down the corridor. We took the second flight of stairs we came to, Malik confidently leading upward as if he had studied the layout of the keep, including its prison in preparation.

The door at the top of the stairs was locked from the outside. It was an extra precaution he must not have anticipated. The guard at the door was asleep, his snoring we could hear through the heavy wood, no doubt courtesy of Meethra.

"Meethra, do you have enough strength?" I lifted the lock pick toward her and pointed to the gap between the bottom of the door and the floor just wide enough I estimated she could squeeze through. I could see she was a little shaky.

"Your power?" She pointed her question at Malik.

"I could use it, but I fear it may draw too much attention this near the exit. I thought it would be better if—" But he was cut short as we heard a *click*. Startled, the three of us turned toward the opening door.

"It would be better if someone had the key?" a familiar voice finished.

Conall was now facing us, holding the key up before him. My stomach dropped. We hadn't spoken, much less seen each other, since the ceremony, and I didn't know what to expect. I knew I wouldn't hurt Conall if he stood in our way, but I couldn't predict Malik. "Conall?" was my only response. Malik was eyeing Meethra now for a clue.

"You didn't think I was going to allow him to execute you, did you?" Conall glanced between Meethra and the sleeping guard, who was covered in fine translucent dust. "Your work is impressive."

She twinkled at the compliment, and a blush I could barely make out in the dim light turned her pale skin pink. "They won't remember a thing." Her voice was feminine and soft. I realized I hadn't heard it out loud before. In the forest, we had only spoken with our thoughts.

I made a mental note to ask her about that later and looked at her raising an eyebrow before nodding to Conall. *Really?* I sent her a thought so only she would hear. I had trained myself to ignore Conall's handsomeness, knowing that in playing the role of his sister, he would always be off-limits. I had done such a good job I didn't even notice his good looks now.

"We need to go quickly so we can get out of the city while there's plenty of darkness left. And before they know we're gone. I have three horses prepared for us," Conall said.

"Us?" I asked, stunned.

"You aren't the only one that gets to have epic adventures anymore." He paused, deciding his next word carefully. "*Nayla.*" He was seeing what my name felt like on his tongue. Satisfied, he continued, "I'll be joining you this time." And he motioned for us to follow.

Conall led us through the maze of the keep, out a set of wooden doors in the building's rear. We were in the gardens I liked to frequent. Conall guided us past the ornamental hedges and flowering bushes and through the rows of tall crops that hid our presence from the guards in the keep to the wall that bordered it. There was a small shed I had never noticed before where three horses with loaded packs were tied to a hitching rail, waiting. The animals looked strong and swift. They must have been the best three horses in the city by the looks of them.

He pointed at the deepest black mount of the three females. "She's yours. I had Felicia pack your things. She said she'd take care of your plants."

"Conall," I pleaded. A mix of emotions in my voice. He hadn't come to see me in my cell, and he wasn't at the trial, so I thought I had misjudged how he'd responded that day at the ceremony. That he wanted nothing to do with me. Guilt ate at me.

"Later," was all he said and threw bundles at both Malik and me, pointing to the little shed. "You can't wear your prison clothes. Too recognizable. Change. *Quickly,*" he ordered.

I hurried into the shed, undoing the bundle Conall gave to me. My favorite black leather boots were inside, with riding pants and a tunic, all wrapped in a cloak with a large hood, all a deep midnight. I ditched my prison frock and slipped into my new attire. It felt good to be in pants and boots again. Surprisingly, it was all only a little loose, which once I'd recovered from the last month, I was confident I'd fill out. Felicia must have tailored it in secret.

When I exited the shed, I saw Malik had opted to change outside and was sorting through a collection of weapons Conall had neatly arranged leaning against the shed. Malik was contemplating deciding on the single pair of horn-handled elongated fighting knives when I pounced, beating him to them.

"I forgot you favor those." He winked at me in the starlight, selecting a mismatched curved pair instead, and gestured to a short sword. "Might as well load up." The three of us picked through the weapons, attaching as many as we deemed reasonable to ourselves. We all ended up looking like mini weapons racks. I laughed aloud at the thought, and Conall, reading my mind, attempted to suppress a smile as he shushed me and shook his head disapprovingly.

I surveyed the three of us. On our dark horses, we would seamlessly blend in with the night. Conall looked toward a gleaming Meethra. "You know where to meet us." She nodded and shot through the sky, her light fading in the atmosphere. It occurred to me that they had been working together this last month while I'd been in my cell. My questions would have to wait.

Conall mounted and nudged his horse forward. We followed suit, tracking the perimeter of the wall until we approached a pair of large doors on a little mound that looked discreetly like a root cellar. He dismounted, motioning for us to do the same. He and Malik got the doors opened, and I saw a sloping ramp that gave enough room for a riderless horse to be led under the ceiling of the tunnel. He motioned for Malik to go first.

"Fair enough," was all Malik said as he grabbed the reins of his mare and led her down the path into the dark. I knew Conall motioned me to follow. It took me a second, but I finally convinced the horse to follow me into the cramped, dark space and down the ramp that proved to be steeper than it looked. When I reached the bottom, Malik handed me his reins, and I found Conall's horse had followed obediently right behind. Within moments they had the large doors quietly closed behind them, and we were standing in pitch black. The ceiling had opened up a little, but not enough to ride.

"We need to travel a bit before we risk light if we do at all. It may not seem possible, but it can be seen glowing through the doors from the towers, and you never know who may be watching. It is best to place your left hand on the wall and follow it, holding your reins in your right. I'll let you know if it is safe to use a lantern," Conall directed us.

The horses didn't hesitate as we led them along with us. The deeper we went into the tunnel, the colder and damper it became, and I was grateful for the cloak. The wall was a smooth stone, and occasionally my hand would run across a trickle of water created from the condensation. We had been walking in silence for about an hour when Conall said, "Be still. Listen." We stopped, barely breathing, trying to pick up on what he heard. "Water. Do you hear it? We must be approaching the river."

"Yes, it is still miles away. How much longer does this passage go on?" Malik asked.

The sound of water was only faint when I was focused on using my power to enhance my hearing. Conall must have known to begin listening for it.

"It goes all the way to the river, but we probably have about another mile under here before we exit. There are four exits total. Three between here and the river, but the next one will leave us deep in the southern forest where we should be safe—enough. The other two exits spit you out nearer the river, and the land is more exposed."

"How did you know about this tunnel? And how many times have you been down here without me, Conall?" It wasn't fair, but I couldn't stop myself. I felt there was a looming secret he'd been keeping from me. I realized that must have been how I'd made him feel. More so. My offense must have come through in my tone because he responded defensively, "Only once, a few weeks ago. I heard the ancestors built an escape path from the keep, but no one ever spoke of it. I searched the grounds and found it. I had Felicia keep watch while Meethra and I explored it."

"Felicia saw Meethra's light. That's how you knew not to use lanterns."

"They wouldn't let me see you. Besides, it looked better if I showed no interest. No one paid any attention to my snooping around."

This far in the tunnel was so devoid of light that I couldn't see him when I glanced back, but I could feel his eyes focused in my direction. It was hard to judge how he was taking the conversation, but I could hear his guilt. These were the first words we'd spoken to each other since the truth of my identity came out.

He continued, "I heard about what they did to you. I'm sorry. I couldn't—" He trailed off and was quiet for a long while before he continued. "Felicia wanted me to tell you she knew. That when you first arrived, sometimes she'd catch you. When you'd fallen deeply asleep, you'd drop a shift and shift a small feature back. But once she came into your room, and it was your dark hair on Vera's body, that's when she knew. So, she protected your secret after that. She realized Vera must have died, and my parents, the Regent, and his wife were doing what they had to do for their territory, their citizens. But when you were sentenced to take the fall for their mistakes after everything you'd been through and given up, she couldn't take it. She came to me immediately and told me she knew. She wanted to help you."

Deep down in a forgotten tunnel, the realm stood still for a moment. I must have stopped walking because Malik broke the silence. "We should keep moving." So, we did.

After another twenty minutes or so, the feeling of the ground we were walking on changed. Previously the stones had been so smooth they were almost slick, but here it was gritty like sand had been spread across them. Conall halted us, "the exit should be near here. The sand, I put it down so I'd know when to start looking for the break in the wall." I could hear him moving around up and down the tunnel as we waited.

"Here," he called from a little ahead of us. We walked toward his voice, his horse following. Again, Malik handed me his reigns, and they went to open the door. The sun must have been making its ascent because I could see a tiny sliver of light make its way through the cracked door. My eyes adjusted, and I could see Conall and Malik peering through the opening, surveying the surroundings. They must have deemed it safe because they opened the door, and my eyes were momentarily dazed by the morning light flooding in. We lead the horses up the ramp and out of the tunnel, securing the door behind us.

"Are you both comfortable to go a little longer? We can ride, and there's breakfast in the saddlebags. I'd like to get a distance away from the tunnel as a precaution."

I gave no thought to my hunger or need for urination, but since Conall had mentioned it, both urges surged to the forefront.

"Yes, and yes, I've got to pee." I pressed my horse's reins into Malik's hand and ran off behind a tree.

When I came back, they were both smiling at me, "better?"

"Much. You guys have it so lucky that you can just whip it out wherever." I rolled my eyes at them. They must have already satisfied their needs, I figured. Conall was combing his eyes through the surrounding forest. "Meethra is supposed to meet us here or near here, anyway."

"I have a feeling she'll find us when she's ready."

CHAPTER TEN

AFTER WALKING ALL night, it was nice to ride in the saddle for what little rest it afforded. Though several hours later, my lower half was aching from adjusting to it. At first, moving through the forest was painfully slow due to the dense patches of thorned bushes that seemed to pop up around every turn. Each time we'd encounter one, it appeared to stretch on endlessly, leading us out of the way as we rode around it.

With the more ground we covered, the trees changed from thick-trunked specimens with broad-fingered leaves to elegant tall pillars with sharp needles protruding from their branches. The needles created a bed on the forest floor that hushed any sound our passing made. I could feel our elevation begin to rise, and we encountered numerous streams and creeks meandering their way through the forest.

At a place where two small streams met, I realized I recognized the land we were traveling through. The forest sounds coming from the trees creaking in the wind and birds and insects brought me back to that little cottage where Vera had spent her final days.

"Conall, I think I know where we are." I broke the silence that stretched on for miles. "There's a cottage, only a day and a half's ride from here. We could make it there before nightfall tomorrow. It will be a good place to regroup for a day or two and devise a plan. I believe it was abandoned after—" I hesitated. I didn't quite know how to say why it had been abandoned to Conall. "I went there when Torin and Lathrais first brought me here. It's where I began my training."

Conall eased his horse beside mine as the three of us stopped to consider. He looked at me, understanding showing in his eyes. "Is this where she's buried?" he asked. Conall's ability to get right to the point was a character trait I always admired, but I wasn't entirely prepared for it. We looked at each other for a long moment. His eyes were glassy, and the eye contacted seemed painful for him, though he forced himself to hold it. I saw he needed me to match his frankness at that moment. "Yes, I can show you where she is if you think we have time."

He nodded, looking away. "Lead us to the cottage, Nayla. We will make our plans from there."

"You're confident it's safe? They won't think to search it?" It was the first Malik has spoken since we exited the tunnel.

"I believe the depth of Torin's denial has pressed its existence out of his mind entirely. Darius has no reason to know of it either. Unless it has been taken over by someone who had stumbled upon it, which seems unlikely, I imagine it should be safe enough. From there, I can lead us to the border of Arborvale. The best strategy may be to hug the Swath in case we need to escape into it." They both looked at me, disbelieving.

"Let's just get to the cottage. We can discuss it tomorrow." Conall exhaled wearily as he made the decision.

✦

We reached a good place to stop for the night. Malik left Conall and me to set up a little camp while he went in search of some light game to sate our groaning bellies.

When Conall and I were alone, I cornered him. "You're mad. Don't lie to me, I can tell."

"So, what if I am?" he asked. His shoulders were slumped, defeated.

"Well, on one hand, I understand. On the other hand, it's not fair because you *know* I couldn't tell anyone. Believe me, it was a burden to me more than you realize."

"Obviously." He flung a steel box at me, and I narrowly plucked it out of the air. "Here, I figured you missed each other." It was the ember.

"Holy shit!" I hadn't even thought to ask if we carried it with us or ask where it had gone. I wondered if Malik had either.

I looked at Conall again as I slipped the ember into my inner breast pocket. He was pissed alright. Nothing so deep a little exercise wouldn't help ease, I sensed. "Are you going to tell me how you got that or am I going to have to beat it out of you?" It might not have been fair, but I was desperate for things to get back to normal between us, though I was unsure if they ever could.

He huffed an angry laugh and motioned to our blades, "I think kicking your ass will make me feel a lot better, if you don't mind."

"As you wish," I said, grabbing the two blades I had selected with shaking hands and took a left-hand fighting stance.

He raised an eyebrow at me, "What are you doing, trying to make it easy for me? Feel that guilty, do you?" He was practically snarling.

I laughed. "Vera was right-handed *brother*," I taunted, testing the water, "but I'm ambidextrous."

And with that, I lunged. I respected his right to be pissed. I was pissed too. At everything, fate, our parents, Darius, and even Conall for never making me tell him the truth. I had spent ten years living a lie when for most of it my best friend had all but known. For the next hour straight, we went blow for blow, becoming bruised and bloodied with little nicks and scrapes. Nothing permanent. Just enough to express ourselves sufficiently.

I saw an opening where he had gone back to old habits, fighting Vera right-handed, and I swung the side of my blade lightly smacking his fingers against the pommel of his sword which he promptly dropped shaking his hand. Taking advantage of his distraction, I swiped a kick behind his legs sending him on his ass and I tackled him to the ground. I had dropped my blades and had the collars of his tunic in a death grip before I realized what I was doing.

"When did you figure it out?" I pressed him, voice trembling. His face was blank in response to me. A little pale, even. "Makers be damned, Conall, fucking tell me!" I was shaking him, tears freely flowing off of my face onto his. In ten, no, fifteen years, I couldn't remember ever crying once. The floodgate had opened. I couldn't stop myself and he was staring up at me as shocked as I was. I felt his hands circle my waist.

"It's okay, it's okay," he urged as he stroked my back.

I met his eyes and sobbed, "It's not okay. None of this has been okay. It all fucked up." I wasn't vain, but I knew my face had to be hideous. That only caused more sobbing. He moved his hands, pulling me toward his chest, and I let him. He wrapped his powerful arms around me as I cried into his chest.

I don't know how much time had passed when I heard Malik grunt to alert us of his presence. I couldn't imagine what we must have looked like to him, weapons lying around, scraped up, me straddling Conall, crying into his chest. I reluctantly sat up, embarrassed.

Malik came over to help me up, grabbing me under my arms. "You guys were supposed to be setting up camp." He was shaking his head, "I've never had a sister," he said wistfully, and left it at that. He had been successful hunting I saw as he went to retrieve the rabbits he had collected. Conall cleaned up the mess we'd made in our little campsite and came over to join Malik and I preparing the rabbits for dinner.

Conall broke the silence. "After my mother died, I knew she had taken her own life. She was never right after she came back and told us Vera had been cured and was healing. I was young, but not stupid, Nayla." He was only now getting comfortable saying my name. "I knew having lost her daughter and being forced to lie to her son must have weighed on her terribly. And the Regent became more distant with her, I think. So, she had no comfort. Only her pain and her duty."

I had seen the unending sadness in her eyes, which had been telling the day of my adulthood ceremony. "That is when you stopped obeying Torin. And he must have known too, because he let you get away with it." I said, drawing my own connections.

"Vera and I had spent almost every day of our childhoods together. I thought she seemed different, but I chalked it up to her changing from the illness. It was what I had wanted to believe. One day I even saw you slip up with the eye color. I convinced myself it was my imagination, but

I think I knew. When I saw you look up at me with those eyes that day at the ceremony I couldn't move or think."

Conall and I told Malik our parts of the story. He listened. Talking about it, saying it all out loud lessened the burden. I could see it was true for Conall too. As I came to a part in the story that was obviously upsetting me, Malik reached a hand out to place it on my arm sympathetically. I flinched.

I hated myself for that uncontrolled reaction, that weakness. When I looked at Malik, it made me think too much of Darius. I saw the hurt in Malik's eyes. Our understanding of each other had changed since we'd met in Drakestone. It bordered on a budding friendship, so he couldn't make sense of my reaction. He moved his hand away.

I don't know why I was making this choice now, but I steeled myself, "I need to tell you guys something, and I don't want you to freak out. And you can never tell anyone. Swear it?"

"How can you say that and expect us not to react?" Conall asked.

"True," Malik said, "but we'll try." He looked at Conall narrowing his eyes.

I took a deep breath. Today was already emotionally brutal, so what was another admission. I refused to let what Darius had done to me steal the comfort the touch of a friend's hand brought.

"When I was in the prison, Darius came to visit me. In the middle of the night. He was so drunk. They had kept me shackled to the wall until I had passed out, and I woke in my cell with my head in his lap. He was... *cradling me.*"

Realization of what I didn't need to say shown in both of their eyes. "He didn't?" Conall couldn't complete the thought. Malik was speechless. I felt ill, bile rising in my throat.

I nodded my head, but I needed to say it. "Almost," I forced out. My voice shook with the admission. I would have cried, but I was out of tears. I didn't know why I told them. "I think it's what he intended. But someone came to the door, and he stopped. Then he just held me and cried. It was my fault, though. I was so stupid. I should have never—"

Malik cut me off, "It wasn't your fault Nayla, you cannot blame yourself."

"But if I had focused on the ember, my task and not got involved, but something about him had drawn me in. I was naïve to think…"

"Stop it, Nayla, you cannot do this to yourself. You may not believe us now, but you in no way deserved or caused what he did to you." I could see Conall's fists clenched tight, shaking with rage.

"He seemed so gentle when I'd been with him in Drakestone. I keep asking myself how I could have connected with a Skyborne who could do something like that."

Malik shook his head, running his hands through his dark hair. "A bit of a mad streak is known to run the Dsiban line. You only saw one side of Darius. The side he'd wanted you to see." Malik's voice was calm, but he was as white knuckled as Conall.

My companions were respecting my wishes and suppressing their emotions, though I could see their anger welling nearing its breaking point. A barely perceptible energy throbbed off of Malik in pulsing waves. Outwardly his eyes narrowed, grimacing.

"I *will* kill him," Conall growled through gritted teeth.

I picked up my knife, twirling it, and stabbed the dirt. I was calm as death. "Not if I get to him first."

❦

I spotted a dim light high up in the sky as it became brighter and brighter. I pointed to where I was looking, "Meethra!" She landed on a large rock near where we were sitting as the sun receded.

"You're safe, I see! I'm so glad. That Skyborne from the trial, Darius, and some others, I couldn't see how many, went in search of you. The energy at the keep was frantic after they discovered that you'd escaped. The Regent," she looked at Conall, "when they told him you'd helped, he became loud and enraged. He is a very unpleasant Skyborne." Her look was sympathetic. She spent the next half hour telling us the details of what she'd seen. Finally, she asked, "Where do you go next?"

Conall told her about the cottage. "What about you? Will you go with us?"

"I believe our paths align, but I have to believe I am not the only one of my kind here in this realm who survived. I must search for them. I am hopeful to find them. I've heard whispers of their energy since I left the Swath." Her voice was so bright with hope. "When I locate them, I will find you and we will join you."

She zipped out of sight eagerly before we could respond. Malik, face filled with contemplation, looked like he'd been about to say something to her. "Malik?" I asked.

Malik glanced sideways; face hardened in concentration. I felt an invisible wave of energy pulse out from him into the realm. "I called her back. I don't think she is going to like what she finds."

CHAPTER ELEVEN

THE SUN WAS setting as we arrived at the mountain cottage. It was overgrown as if it had sat untouched for the ten long years since Lathrais and I had finally left it. What had once been decorative vines with bright green arrow-shaped leaves climbing neat trellises now covered most of the cottage's weather white stones. Several of the windows were nailed shut, but one stood ajar. The door looked clear, though. Malik raised a hand to halt us. He looked toward the little building, and I could feel a shimmer of energy licking across the ground into the open window. He seemed to test it, tasting the stream of energy with his mind. "Empty," was all he said.

Weeds and wild grasses clogged the little courtyard, and Malik led the way, hacking down a path with one of the curved blades he collected. We approached the front door. Locked. I pulled out the pick I had stashed in a pocket and, in a moment, had the lock open. The air in the little house was stale, and a thick layer of dust covered everything. Malik entered the house with me while Conall said something about seeing to the horses and plodded away.

I must have appeared annoyed with Conall because Malik squeezed a gentle hand on my shoulder. "Don't be too hard on him. You and I have had much longer to adjust to this, to *you*." I knew his intention was comforting, but I couldn't help but feel my skin burn where he had touched my shoulder, even after what I had confessed to them. "I hate this strain between us. I miss him, you know?" I was speaking more to myself than to Malik, but he indicated his comprehension.

Malik and I went through the cottage, making an assessment of any useful items we found. We shook out linens and placed them on beds in the three rooms and started a pile on the table in the primary room of our inventory by the time Conall came in. His face was red, but there were no signs of tears. He was carrying our packs and set them by a smaller table in the sitting area.

"Do you want me to show you—" I offered before he cut me off.

"It doesn't matter, Nayla. We are here now because it is convenient. Besides, she and I had never been close, not like you and I were. When she came back, I thought maybe she had changed, or it was our age, that we had bonded more."

Were, he said. I felt the sting of the word and did my best to heed Malik's words and ignore it. I knew it wasn't easy. It wasn't easy for any of us, but Malik and I had no choice in the matter. Conall had chosen to abandon everything he knew, every plan he had, and come with us to save me and help us uncover what to do with the ember. Even after yesterday, he needed time. Wordlessly, I went to get the supply packs and sort through the food Felicia packed. I was starving, and I knew feeding us would ease much of the tension.

Malik took his pack to his room, pointing to the two others directing Conall to deposit our things. When they came back, I brought in a bucket of water from the well and rinsed some dusty dinnerware. I took some small pleasure in laying out the assorted herbed flatbreads, dried fruits, and cheeses that were packed for us. I was staring at the spread as my companions entered the room and smiled at my display. "Sweet Makers!" I exclaimed as I remembered the surprise I hoped was still there. I knew I alarmed them, but I didn't care as I rushed outside and around back to the root cellar.

I was so excited I fumbled hopelessly with the lock. Giving up, I reached for the pulsing energy in my veins, partially to see if it still existed, but mostly out of impatience. I held the lock in my hand and released a sliver of energy into it, connecting with its own. The edges of the metal lock shimmered in space, and I squeezed. There was a loud pop, and it cracked under the pressure of my fist before it disintegrated in shards in my palm.

Conall and Malik followed me in my haste outside to see what caused me to start. Malik was standing there, looking at the metal fragments in my hand. I cockily tilted my head toward him, shrugging as if it had been no big deal.

The cellar door was heavy, but I managed it, shooing them back. I entered the darkness of the cellar, going in deep. I used the common power to find a small lantern and light the space, but not until I was deep enough so they wouldn't see what I was searching for.

"Score!" I yelled, giddy. I set the lantern down and put a bottle under one arm, and took two with my free hands. I let the light extinguish as I walked away into the ebbing daylight of the entrance. Conall's smile was immediate as he realized what I carried. The first bottle I extended to him, a peace offering of sorts. "One for you." He took it, shaking his head in disbelief. "And one for you," handing the second one to Malik. I held up the third, "And one for me."

They both laughed at that. "Please tell me you didn't lead us all the way to his overgrown cottage just for wine?" Malik grumbled.

"I bet that is exactly what she did," Conall chimed in.

"Oh, don't be such spoiled sports. Lathrais kept the best vintages when we were here. You both appreciate me when your belly is filled with its warmth in about an hour."

⸎

As predicted an hour later, after a healthy debate on the safety of drinking while being hunted, we were each of us a glass or two in. The tension was decidedly relaxed.

"How long do you think we can stay here?" I asked.

"Probably need another night here, then we should be off." I must have looked disappointed because Conall continued, "There's *that* much wine down there?"

"We don't even know where we're going or what we're doing, for that matter." The mood became more serious at my questioning.

"I think the wisest course of action is to take this opportunity tonight to rest and enjoy the rest of this fine vintage." Malik raised a glass. "We are owed a little pleasure from the Makers, after all. Hopefully, Meethra will come back by tomorrow. I'll fill you in on what I know, and we can decide the best course of action and make our preparations for an early departure the following day." Contemplative silence hung for long moments when he finished his thought. I was beginning to appreciate Malik as the voice of reason in our little band of escapees.

≼

His third glass was well in effect when Conall said, "Show me. Nayla, show me how you do it." Malik tensed as I studied Conall, searching his face for his intention. This could go either way, but I knew if I was going to rebuild what was broken, I had to trust him and his intent.

"Okay, I will. I don't think I can show you how to do it, but I can show you how I do it. What do you want to see?"

Malik eased. "How about something benign? What did you say your attendant's name was? Felicity?"

"Felicia," Conall replied. "No, not her. Torin. Become *my* father."

I nodded, inhaling deeply. Since I dropped the shift of Vera, I hadn't taken another appearance. It was a month of living and sleeping in my own skin. I became so accustomed to it I didn't realize what a constant drain it was to keep the appearance of another continuously. Closing my eyes, I put Torin's face in my mind, his body, his hands, his unfeeling steely eyes. Conall quietly gasped and saw my outline blur before he saw Torin sitting across from him.

"You look real. You are him. I knew you did Vera, but can you do anyone? Could you do—me?" He reached a hand across the table and touched my face and the beard I knew I now wore. "It feels real."

"Well, it is real, in a way, I suppose. And yes, I can do you, though I'd prefer not to if it's all the same to you."

"Agreed, this is weird enough for one night." Malik reinforced my hesitation.

"You used other's bodies when you infiltrated Drakestone?"

Conall had never seen me change, but he now understood how I'd gotten away with stealing the ember. I mastered it before Lathrais brought me back to Eastdow. Before I met Conall. "Not their actual bodies. They still existed. I just appeared to be them. And, yes, all the time. I became whoever I needed to be in the moment. When Vera was in her guestroom sleeping or reading, when I knew no one would come looking for her, I would sneak out as someone else to search. Mostly, I chose keep workers who would likely go unnoticed in the hallways. Especially at night. It is a useful tool."

I shrugged, knowing I made it sound nonchalant, which to him it was anything but that. It was how I saw it, though. It was how I saw all power, useful, yes, but only a tool. The object in my pocket buzzed in discordance.

I dropped the shift, and Torin's image faded in a blur until I once again sat with them. I drained the last of my glass. It was full-bodied, dry and subtly burned as it warmed me. "I'm going to bed. I'll see you two in the morning," I said as I padded off toward the room they had put my things in, looking forward to the rest I was soon to get.

The beds in the cottage weren't anything fancy like what we had at the keep in Eastdow, but compared to the pallet of hay that had been my bed for the last few weeks, they were a dream. I tugged off my boots and outerwear and was out as soon as my head hit the pillow.

Sleep that night was a confusion, my imagination loosened in part by the wine and in part by the ember I carried in my breast pocket even as I slept. Before, when I had carried the object, it was the same with the dreams. It was like the ember was imparting its own visions into my dreamscape. Inescapable dreams would flood in.

In my lucidness, I would see a white glowing orb, similar to the darkness of the ember, hovering on a simple sandstone pedestal and a Skyborne sitting in front of it on the ground, legs crossed and eyes closed. Guarding it or praying to it, I couldn't tell. I was being drawn to the light of the object. A few soundless steps so the Skyborne wouldn't sense my presence, and I was reaching for the energy on the pedestal. The mirror opposite of the ember I carried. But right before I'd touch it, the Skyborne's icy blue eyes would snap open, sending dread down my spine, and I'd wake, gasping. I could never see the Skyborne's face clearly, or I couldn't remember it, but his shining blue eyes... I could still see every detail of them.

Tonight, I stood in darkness before a large opening in the ground. A portal, it seemed. Darkness blurred and hummed around its edges. As I walked closer to it, the humming intensified, linking itself to the rhythm of my breathing. The passageway looked and behaved like the ember. When I reached the precipice, I knelt before it and cautiously reached my outstretched hand down into the pulsing darkness. It didn't feel like anything. I expected to feel a vibration at the edges of the hole, or like how my power felt in my veins, but it was a void. I leaned my body toward it, pressing my face into the darkness.

Slowly, my eyes adjusted to a familiar scene. In the distance, I saw the Skyborne sitting, but this time I was behind him, and he was between me and the white pulsing object. Before I realized what was happening, its pull nudged me forward enough I'd lost balance, and my hands slipped. I tried to throw myself back to regain my balance, but it was too late. I was falling faster and faster. I couldn't see the Skyborne anymore, only nothingness all around me. My stomach was in my throat as I fell and fell, still gaining speed as I careened down an endless dark tunnel.

I shot up in bed with a breathless scream in my lungs, cold sweat making my undershirt cling to my skin. Conall's broad frame was standing over me, staring. I reached for him, but my hand went right through him. He wasn't there. I must have fallen back asleep. Or was I awake? I couldn't tell.

I frantically looked around, taking in the space. One moment, I was in the bed in the cottage, the next... I felt the surface I was lying on. Hay. *Click*, I heard the door to my cell open—a soft creak, then footsteps. And I knew whose too. I could hear his breathing, feel it almost in the cramped space of the cell. His familiar scent, the one I had clung to my hair after the nights we'd been together in Drakestone, filled my nostrils. Instead of the clenching heat I'd felt between my thighs before, I felt a stiff dread. Panicking, I thrashed, trying to rise, so I could defend myself this time, but some invisible force was holding me down. Darius stood over my restrained body and laughed as he reached his hands toward me.

I felt hands on my shoulders, shaking me almost violently. *Nayla,*

Nayla, a voice, *no* two voices in the distance called. The voices pulled me from the sticky terror I was submerged in. I awoke again, lying still, panting, willing myself not to fall back asleep. The hands at my shoulders helped me into a seated position as a soft light filled the room. Conall was sitting on the bed next to me. *Real now,* I thought as I brushed my fingertips across the firm hand still gripping my shoulder. I touched the hand on my other side. Malik was seated on the other side of the bed. Both of their eyes were wide with questions.

The wind howled outside, and the chill of the night flowed in through a draft in the vacant fireplace. The light blanket I now pulled up around my knees was not enough to calm the trembling caused by the cool air on my damp skin and also the residual nerves from my dreams. When I passed out, I hadn't bothered using my power to warm the room. I forgot how brisk nights could be up here.

Conall followed my gaze toward the fireplace and lifted a hand, and a dancing flame took seat in the hearth, the yellows and golds twisting and growing, devouring the crisp air from the draft. The balmy heat it produced radiated toward me, comforting tendrils of warmth hugging me soothingly. "You don't have to do that, you know," I said, looking from Conall to his hand.

"I know, but I like to. It makes me feel more... *powerful.*" His grin turned serious. "You were screaming. Are you okay?" he asked tentatively.

"You sounded as if someone was murdering you. I've never heard a scream like that, Nayla. It chilled my blood," Malik echoed.

Conall now had my hand in a death grip as he spoke. "I've never heard you make so much as a sound while you slept. I mean, besides that one time, you got really drunk and started snoring."

"Shut up." I smiled, trying to jerk my hand away to punch him, but he held it firm. Faint dawn light was slowly creeping in through a small crack in the wood of the closed window. I sighed, frustrated that sleep hadn't come as restfully as I'd hoped. "I think it's the ember, maybe. When I carry it," I patted the pocket of my undershirt, "my dreams are more vivid. Lucid, even. I think I see some other realm that's real. It's really strange. I don't know if it's sending me images on purpose," it subtly pulsed in my pocket, "or if its power is strong enough that being so near it my own power is more active. Like just then, I swear it responded to sending me images. And it's done that on other occasions like it has an opinion on things." I surveyed them to see if they thought I was as crazy as I thought I sounded.

"Maybe another night's rest is all you need. And less wine," Conall said.

So Conall thought I was crazy.

I looked to Malik, pleading. "I think it could be possible. The way it reacted that day during the ceremony. It did not want that high priest to touch it. My power could feel it," he paused, searching for the word, "*protest*. Since you took it, it has definitely been more active. While my family kept it, I don't ever remember it being animated like that."

"Did you see it often?" Conall asked.

"No, but I was curious, I'll admit. I did look in on it occasionally. And our priests didn't have a better grasp of it than yours." Malik turned to me. "You think it's sending you images? What kind of images?"

I wasn't going to tell them about my nightmare about Darius. Those dreams were coming from my own demons, and not the ember, anyway. So, I told them about the recurring one, the Skyborne, the portal, and the sphere of light that was the ember's mirror. And how I fell and fell this time. My companions listened and tried to understand. Conall was still skeptical about the ember sending the images, but Malik was evaluating in his quiet, contemplative way.

"It could be trying to lead you somewhere or show you how to use it?" he puzzled.

"I think it wants me to find that Skyborne. He is in every dream."

"I don't know, Nayla. It killed Lathrais, and it's sending you dreams that end with you waking with unholy screaming. Are we sure it isn't a sinister force? I mean, it is a bottomless *darkness*. Maybe the male wants its power and is sending you those images to lure you to him. And if it would let you use it, to what end? We know nothing about it, and our best seers don't really have a clue either. We don't even know where we're going next." Frustration was ripe in Conall's tone.

"First," Malik's tone was authoritative as he spoke, "there must be some truth to be sorted out from all the prophesies. Each territory seems to have a different version, but they all have a similar thread. All of them end up with, in the most basic terms, an individual using the ember to create a portal to bring us back to Idia. Whatever penance that sent our kind here is over, and the way back is accessible now, granted through the remnant of the force that sent us here, the ember. So, I don't think it can be a coincidence that some of us are able to sense and wield more power right when the ember has become more active. Not to mention that Nayla has all but used it with no ill effect."

Malik's jaw was firm, resolute. He was by far the most serious one in our group.

"And second?" Conall asked.

"Second, I have friends in Seabrook who will help us. Before Darius found me, I had gotten a letter off to Seeley, the Regent Femi's son, informing them of what had taken place at the ceremony. He will expect us."

"How did you know I'd come with you? I practically thought we were on opposite sides." I trailed off.

"What?" he rebuffed, clearly annoyed, "Of good and evil? Everything is not so black and white as you think. There's darkness and light in everything. And I saw you, Nayla. I saw your shift for what it was the day we met in Drakestone. I've already told you as much."

I remembered, then, his inquisitive look when he bowed at our introduction. "Why didn't you reveal me?"

"I can feel things that are hidden. I sensed you were hidden beneath her. I didn't reveal you because I wanted to let fate play out, among other reasons I've already told you. Besides, where would the intrigue be if I went around exposing everything I knew? Besides, I had a feeling we'd end up on the same path, eventually. When Lathrais was dead, and I saw them look toward you, I left to send the letter. I hadn't expected to run into Darius after on my way to collect you."

That explained where Darius had slinked off to after the ceremony, I thought. "And Conall, in all the chaos, you stole the ember. And here we are."

"Right. So here we are," Conall repeated. "I don't have a better plan. I got us this far. What about your family, Nayla?"

"I haven't seen them in almost ten years. The day they sent me away, sold me to Torin and Lathrais, for all I know, so I'd rather not waste another thought on them. I believe both my parents and my three younger sisters are still alive, but I don't think we'd be welcome. They'd likely sell us back to Torin."

Conall nodded, looking toward Malik. "We will go to Seabrook to seek shelter from your allies there."

I inclined my head in agreement. I knew it took Conall a great deal of faith to trust Malik, considering their territories had been adversarial ever since Drakestone had failed to release the ember at the end of its guardianship. We were all performing an exercise in trust with our fledgling alliance.

"Do you guys realize we're all former heirs to territories?" I asked with amusement. Conall looked deflated, though good-humored enough about it.

"How much wine did you say was down there? We may need it after all." It was Malik's turn for humor. "Well, there's no sense sleeping more. Conall, you didn't happen to pack a map, did you?"

"Obviously," Conall huffed.

"How fortuitous," Malik roguishly replied.

"I did spring you two from prison, if you recall."

I hoped the mild bickering was not the start of a new dimension of their relationship. "Enough, get out of my room. I need to freshen up, and your voices are grating on me." I feigned irritation expertly.

"So charming," Malik winked as he left my bedroom.

Conall lingered for a moment. "You *are* okay?"

"I'm okay. They're just dreams." I squeezed his hand. I realized he hadn't released mine during our entire conversation.

⁂

It took me about an hour to sort through the items in my pack and get presentable for the day. Conall had knocked on my door a little after he'd left and given me a warm bucket of water to clean myself with, so I was feeling more alive and prepared to think.

When I joined them, Conall was cooking eggs over a fire produced by his flames. "Where did you find those?" I asked as I noticed the godfly had returned and was perched on a shelf *very* near Conall. I smiled at her in greeting. She returned the smile, though half-heartedly. A nervous reservation gleamed in her tiny eyes as she warily watched Malik.

I gestured to the fresh eggs, and Conall pointed the wooden spoon to Malik, who was hunched over the map Conall had brought. They had a string positioned in what I assumed was the proposed path.

"How does your power work, Malik? Is it how you found the eggs?" I studied him with a level gaze.

"Yes, there were some waterfowl nesting near." He hesitated, rubbing his eyes. "Do you really expect I'll tell you all my secrets?"

"Trust goes both ways, Malik." I locked eyes with him urging him on.

Malik sighed, relenting. "Same as yours, I suppose. I sense the energy in things, like a woven vibrating tapestry covering everything. And I can focus or send my attention in a specific direction and feel its essence. Or I can fade my essence, so I'm more difficult to detect. I'm sure you can imagine the advantage that has when trying to collect information."

"Spy, you mean?" Conall interjected bluntly.

"Yes, if you *must* put it that way," Malik huffed. "In a basic way, it's the same thing you do when you warm a room. Skyborne do the things we refer to as the Common Power as a natural-born instinct, so we think nothing more of it. Anything more difficult, those of us who can, learn it. Isn't that what you do, Nayla?"

"I guess so. I'd never thought of it that way." I thought of how I'd known how to crush the lock last night. "I could feel the lock's make-up and knew how to change it so it would be weakened enough to collapse under the pressure of my clenched fist. And when I move things, I feel what their make-up is and use that to compel them toward or away from other nearby objects. That took a lot of practice at first since you kind of have to think backward depending on the direction you want the object to go, but now I can do it without thinking. But changing my appearance was simpler than that, though. Instinct as you said."

"We see essences," the godfly interjected. She directed her attention at me, "When you were the blond-haired girl, then with your dark hair, I saw you as the same essence. The same way you see each other in different clothes. I feel the essence of the trees, the rivers. Anything that has energy, really."

"Interesting," I said. "I had been led to believe my extra skills were unique, but if you have them, and if Darius is more powerful than you—"

Malik sneered, "Darius is very proficient at using the common power, so he leads everyone to believe he has more. Yes, he's faster and stronger. All that. He's nothing special."

Conall cleared his throat, looking at him.

Malik chuckled, holding up his hands in deference. "No offense intended, Conall."

"Malik and I have an idea of how we'd like to travel to Seabrook," Conall said, changing the subject as he handed me a plate with a portion of eggs and a piece of bread. I stuffed a bite into my mouth as I turned to study the map. They had it laid out for us to stay on this side of the river and hug the coast. I didn't like it.

I shook my head at the map. Meethra flew from her perch and landed on the table atop the map. With a mouthful, I said, "No, no, inside, we should hug the forest. I told you guys."

"Ever the lady. We have all day, Nayla. Feel free to swallow." Malik pressed his lips into a smirk. I would have stuck my tongue out at him, but I elected not to gross him out further. "Did you make friends while you were in the Swath?"

"Not friends exactly, but I did gain the acquaintance of its inhabitants and they with my shields. Crossing the river undetected will present the biggest challenge, but I think not only is the distance less to Seabrook if we take that route, but we also can seek the cover of the forest if needed. I think if I conserve my power, I can shield all four of us."

"Okay," Malik mouthed as if not entirely confident.

"She shielded herself and Meethra for days when she was exhausted." Conall jumped in, defending me.

"Not for days, but yes, it should be doable."

"She didn't shield herself exactly," Malik clarified. "It seems the ember interceded on her behalf. I determined that the morning of the ceremony during our little chat."

Conall was incredulous. "Excuse me?!" He looked back and forth between Malik and I.

"He was in my bed when I woke up," I blurted out. That didn't make it sound better. Malik grinned salaciously. I rolled my eyes.

"He was in *your bed*? Do you realize the danger you were putting her in if someone would have caught you?" Conall demanded.

Malik looked Conall dead in the eyes, "Jealous?"

I squinted, furrowing my brow at him, half amused despite myself and half pissed he was taunting Conall. Beside me, Conall vibrated, patience ebbing. I held Malik's stare, raising an eyebrow, "That's enough, Malik."

Malik threw his hands in the air, exasperated, "No fun, you two." He turned toward Conall, "You're going to have to learn to trust me at some point. Besides, it's a poor use of time trying to find all of my character flaws. It will take you too long."

I couldn't help but smile, though I knew Conall was still struggling to trust him. Malik's little jabs weren't helping. His self-deprecation was a good gesture and also revealing of his own low opinion of himself. I not only had come to like Malik, I think I was beginning to trust him too.

I moved to his side of the table and stroked Malik's back gently, "There, there, not to worry, little one. Conall will learn to trust you, won't you, Conall?" Conall howled at that, and Malik shook his head, trying his best to suppress a grin.

It only took me and the godfly, who'd sided with me, a few more hours of rigorous debate to convince them the forest's edge was the safest bet. We wouldn't have the protection of the Covenant between the territories now since we were confirmed fugitives. And no one in their right mind would enter the forest. So that is where we would go.

CHAPTER TWELVE

THAT AFTERNOON WE took a much-needed break. Conall reluctantly approached me and asked that I take him to his sister's grave. It was likely the only time we'd be here, so I was glad he did. After everything that had happened, visiting the girl whose image I'd worn for years would be cathartic.

I led him up a long-overgrown path behind the cottage that led up into the trees. It took me longer than I'd expected, but eventually, I found the tree with a uniquely gnarled trunk we'd buried her underneath. I cleared the grass and weeds off of the smooth river rock that we'd made her headstone and looked back at Conall. We hadn't spoken as we'd walked there.

"You got to spend time with her before she died?" he asked, staring at the ground.

"Yes." I didn't know what else to say.

"Did you like her?" His voice trembled as he spoke.

It made my heart ache for him that his family had kept this from him. Had not trusted him to be able to keep this secret. I kneeled down at the foot of the little mound, and he came to sit beside me. I reached for his hand and answered him.

"Yes, I did like her. Very much. I admired her strength. And I promised her I would carry out her task. It is often what kept me going."

I angled my head to look at him. Tears were running smoothly down his face. I watched him, waiting for him to speak.

"I know I was young, but I wish they would have trusted me. I keep thinking, I've done everything that has ever been asked of me. I've never balked at the position I was born into. I don't know what it was about me that made them not believe I could keep this secret. Especially my mother. Especially you."

I think my heart fractured a little when he said that. I considered what to say, but he continued. "I understand you did what you were made to do. I'm not angry anymore, Nayla. This has been so confusing. Part of leaving with you and Malik is me wanting to rebel, as childish as that sounds. It's not like being the faithful Regent's son got me into the party. I felt like it was time for a change. By now, my father knows I helped you escape. He'll find a new wife. He's young enough to still have children. Or I could go back and still be the regent, you know. I'd have to do something to prove my loyalty." He looked at my widened eyes as he said that and laughed under his breath, squeezing my hand. "The other reason I left is that I apparently have a traveling home."

"I don't understand," I cautiously told him.

"*You're* my home, Nayla."

When Conall and I got back to the cottage, Malik had arranged a spread for dinner, and Meethra was perched on the back of a chair waiting impatiently, two long graceful pairs of wings behind her. I got a really good look at her. She was a beautiful being, something between a Skyborne and an insect. Her translucent veined wings were the most insect-like characteristic, similar to the long-winged bugs that landed on the surface of ponds.

I looked disappointed at the lack of wine glasses on the table. If I'd thought getting through the conversation this morning with three Skyborne who'd all been groomed to be Regents was difficult, my gut told me that was nothing compared to the conversation we were about to have.

"So why did you call me back, Malik?" Meethra uttered, anxiously shifting on her perch once we were all seated.

"The rest of the godflies were systematically rounded up over the years. They're being held in a mine somewhere in Monterra," he answered her directly.

Meethra's light dimmed at that. "How do you know?" she asked, stunned.

"I've seen the mine. And I have seen the result of what they are using them for." Malik pulled out a small red-pink crystal from his pocket and set it on the table. "I don't know the details of how they can use this." He held it between his thumb and forefinger and squeezed. It crumbled.

"Did you feel that?" Meethra asked.

Conall and I shook our heads.

She flew onto the table and crouched down next to the remnants of the stone, observing it intently. "I felt something when it was crushed. Like in the process of being broken down, it released some of its energy. Do you think they're harnessing it somehow?"

"It seems likely. Here's what I know," Malik answered. "Monterra's Regent, I mean *Regius*, is Kymar Shal. He has a daughter about Nayla's age called Emerson, who has strong healing gifts. Since she came of age, Kymar has been making her do terrible experiments involving the godflies and this stone, ground up into a fine powder. It's what Darius referred to during the trial," he said, watching me turn a second fuchsia stone in my hand. "Emerson took to the work as naturally as you took to shifting your appearance. Kymar had other healers working on it before but with little progress. Since Emerson took over, she's been able to create a new species. This hasn't been done since the Makers created the Skyborne, and we've all been taught the cost of that."

"What do you mean, the cost?" Meethra asked.

I'd always regarded those stories as just that, stories. I realized the godfly probably didn't know the history of our kind.

"You've heard us refer to the Makers, right?" I asked her.

She nodded, "We call them Etherra in my realm."

"The story of the Makers' creation of the Skyborne is taught to us as children, in a very reverent sort of way. So it goes soon after the dimension of time came into existence, the Makers evolved. They were the first species that developed enough to develop language and society and all the other signs of intelligence. Soon they learned how to manipulate the energy surrounding them to their will. They mastered it so well, they moved through realms."

Meethra glanced at my pocket, holding the ember. *Realm Walker,* she'd called me. She'd said she saw the essence of things. The ember became heavy.

I shook the thoughts away and picked up Malik's story, "The Makers sold themselves as gods to the species in each realm. Really, they're glorified meddlers as far as I'm concerned. The dependence they'd created upon themselves became monotonous over time, and in their boredom, they tested their power. They identified a large-brained bipedal species on a planet called Earth as one of the more intelligent and adaptable species in the greater multi-verse they reigned over and began depositing them in different realms to see what type of new species time could create." No doubt what Uden had referred about being distant cousins that day in the Swath, I thought to myself.

"Eventually, that species, called humans, merged with other species in the various realms, and the Makers, being proud parents, wanted to reward their chosen pets for being so adaptable. They signed an agreement with the humans, the Ukarid. The humans, greedy for the Makers' knowledge and power, offered themselves up as the subjects for a new experiment."

"There was a catch, though. The Makers couldn't harness enough energy to convert the entire human population. So, they used the life energy of the humans who would not make the conversion. The cost was the extinction of the rest of the species entirely. Their realm was destroyed in the conversion, and the Skyborne were created and given a new home realm, Idia. The Makers gave their children the ability to sense the fields of energy around them and taught us how to harness that energy to create our own power. The one gift they never gave us was the ability to walk between realms. They reserved that for themselves. It is just a story, though."

Realm Walker, I thought.

"What was the cost to the Makers?" Meethra asked.

I looked to Malik and Conall to see if they had the answer. Malik shook his head, "I don't know. I only know that Emerson has done what only the Makers have done before creating a new species using this stone and the godflies. There are hundreds of them by now. Creatures are a mix between a godfly and Skyborne child. They tried with other animals, but Emerson preferred the result of that particular combination."

"There are godflies still alive?" she asked Malik hopefully.

"Yes, but I don't know their condition. Because of the connection between our families, I've been to the mines, but I never was shown where the godflies were kept. Emerson guards her work closely. I'm sure you can imagine what type of person would relish in the horrors she creates."

"She uses her healing abilities to create monsters. I think that says enough," stated Conall as he nudged out dirt from under his nail with a small knife.

"My father, Drakestone's Regent Karish, and Regius Kymar think that if they can open a passageway between realms, they can send Emerson's creatures into Idia. The creatures have the ability to obstruct the Skyborne, who were left in Idia's power, like what happened to you during the ceremony, Nayla. Then their armies will go in and do the rest."

"And let me guess, we're going to stop them?" I asked.

Malik nodded, giving me his best conniving smile.

"Well, that doesn't sound daunting at all," I grinned.

CHAPTER THIRTEEN

W̲E̲ F̲O̲L̲L̲O̲W̲E̲D̲ T̲H̲E̲ forest for as far as it would take us. Meethra scouted ahead. We made it to the two little mirrored towns at the narrowest part of the river, at the border of Arborvale and Eastdow, where we decided we'd cross without any trouble. There were ferries and bridges at different places along the wide-roaming river. The towns were a hub of trade between the two territories. There was a large bridge that separated the towns, and there was always plenty of traffic to blend in with crossing it. We waited until dusk to enter the little town on the Eastdow side. Our biggest risk would be in crossing the bridge, which we'd decided to do in the morning. Lookouts were stationed monitoring the passage between territories, so crossing with the morning traffic would be much less suspicious.

I was familiar with the small inn at the edge of town near the bridge where we would have to cross over to Arborvale. Malik and Conall kept to the shelter of their hoods while they tended the horses outside and unstrapped our belongings. It was decided it would draw less attention if the godfly stayed out of sight and met up with us at the edge of the forest.

I approached the innkeeper wearing the facade of a young, well-bred-looking female, traveling with two guards to visit my acquaintance, the Regent's heir, Carina Kalederan. The squat Skyborne was all, "but of course," and "the only best milady."

We entered the large room with a pair of matching beds, and I couldn't imagine the fake lady I portrayed would be too pleased with the accommodations.

I shook her image off with a shiver.

"You, the real *you*, is beautiful, you know." Conall looked at me as if I were still make-believe.

"You really ought to stop gawking. You're starting to freak me out," I said as I turned to study myself in the small clouded mirror that sat atop the little dresser in the room. It was me, the figure I had so rarely seen in the last ten years, staring back. I didn't know how to see myself as beautiful. I looked in the mirror and saw myself as a tool. It was sad, really, I thought as I cocked my head to the side, assessing myself.

Malik wandered over to me, tossing off his hood. "He's right, you know. Your eyes could slay a dragon, Nayla." He was winking at me and chuckling to himself. I rolled mine at him exaggeratedly. If he had said that to me three months ago, I would have sworn he was a creep, but now I was acclimated to his humor, so I laughed with him. A little sarcasm sprinkled with truth. That was Malik.

I indulgently looked at myself in the mirror once more. You know what, they're right, I decided, as I stood a little more upright, shoulders back, more proudly than before. And as a smile escaped my lips, a pillow smashed into the side of my face.

"Jerk!" I yelled at Conall under my breath, trying to keep it down to prevent a scolding from Malik. I casually waltzed over to Conall and slipped in a playful yet solid punch to his ribs. "You deserved that, don't say you didn't." He rubbed his side and laughing.

I scanned the room and noticed a small writing pad and an inkpot. The drawers I opened were empty. I hadn't seen my sisters in over ten years. We hadn't even been allowed to maintain any correspondence. I assumed they thought I was dead, overtaken by some mysterious illness in a foreign territory like Vera, no doubt. I thought to hassle the innkeeper for a pen, to compose a message to Carina, but reconsidered. With my father still clinging to the regency, after the way he'd so easily passed me along, the risk was too great.

"Before it gets too late, we should go get some provisions," I told them. "Conall, you stay here and guard our stuff. You have more coin, right?" He nodded, handing me a small pouch. "Malik, you come with me and do your shadow thing." I slipped back into the lady shift and walked out the door, not waiting on Malik to follow.

An hour later, we came back, Malik struggling to carry the awkward packages we'd procured. "You couldn't have helped him carry anything?" Conall asked, taking a pouch Malik looked like he was about to drop.

I spun, "Not as the lady." I said, batting my eyelashes playfully. "This should be enough to get us to Seabrook. Malik says there isn't much in the way of supply outposts in Sundale."

"Tonight, we'll keep a rotating watch. This is probably the most exposed we'll be. I'll take the first." Malik walked over to the desk chair and picked it up, bringing it over to the door.

"I guess I'm just here for ornamentation then?" Conall snipped.

"We are trying to contribute, Conall," I said. "And you have made a point to mention *you* did spring us out of prison."

"*Several* times," Malik coughed. I gave him a conspiratorial grin as we silenced Conall's pouting.

❧

We left early the next morning, quietly padding through the common room toward the exit. The innkeeper caught our attention, loudly clearing his throat.

"Yes?" I asked.

"Some soldiers came through here late last night asking if I'd seen anything suspicious. If I had any odd guests staying here last night," the gruff Skyborne said.

"And what did you tell him?" I batted the lady's eyes with intention this time.

"Depends," he shot back, crossing his arms in front of his chest. "I told their leader I'd let them know."

"They're still here?" I asked, trying to stop my voice from cracking.

"Their leader and two of his men took my remaining rooms upstairs, and the rest went to an inn down the street."

I swallowed. "I see." *Shit.* That meant Darius was upstairs right now and might come down at any moment.

Conall stepped forward. I flinched, looking at his exposed face. He was well respected among the territory's citizens, and Darius was clearly not from Eastdow. "As far as I'm concerned, you've seen nothing suspicious. Just the normal travelers, going about their business. I'm sorry that those foreigners are here giving you a hard time. Here's a little extra coin for your trouble." Conall said, pulling a few pieces out of his pouch and handing it to the innkeeper. "Thank you for your hospitality."

The Skyborne stood, blinking at Conall. It was a gamble and a possibility the innkeeper would sell us out still. "I… uhhh, thank you, sir," he said, closing his hand around the coins.

Conall smiled tightly at the innkeeper and nodded to us right as footsteps sounded at the top of the stairs. "Let's go."

"Stay safe!" the innkeeper called out after us. I'm pretty sure all three of us winced.

We filed out the door with haste, hoping our horses were still there. As luck would have it, they were. We quickly packed our saddlebags, mounted, and headed toward the bridge, nervously glancing back toward the inn.

"That was exciting," Malik broke the silence.

"You *would* have enjoyed that," Conall chided.

"Will you two shut up," I demanded. I was not in the mood.

We spotted a large group of riders on horseback approaching the bridge and slipped alongside them, hoping to blend in. Once safely across and with no sign of Darius, I exhaled.

While we rode, the skin on the back of my neck prickled. I kept getting the feeling we were being stalked and not by our flying friend. *Malik?* I whined again.

Nothing within the range of my power, Nayla. Still. An edge of humor traced Malik's thoughts.

From the twin towns, the barrier of the Swath came into view as afternoon gave way to evening. There was a small cropping of boulders midway down a shallow hill that looked placed there by a lazy god. We had enough light to get situated, and it looked as good a place as any we'd seen to stop for the night. The Swath was still a long sprint, but if danger did come, that feeling that had been trailing me, we'd be able to make a break for it. As long as we outran our attackers, we'd make it inside the boundary of the forest.

I took a bite of the dried salted deer as we sat in the dark of our campsite. It was chewier than I liked but gamey and fresh still. "Do you guys think Darius was really in one of the rooms right next to us last night?" I asked; the thought gave me the creeps.

"That's what the innkeeper said," Conall replied.

"Malik!" I demanded.

"I can't keep sweeping power out every five seconds just because you are nervous. Besides, it's not that easy with all these boulders." I'd annoyed Malik now.

"I'm sorry, but I just can't shake this feeling. Like that, did you guys feel that? Shh…"

We stopped chewing. I could hear our breathing mixed with wind. My mind deciphered the pattern. My power poked me gently. *Listen.* It took control of my senses, pilfering through the sounds. There was a fourth set of lungs working in our vicinity; *I knew it.* I held up a hand to keep them from making a sound as I worked to find its source.

They understood what I was doing and followed suit. Within a moment, Malik made a subtle nod to a pair of large boulders leaning against each other to my left. He closed his eyes, and I felt energy sweep from him toward the boulder.

"It's a young girl," he mouthed to us a moment later.

I noticed a small crevice between them. "I have to pee if you'll excuse me." I rose to my feet, casually walking outside our god's strewn shelter. Our guest's breathing quickened as I worked my way behind the rocks she was taking shelter between. My back was against the boulder as I slid my way silently around to the opening on the backside. I knew… because *I knew* that Conall and Malik were covering the opening. This girl, whoever she was, either had a death wish sneaking up on three persons such as ourselves or had a considerable reason to do so. She must have known she was surrounded because there was a change in the rhythm of her breathing.

The rock I was leaning on trembled.

"Come out! We know you're in there," Conall's confident voice called from the other side of the boulder.

I glimpsed around the bend of the rock. The girl pounced toward Conall. They were a whirl of movement and blades. Blow, parry, block, blow, parry. It was almost so fast I couldn't see if either of them had landed a shot. They both were fueling their speed with power.

Watching skilled fighters was always enamoring, and Malik and I were clearly taken aback by the girl's unexpected prowess. And I wasn't worried about Conall *yet*.

Catching a stray blade by jumping in the fray moving that fast was a risk. Malik and I circled their action, waiting for the girl to make a mis-step. The girl saw an opening, a false opening I knew from sparing with Conall, a trap. She heaved a burst of energy toward it, flattening her blade as she went for it. But he spun in anticipation, throwing her off balance. I struck in a single swift motion, a light smack to the back of her thighs with a stick I had picked up, and down she went. Malik and Conall had her unarmed and pinned before she could take her next breath.

Conall looked at me, "A stick is what you bring to a sword fight, *seriously?*"

"What?" I shrugged my shoulders. "She's only one girl. And I'm pretty sure I'm the only girl who can take you." I winked at him and looked at the *only one girl*. One very specific girl, I realized. There was only one very specific girl who she could be too. Carina was too prim and was more suited to battling with words than weapons, and our middle sister, Balene, would have been unlikely to develop into the petite animal I was staring down now.

"Hello, Judith. Remove the lady's hood if you don't mind," I said. Malik pulled off the dark cloth, illuminating her shadowed face as I directed. Sure enough, sweet little Judith, my youngest sister all grown up, was looking up at me, smirking with a boyish, no longer innocent, grin.

"You could have caused permanent damage, Nayla. Now tell these smelly brutes to get their hands off of me." She was jerking her shoulders in disgust, almost, trying to break free. It was an odd way to greet an older sister who you hadn't seen in ten years and likely presumed dead.

"Who sent you?" Malik growled.

"I sent myself," she growled back. "You are Malik. Which makes you, Conall. Now let me up before you piss me off."

Malik and Conall shared a look before they eased off her, finally agreeing on something for once.

She casually got up, smoothing back her shoulder-length dark hair and brushing off her tunic as if all of this was totally normal. She walked over to gather her weapons and sheathed them at her sides, and took her place on a stone by the fire.

"You guys are just going to let her do that?" I motioned to my sister.

"As you said, she's just one girl," Conall retorted.

"Got any food? I'm hungry," Judith practically demanded.

Conall and Malik looked at each other for a clue.

"Refreshments sound nice. But first, you need to tell us how you found us here and what it is that you want." I motioned to my pack for Conall to grab a portion for my sister. Malik sat cautiously across the fire from her. Conall had drawn a wineskin as well and took a swig, passing it to me, and I followed. We joined them sitting.

"It is rude not to offer your guest the first drink," the young lady spoke.

I handed the skin to Malik, who pulled deeply from it. He held it in her direction, but as she reached out, he pulled it slightly out of her reach. "Are you even old enough to drink, *Judith*?"

She grinned. "Jude, preferably. And yes. My adulthood ceremony was last year."

He continued, "Okay, Jude. Why don't you tell us a little story, and we'll share our wine with you. And maybe even our camp."

I had seen the flat edge she deftly swept toward Conall. This sister of mine was no enemy. I walked over to Malik and snatched the skin, and handed it to her.

"Jude, it is now? I like it." I turned to her in seriousness, "It has been a long-time little sister. Too long. And I'm sorry for that." My heart ached seeing her, but we both clearly still had our guard up. Seeing the strong and adept young female she'd grown into made me regret the years I'd missed watching her mature. I had so many questions. The main one now being how she'd learned to fight like that.

She looked back and forth between Conall and Malik as if they hadn't been there; a damned-up lake of information would flood out of her. "I trust them with my life. Now spill," I said. I didn't miss how my words caught Malik off guard.

Jude nodded, understanding the freedom to speak I granted her. "Mother told us after my adulthood ceremony. She gathered the three of us and told us everything. That you weren't dead, where you'd gone, and what you'd done. Everything. I could tell keeping that secret had been a burden to her all those years. She seemed lighter after she'd told us."

I thought wistfully of the similarities with Conall's mother.

"They told us you'd been kidnapped and were missing, presumed dead. We had a funeral and everything. But you see, when you left, things started changing. We changed. Nayla, we knew it was a lie," she said urgently. "Balene, Carina, and I would meet and come up with our little schemes to get you back. But we didn't know anything. So, Carina set us a course of action. She studied under mother and father harder than she ever had before. She read every book in our library, I think, taught herself old languages and histories. She learned how to influence Father in a way that he would listen. Nayla, he listens and obeys her. And Balene has water in her veins; she can heal. Heal like you never could. I've never seen anything like what she can do."

"And you, Jude?" I interrupted. I looked at her with pain in my eyes. It was pride and the pain of another lost child I saw in her—pain in her strength and burden.

"When I got older, I realized what they had. I couldn't feel anything different, though, so I begged Carina to make Father have me trained to be a fighter. Carina was never going to do it, so I would. And I was fast, power fast. The old men in the Arborvale keep don't know what to do with me." She was smiling proudly now.

"I can see why." Conall was rubbing his shoulder now, a hit he must have taken we hadn't seen.

She continued, words tumbling out of her. "Father has been tiring,

gravely, so Balene believes, so Carina has been handling all of his correspondence. We heard about what happened at the ceremony. The price
on you all now. And I knew you'd come through Arborvale, so I searched
for you." She finally took a drink from the skin and passed it to Conall.

"How do you know we want the same things, Jude?" I asked, testing her.

She looked at me funny then like she'd never considered it. "Well, I
know you, Nayla. You're my big sister. And Carina said…"

"What did Carina say, Jude?" I pressed.

She squared her shoulders. "Carina said that you would do it. And
you did. And together, we are going to make this world a better place. I'm
still hungry," she announced.

Makers, she was naïve. But well-intentioned. I turned to Conall and
Malik, "Well?" I asked them. They both looked at each other, before
Conall apparently losing the staring contest, got up to get her something
to eat. Even with all her fighting grace, she clearly was still accustomed to
a certain lifestyle.

"So I have a rough idea of what happened to you, rumors and all. So
what's next? What do we do now?"

She was so young, I realized. They had been training and waiting,
wanting to help, to do something. I empathized, and I had so many more
questions about Carina and our mother. About why she had told them,
but they would have to wait.

"We need you to take a message back to Carina and Mother," I
told her.

"You don't have a plan?" She was shocked, almost appalled.

Malik interrupted. "Of course, we have a plan."

"I'm not a child if that is what you are thinking." She paused. "Do
you not trust me? Is that it?" The words were quick off her tongue. She
was a flurry of energy, propulsion, in a girl. I feared to think of the heav-
enly fury she'd be in a real battle. She glared at Malik before she met my
gaze squarely. "Well, you ought to trust me because you've got a few hours
before those Skyborne who are after you catch up."

That woke us all up.

"You didn't know?" she asked, leaning toward us. "They followed you from the twin towns, I think. I tracked them, but I'm way faster. Don't worry, I'll do what I can to throw them off your trail." She smiled slyly. "Now your turn. Spill."

Malik started laughing. "Makers, if this is what the two of you are like, I fear the thought of all four Kalederan girls together. Alright, Jude, here's what we know."

He told her about the horrors being created by his father and Kymar in the mines. About the godflies. And about Torin's fledgling new alliance. "We are making our way to Seabrook. I have friends there. From the Territory's seat, we will lay out our plan. I have some ideas of how to we can take the mine." Conall and I glanced at each other. This was new news. "We need allies, Jude," he continued. "Can you bring either your mother or Carina to Seabrook? When we arrive, Femi, the Regent there, will send a request for a diplomatic meeting. I know your father is fading, but one of them must come."

Her eyes gleamed with purpose. "I'll make it happen." She jumped up, walking over to me awkwardly, then threw her arms around me, a small sob escaping her tight control. I just stood there, stiff in shock.

"Now make haste!" My little sister ordered, staring us down until we were moving quickly enough for her.

Once satisfied, she said, "See you soon."

"Thank you," I replied, but she had already slipped away fearlessly into the night.

We rode hard through the night and into the morning. We rode until the horses were slipping on the sand-covered stones in Sundale and could no longer manage a canter.

"We have to stop," I begged.

"We can manage a few hours," Malik said.

A few hours reprieve was all I needed. We found a small stream and a patch of grass where the horses could graze. There likely wouldn't be another before we got to Seabrook, so we needed to take advantage.

The letter Jude handed to me before we left nagged at me. I rolled out a pallet and took advantage of the waning light to read it. Carina's voice was there in the letter but formal as if she was unsure of who her reader was now. I could read the sorrow, hope, and resilience in her words, too. Hers was the voice of a leader, a guardian. A Regent. She vowed to support me, unlike what our father had done. I thanked the Makers Jude hadn't gotten caught with this, as it would have certainly meant problems for them.

I briefly flipped through a few pages of the book our mother sent. It seemed to be some type of early historical volume with ink-drawn images and charts that looked like lineages or timelines. I put it in my pack for later.

Balene's package was another mystery, however. It was three vials of a dark blue powder with a poem. A bad poem. A poem with a hidden message.

A lover's bite at night
The mark he left today
A mix of dark and light
And never it will stay

As far as anyone reading it would ever know, it was a love potion. Or an elixir to rid oneself of an unwanted pregnancy more like. I knew, however, my sister, who I hadn't seen for ten years, would have little interest in my love life. It was a cure, a remedy. A mix of dark, the power, and light, milk, water, I wasn't sure, but I knew it must be important enough that she sent it because I'd need it.

CHAPTER FOURTEEN

THE NEXT DAY we made a good distance into the next territory, Sundale, and were deep in the Bare Lands, a stretch of rough rolling desert that bordered the forest.

Traveling on the path through the scrublands, where the arid expanse transitioned into the Swath, left us exposed. It was better than trying to force the horses to walk through the hot sand to seek shelter in the desert caves which lay further south. Not to mention avoiding the small animals that lived in the sand that bit to leave nasty little wounds.

Over the years, I had never spent any time in Sundale or seen much of the desert territory, but I heard that it was beautiful the closer to the coast you traveled. The two principal cities, one of which was the seat of the territory, are set in large bays that provide sea access for trade and excellent saltwater fisheries in the nearby waters. The territory also produced a kind of hard sandstone material you could build with, though in eastern and northern territories, the stones and timber from the mountains were preferred. Had my path been different, I might have liked to travel there to see Sundale for myself.

We stopped to rest for a few hours at an unexpected spring and were taking advantage of watering the horses. I moved through a series of stretches when I heard the horses whinny and stomp. I looked toward where they were tethered.

"What's agitating the horses?" Conall asked, doing his own routine.

"Stingers probably," I said, thinking of putting a shield around their ankles.

I felt a sweep of energy chase out, then recoil. I looked a Malik. His eyes were wide, and he nodded to the long knives I laid next to my makeshift pallet.

Damn it. My heart thundered.

Only a few breaths later, Conall and Malik jumped up from where they'd been sleeping, arming themselves. We were standing back-to-back, weapons drawn. Twelve armed Skyborne surrounded us.

Doable, if it wasn't for Darius.

They pointed an array of sharp objects in our direction. Darius stepped forward. He looked at me, smirking. His eyes did not betray his recollection of what he'd done if he even remembered. His gaze flicked between mine and the pocket where I carried the ember.

"Don't even think about it," he emphasized, lip curling triumph. "We both know you'll lose. So surrender."

He was turning something over in his pocket. A vial of that red powder, I realized. He'd probably carried enough to dose the three of us.

We can't risk one of us getting injured or killed, Malik spoke to my mind. *We'll find another way.*

Surrendering to Darius made me sick, but it wasn't worth one of us getting killed or injured. Malik was right. I slowly put my weapons down, and Malik and Conall followed suit. Darius's men seized us, removing the smaller weapons attached to our persons and bound our hands and ankles. Darius sauntered over to me. He reached a finger toward the hidden left shirt pocket where I carried the ember tapping the box through my shirt three times, verifying its presence. Then he held his open hand out to me and raised his brow, waiting. I lifted my bound hands toward him, smirking, but he called one of his soldiers over. He pointed to the place he had tapped as if I was something dirty he didn't want to touch.

"It's there."

The Skyborne tugged at the V of the tunic, tearing it enough so he could reach his club-like hand inside my shirt and fetch out the ember for his commander. The box shuddered as it lost contact with my skin. The hole it left was immediate.

Darius let out a sigh of relief as the Skyborne placed it in his outstretched palm.

"What a productive day," Darius crooned, pulling the vial from his pocket, replacing it with the ember. He handed it to the Skyborne nearest and gave a once over to his brother, Conall, and I. "Dose them, as a precaution," he commanded.

After we recovered from the coughing fit caused by the powder, they hoisted us over our horses, stomachs on the saddles and head and feet hanging down on either side of the horse's flank. They secured us in place.

Darius drove at an unrelenting pace. We were halfway across the territory by nightfall. By the time we stopped for the night, I was thoroughly exhausted from the beating I experienced from the ride.

A soldier unstrapped me, and I fell with a thud onto the ground. The burly Skyborne who'd reached into my shirt came over and yanked me up onto my knees, then to my feet. He undid the binding at my wrists and retied my hands behind my back. "Sit," his gruff voice demanded. I lowered myself to the sand, and the soldiers arranged us in a little circle, seated backs facing each other. They laced a stake through our tied wrists and hammered it into the ground. My shoulders barked at the stretch.

"What exactly was your plan, Malik?" Darius paused to take a bite of the hard cheese one of his fighters handed him. He spoke to Malik, but he didn't take his eyes off me. My stomach lurched as I glanced toward his pocket and the object within. I could feel its attention on me too.

Darius looked at his brother. "You were helping her that whole time. Did you know she was playing me? Your own brother?" His face wasn't angry though, it had a strange, perplexed look. "You betrayed our family."

He trailed off, returning his gaze back to me, anger returning with it, "*you* betrayed me, too. And all for what? You three were going to stop us? Or did *you* want to rule?"

He huffed a laugh. We said nothing.

He continued his one-sided conversation. "What I'm really curious about is how exactly you were going to do it? Sneak into the mines in Monterra and use your power to destroy all of Emerson's work? I understand, believe me. They make me cringe, too. But they are necessary. Those with a weak constitution aren't meant to rule. Sometimes you have to get your hands dirty. Anyway, I'm taking you three to father. He asked I keep you alive. *If possible.* Not sure what he plans to do with you, though."

Darius shrugged his shoulders and turned to walk away.

"What happens when the creatures turn on you, Darius?" Conall called after him, straining to look over his shoulder and meet Darius's eye.

"Emerson has total control over them, I assure you." Darius carried on, smiling wistfully, admiration evident in his voice. "They are less sentient than you would think. Think of a mindless servant capable of blocking your connection to the energy surrounding you. They can fly, and there are thousands of them. They could render armies powerless. And when we're done with them, we'll use the ember to deposit them in some other realm. It is a simple yet ingenious plan."

"Has it ever occurred to you that you don't even know what you'll find if you ever make it to Idia? *Who* you'll find?" Conall asked.

"Don't engage with him," I whispered.

"Does she hold your leash too, Malik?" Darius taunted, smirking at Conall.

Conall snorted, the jab having the desired effect.

"I'll admit, a Skyborne who can become a limitless number of females, *and males*, has her appeal," Darius said, eyeing Malik, "But, females need boundaries and structure. Husbands and children. Otherwise, they malfunction and destroy civilizations. It's why we don't allow women to hold the regency in Drakestone. Deceitful and fickle. I learned that the hard way."

He looked at me, patting the ember in his pocket. "Nothing I couldn't recover from."

My blood boiled as he walked out of sight. How had I not seen that side of him?

That was educational, Malik spoke to me, silently interrupting my devolving thoughts.

Darius always was overly confident, I replied. It was one thing that had attracted me to him. I kept that to myself.

❦

The night dragged on. The next day they strapped us to the horses the same way. The pace we traveled at was excruciatingly slow. By the third night, we knew the routine and sat ourselves down so they could hammer the stake between our wrists. I couldn't get comfortable, and I was losing hope of ever escaping Darius, who was doing nothing to make it any easier.

I could hardly sleep, not because of our painful position, but because I kept thinking Darius was going to sneak up on me in the middle of the night. He'd certainly threatened it enough during the day.

I had to stop myself from fidgeting and waking up Conall and Malik, who were lightly sleeping, judging by their steady breathing. Out of the corner of my eye, I saw a dim light in the distance.

Meethra! I thought.

What happened? she replied faintly, her voice barely a whisper in my mind.

Ambushed, I responded. *Days ago.*

I can probably put half of them to sleep, but not all. What can I do?

In my bag on the darkest mare, I told her, thinking of my sister's gift. *There are three small vials containing a dark powder.*

A dark powder that did what I hoped it did. The godfly flew over, pushing open the saddle back far enough to crawl in. One soldier nearest stirred.

Still, I told her.

He leaned up and looked around. I closed my eyes, feigning sleep. He shrugged, satisfied it was just the horses moving and lay back down. Within moments, his breathing confirmed he'd fallen back asleep.

It's clear.

Meethra flew the first vial over to me. I was building up saliva in my mouth. I hoped it was enough liquid.

Pour it in my mouth, I thought for her. She struggled with the little cork but eventually got it. Like the lock pick, the vial must have weighed nearly as much as she did. But she got it high enough and tipped the contents into my open lips. I swished the bitter powder with my spit. When satisfied it was mixed enough, I swallowed, waiting.

Meethra went to retrieve two more vials.

So slowly, I could feel the tendrils of energy creep back into my awareness. It was like being able to see again after being kept in the dark for far too long. And this time, it had been less than a day.

Thinking of what Darius told us, I hoped Balene had a lot more of that stuff.

I felt for the energy in the bindings at my wrists. Bit by bit, I weakened the material until a small tug loosed them so I could gently slip my hands free without startling my sleeping companions.

Malik, I called to his mind, trying to get him to open that channel between us. Meethra handed me the second vial. I opened it, sneaking around to Conall, still thinking Malik's name. Conall's eyes were wide open. Waiting on me. I leaned into his ear and breathed, "Fill your mouth with spit." I showed him the vial. He understood. He obeyed.

Nayla, Malik finally responded. I went through the same procedure with him. By the time both of them had swallowed Balene's powder, I had their wrists freed and all of our ankles.

The Skyborne who'd awoken earlier stirred. He must be a fitful sleeper, I thought because I knew we were quiet. "Hey—" he grunted, but Meethra zipped over, dusting a light powder over him that put him back to sleep. It was enough to stir another few guards. Meethra flew quickly to put as many to sleep as she could.

Six fighters still rose.

Where was Darius? I thought.

Conall and Malik snuck over to where they'd stashed our weapons. On the opposite side of the camp from me. One moment we were all assessing each other. The tension in the crisp night air was palatable.

The fighting began under the moonlit sky. I was unarmed. I saw Conall and Malik grab a few blades. Conall tried to toss a long knife to me, but it was short. I went for it, but the Skyborne nearest me advanced, swinging a sword broadly. I ducked and pushed in with a low kick to the Skyborne's kneecap.

Crunch. He howled as his knee collapsed. The soldier was still trying to swing at me from his one good knee. I spun, easily avoiding his blade, and landed an elbow at the base of his skull. He fell over with a thud. I looked up to see how my companions were fairing.

"Malik, behind you!" I cried. I watched long enough to see Malik deflect the oncoming assault. Malik was about to land a death blow when Conall called, "No! Alive. They're only doing what they're told." Deftly Malik adjusted his angle, narrowly missing the surprised soldier's throat. Taking advantage, Malik thrust forward, striking the Skyborne's temple, rendering him instantly unconscious. I took a short knife from the body at my feet and ran toward the action, swiping the longer blade Conall had tossed toward me.

Only two down. Conall was fighting hesitantly, I saw. Scanning the soldiers, I recognized the uniforms on some of them. Shit, I thought. Some of these were his Skyborne from Eastdow.

"Conall!" I pleaded. I'd rather live with the guilt of losing Eastdow soldiers than lose either of them. I knew he heard me, but he still didn't strike to kill, bringing down one of the two engaging him with a swift strike connecting the pommel of his sword with the Skyborne's skull.

I frantically scanned for Darius as I took on the next attacker. It was the large Skyborne with the club-hands. If he'd been covered in hair, I would have thought he was a bear. He was one of Darius's, so I threw everything I had at him.

I blocked a swing that came a little too close for comfort. Our blades clashed—my smaller one quivering beneath his. This Skyborne was more skilled than the other. I couldn't get a strike in. I went in close, jabbing with the knife I'd nicked off the first one I took down. But he expected it. He unsheathed his own short knife and swiped my side. I dodged, wincing at the narrow line of blood he'd drawn. His sweat and blood flicked onto my face when I drove my knuckles into his jaw. It tasted sour like piss smelled.

I caught sight of Darius running back toward the commotion. I spun away from the bear and leading him toward Malik, who was only fighting one soldier.

"Take him," I called as I ran past. I caught the shock in Malik's eye as he slammed his sword against the Skyborne's, which shattered like the cellar lock. I'd been working on that as we'd fought. I smiled when the bear squealed as Malik gutted him.

"Darius!" I yelled. I felt rage, red hot heat building in me as I raised my knives to block his attack. Metal scraped on metal as he held firm, pressing me back. He forced me into a sandstone mound as we studied each other, breathing heavily.

For a moment, over our locked blades, I saw a glimmer of the Skyborne I had known. Beneath the dirt and grime, his smooth open face, deep olive skin, and silken black hair spoke to me. His lips, full and firm. Beneath his aggression, warmth shown in his eyes for a second before they flashed back to dark hate. I saw the Skyborne who came to the cell that night. Those beautiful features I had touched and tasted, twisting into something entirely foreign to me.

Terror filled me. He was looking at me as if he didn't remember. How could he not remember? I screamed inwardly.

"What you did to me, Darius, was inexcusable. You may not remember, but I remember." My voice shook with anger while I held his stare. Slow recollection trickled into his eyes. I felt him shudder through our tangled blades. Regret, that's what I saw in his eyes as he experienced the realization of who his anger and hurt drove him into becoming. I felt the pressure ease. I thrust my blades forward, attempting to push him backward, but he was already retreating.

Coward, I thought. A surge of raw energy coursed through me. Vengeance consumed me.

At that moment, I had no control as I launched myself at him, swinging in a blind fury. He was blocking every shot I took, but barely.

Out of the corner of my vision, I saw Conall and Malik still fighting.

I harnessed my power to increase my speed so that, with two maneuvers, I had Darius disarmed and on his ass. But he was so damn quick. Sand dusted up into the air as his foot swung out, tripping me. We were tangling on the ground. Dirt and sand grated in my gritted teeth. He had the advantage.

Darius grabbed my hair and bit my arm so hard I reflexively let go of the knife. I jerked up and smashed my forehead into his chin, splitting the skin. I had aimed for his nose. With my free hand, I punched the tender spot on the inside of his wrist. The knife he'd taken from me when flying. Afraid he'd get my other one, I tossed it away. I couldn't use it this close, anyway. He lunged for it across my body so unearthly fast, catching it before it hit the ground.

Lying on top of me, he brought the knife to my throat. My surroundings went quiet. I could hear the insects in the surrounding shrubbery chirping, carrying on their nightly routine. Blades of the two remaining men clanging distantly. Moisture from Darius's heavy panting swelling the air above me.

He ran his firm hand through my inky locks and gripped down, smiling. At that moment, it was just the two of us. He was so close I could taste his breath. Icy dread followed the blinding rage—the ember pulsing between our bodies. I couldn't tell if he could feel it too. He jerked my head to the side.

"I think father will let me keep you," he breathed into my ear and licked my earlobe before pulling it into his mouth. The cool night breeze chilled the delicate skin beneath my ear. "I find I rather like this form. Much more delicate than your last one, which seems to suit my current mood. The more delicate, the better." He was like two different males, I thought as he threaded his hand through my hair, pulling exposing my neck further to him. "Mine," he breathed.

One moment, it was sheer panic. The next, I felt energy pulse through me, coming to a defined point. The ember rested between our bodies. On instinct, like it was in the Swath, I drew it toward my center, pulling in as much as I could. More and more.

I violently expelled it. There was a booming crack. A light flared, shocking my vision, and depthless black surrounded me. My eyes adjusted. I was the pulsing darkness of the ember.

I got up, orienting myself, and wandered toward Malik and Conall, who, along with the last two soldiers they'd been fighting, had stilled.

I cocked my head to the side, intoxicated by the tapestry laid out before me. I could feel the details of their very make-up like a map. The energy pulsing down endless pathways from their brain to their tissues. Their sweat escaping their pores, their blood traveling through their veins. I could see every leaf of every shrub, the bugs living inside. Their tiny legs moving, mandible's munching on leaves—every grain of sand, every fleck of dust. I was aware of it all.

I could see how to break the men apart.

Conall was looking at me with wide eyes. *Fear.* Conall was afraid of me.

I looked to the men, then to Conall, and knew that what I could do to them would be an abuse of the power I felt. I wanted to use it though, I deserved to finally have the channels to this expansive energy blown wide open. To feel the euphoria thrumming through my body as it was now—*my* power.

"Easy, Nayla," Conall cautioned. I stared at him curiously. Didn't he want this for me?

The men saw my hesitation and raised their swords again. But they turned to dust in their hands.

I shrugged, turning to where Darius lay unconscious. He had been thrown back. He had the wind knocked out of him, his shirt was in tatters, and there were hand-shaped burns on his skin like he'd been in the sun for too long, but he was alive. Why had I had left him alive? I thought, considering rectifying that mistake.

I strode toward Darius. I heard a gasp of pain, then a steady hand circled my waist, pulling me in to a powerful body. A grounding warmth flooded through me that felt like home. *Conall.*

⁓

When Darius came to, the three of us were surrounding him, weapons drawn.

"Nayla, please," he whispered.

Malik and Conall were by my side.

"I ought to kill you, Darius. What do you guys think, kill him?" I asked them.

"Why not?" was Malik's only response about the life of his brother. His face showed disgust, however.

Conall pointed his long sword into the delicate place where the inner thigh meets the groin, near enough to Darius's manhood that he squirmed. "Or I could disarm him if you'd prefer?" Conall winked, enjoying this part of our adventure.

I cocked my head contemplatively, appearing to be weighing my options.

"How about this? There's already too much killing. We can tie him up, leave him, and *hopefully* someone will find him?" The sooner I could escape his company, the better.

"Nayla, I think he would make a useful prisoner. We could get information from him. There's still more he knows. And I don't know what to make of this new alliance with Eastdow."

I considered Malik's point. The last thing I wanted was to drag this Skyborne, of all prisoners, through the Swath, which was where I'd decided we'd be going next. "What about the risk that places on your friends?" I argued. "And we are *not* going to torture it out of him. I refuse to lower myself to their level."

"There are other ways." Malik gave me his crooked smile and nodded toward Meethra, who'd stayed away from the fray of fighting.

"We agreed to do things justly. We vote," Conall chimed in. "Darius may prove useful, and Seabrook, I imagine, understands their risk. We should take him."

I rolled my eyes. "Fine, he goes then."

∽

I had already searched Darius for the ember, but all I found were broken shards of the already cracked box.

"Where do you think it went?" Conall asked when I showed them.

"It was in you, or on you," Malik said. That is what the power I had felt was. I was prepared to deny that, though.

"I don't think so," I replied. I retraced my steps at first light. It had been too dark to see in the dead of night, even with the moon. The ground was scuffed and scattered with the dried blood where the fight had taken place. I was getting frustrated as the Light Star beat down on us from its position high in the mid-day sky. Desperate, even.

Conall led me a distance from the camp, in the direction where he'd carried me from after the fighting when I finally found it. With the box in shards, I didn't know how I was going to carry it.

"Guys," I called.

They came to kneel beside while Meethra flew down, crouching to get eye level with it. The four of us stared at the little black nothingness.

"Thank you," I said to it. It pulsed an acknowledgment.

"How are you going to carry it now?" Conall asked.

"She is going to pick it up," Meethra answered authoritatively. She was right, though I'd prefer a proper container to place it in. I didn't think I could just scoop it into something random. It would probably get offended, considering it has most likely saved my life twice now.

"You're not going to kill me if I touch you, right?" I asked it. The frequency of its buzzing changed in emphasis. I hadn't remembered it responding to Lathrais.

Conall was looking at me like I was crazy. "Quit anthropomorphizing it. It doesn't have feelings."

I looked at the glowing remnant of power and asked, "What about Conall? Would you kill him?"

I swore its vibration felt like a laugh. Malik certainly laughed. I was grateful because my hands were starting to tremble because of the rising intensity of the moment. If these were to be my last moments, I'd rather bypass the drama.

"Here goes nothing," I said, huffing anxiously under my breath before I reached down. Conall gulped as I cupped it in my palms. I released the breath I'd been holding. It floated up with my hands, not quite touching them, but hovering inside my palms. I moved it to one and wiped the cold sweat from my brow.

As we went back to the camp, none of us spoke. I knew they'd understood the gravity of the moment because Conall had laced his fingers through those on my free hand and held it in a stranglehold. On my other side, Malik's hand clamped lovingly and a little painfully on the nape of my neck. Darius eyed us as we walked past him. His mouth stood agape as he saw the ember in my open palm.

CHAPTER FIFTEEN

"DID YOU GUYS hear that?" I caught the faintest rustling at the edge of the Swath. "Wake up," I whispered. My companions were deeply sleeping like only males and children can, exhausted from traveling and fighting or growing in the case of children.

After our skirmish with Darius and his soldiers, we'd found a safe enough place to camp near the border of the Swath. The location brought us closer to the invisible boundary, but I knew we were still outside it.

Considering who and what was probably hunting us, we agreed our best chance would be to duck into the forest using the protection of my shields, though I'd insisted we go in preemptively as a precaution. I'd just about got Malik and Conall convinced when I misinformed them that the Swath hadn't been *that* terrifying.

Part of me was curious to engage the creature, Uden, again, too. He hadn't killed me when he could have, which piqued my interest.

"Pssttt," a familiar hiss sounded in the air around me like it had before in the Swath. "I've been tracking you since you used the ember. The flare of energy was— *extraordinary*."

I could barely make out the familiar figure as it exposed its location at the edge of the forest, moonlight illuminating its translucent skin. The creature must have had countless opportunities the last few days to contact us but had been waiting until my watch to speak to me alone. I didn't raise the alarm.

A gagged and tied Darius who'd stirred watched me slyly as I walked over to the edge of the Swath.

"What do you want?" I whispered, so he wouldn't hear. "The last time we saw each other, you were threatening to make a meal of me. Do I even want to know how you can still recognize me?" Essence, like Meethra, I assumed. Or my appetizing scent. I shivered away a sudden chill.

It smiled, amused. "I believe we may have a use for each other." Uden paused, waiting for me to consider. I knew what it would use me for, so—then it occurred to me.

"You're planning to offer me safe passage through the forest, so I don't have to use my shields."

"Smart," he commended. "And?"

"And when we figure it out, you want passage to wherever you call home."

"Precisely. More pursue you still. Towing a prisoner around will slow you." The corners of his peeling lips turned down in a disapproving frown as he confirmed what I had suspected. "We could take him off your hands?" Uden asked hopefully.

"No," I said flatly. As much as I hated Darius, I couldn't bear the thought of watching even my worst enemy get eaten alive.

"Just an offer," he shrugged. "I thought you may need a guide." A flabby arm swept in a welcoming gesture toward the forest.

"You expect me to believe you have good intentions?"

"I heard what happened to your High Priest. I doubt that *thing*," he hissed, eyeing my pocket, "would be any kinder to me. *You*, however, hold its favor. Do you deny that?"

I ignored him. I was contemplating my previous interactions with Uden and his insinuation of the ember's preferences. "But I thought you'd said you'd been here forever?"

"Not forever. Longer than your kind, but I did not say *forever*. Like every species who's arrived over the millennia to this place, this realm of the banished, we too are displaced. Our kind should have returned to our realm before you arrived or when the godflies were banished here, but something remains amiss. There are untold realms out there. Realms where even beings such as myself are at home."

I was becoming increasingly conflicted. "When we first met, you sure gave the impression that feasting on the flesh of Skyborne was a satisfactory enough existence. You'll forgive me if I'm having trouble bridging the gap between flesh-eating monster and sympathetic homesick ally."

"Believe me, girl, no one who has ended up dinner for a creature in this forest didn't deserve it. At least *a little*." He snickered.

I thought back to what I knew of the early conflicts after the Crossover. What the Skyborne must have felt finding themselves displaced and with only the supplies on them; what it would have turned even the most moralistic Skyborne into. I shuddered.

"So, first, I get to trust *you*. Your part of the bargain seems much less risky."

"There are places you could send me that I would find a fine hell, so I would disagree."

This conversation had already been enlightening. "If I took your offer for a bargain, I'd add the stipulation to create trust between us, of course, that you share with us everything you know about the history of this realm. Answer all my questions, *truthfully*."

His bulbous head tilted, weighting my request. "I don't see what it would hurt. Bargain then."

"Bargain." I didn't know what Malik and Conall would think of me making a deal with Uden, but if he wasn't lying, it would get us through to the border of Seabrook safely, and I wouldn't have to worry about shielding us. We might even get some valuable information from this long-lived creature along the way.

I moved my attention to the ember, waiting for it to weigh in on the decision. No change. I had begun picking up when it didn't like a situation. There was no warning hum. Good.

The creature tilted its nostrils skyward, inhaling the cool night breeze deeply. It exhaled slowly, tasting the air. Accurately assessing my thoughts, it motioned to my companions, "You have hours, if that. The ember will be easy to pick off you now. This part of Sundale is essentially unregulated with the population centers so far away. More of your kind and their creatures follow your trail. Their lust for the ember's power urges them to travel without rest through the night. Enter when you are ready. No harm will come to you. I'll meet you shortly thereafter."

It turned, retreating into the shadows of the forest.

～

"Why didn't you wake me for my watch." Conall was already grumbling at me. He threw a piece of bread in my direction, scowling.

"We all need to share the burden, Nayla. If one of us tires, it puts all of us at risk," Malik scolded, chiming in.

I raised my eyebrow at him, preparing to contradict him, but thought better of it considering the news I had to tell them. "You're right, sorry," I mumbled. That apparently was the exact wrong thing to say because they both stopped what they were doing and turned toward me.

"What is it?" Conall accused.

"Nothing," I replied innocently. I loved, and hated, that he could read me so thoroughly. It was comforting yet disconcerting to be known like that.

"Since when are we right and you sorry? What have you done?" Malik impressed firmly.

"Well, it's just that while you were sleeping, I might have made a little arrangement with the Uden for our safe passage to Seabrook."

"And who is *Uden*, Nayla?" Malik had come over to kneel near where I was sitting for this conversation.

Conall got up and began pacing, answering on my behalf. "Uden is the creature who tried to kill her when the ember transported her into the Swath. He's one of the oldest beings in this realm and possesses quite the appetite based on Nayla's description." Conall turned to me, putting his clenched fists on his hips, "So, he's going to let us pass through? Why would he do that?"

"What did you offer him, Nayla?" Malik said, tone full of rebuke.

"First, he and the rest of the creatures in the forest aren't even from here. He told me that there were untold realms, one of which they called home. And he implied the ember doesn't just open a path to Idia, but to many other realms too."

Malik interrupted, "And when we learn how to use it to open portals, he wants to return home, is that it?"

"More or less."

"Why do we need his help if your shields can protect us?" Conall asked.

"They're still weak, and my control is, umm, questionable. And I'd rather not call upon the power of the ember again. You saw what happened before."

I remember standing there after the fight having the most graphic visions like I could see a vibrating webbing connecting everything. I could see the very particles of the steel in the fighter's swords change and shape to my will. Like what I'd felt with the lock, but this time so much more clearly. It took a little tug of the right energy, and they crumbled. I lost track. I woke a short time later as Conall was carrying me back to the camp.

"We're safe enough for now without you needing to make a deal with that creature." Conall was pacing. From his body language, I saw he was going to present more of a hurdle than Malik. I knew the bedtime stories he'd been fed as a child about the horrors in the Swath.

I directed my attention to him. "It's all true, flesh-eating monsters, scalding pools, a barrier that holds bad children inside." I knew I shouldn't tease, but I couldn't help myself. "By now, they'll know we have Darius and recognize the surge of power from the ember. Uden says they travel day and night, Conall. And I'm not convinced we are to be taken prisoner this time. Uden sensed them hunting us. We need to gather everything and move now. The deeper we can get, the more likely they'll lose our trail."

"We will fight them." Conall rotated his shoulder around and winced. He must have strained it during the fight. I made a note to heal it, and our wrists, which were chafed raw when we stopped to rest.

"Conall, we can't fight them. There will be too many."

"And what of their creatures?" Meethra's voice shook.

"There can't be over ten if they move that quickly," Conall argued.

"We used almost all my sister's antidote to escape. If they have more of that compound, or if what Malik said the creatures can do is true, we won't even have our speed. If something happened to either of you—" I trailed off; the thought made me sick. "I can't let that happen," I said firmly.

"So, what, you're making the final decision, is that it? Because you have the ember, you make the plans?" We spent ten years as siblings and never even snapped at each other, much less argued. Since Malik and I escaped from Eastdow's prison, Conall's temper toward me had grown. Or since he learned who I truly was.

"Look, you know that isn't true. But if there are soldiers from Eastdow, you don't want us to kill them. I saw you hesitate back there. Trying to only incapacitate them is too risky."

I saw on his face my words had their intended result, but Conall took a fresh approach. "Are you so sure your forest friend isn't trying to lure us into the Swath to take the ember for himself? Or worse, make sure Darius knew where to find us?"

"He knew what happened to Lathrais. And that is impossible. You know he can't leave the barrier—"

"Again, we vote," Conall cut me off. He looked at Malik, assessing. "I see I'm going to lose this one, and that's fine. But from now on, we vote. That's the only way this will work. Malik, what is your say?"

"It sounds like the forest is the most prudent decision. She trusts this creature, and her shields and the ember will be our backup." He shrugged nonchalantly and gathered his pack. Conall looked at Meethra.

"I— I can't," was all she said. Her yellow skin had paled to a parchment white. She stared at me, begging me to understand.

"Find us in Seabrook, my friend," I relieved her.

"The Swath it is." Conall was shaking his head as he kneeled to gather his things.

The giant domed shield that rested over the Swath was difficult to detect without using our enhanced vision. I knew we were getting close and motioned for them to slow. A few feet in front of us, there was a wrinkle in the air. As we approached the perimeter of the forest, the ancient power of the barrier gave a slight quiver. I reached my hand out, waving it through. The border rippled where my hand passed.

I looked at Conall, "You ready?" I stepped through, turning to them. Malik shrugged, following in his nonplussed way. Conall, more uncertain, inhaled deeply and took a gigantic step as if he was trying to clear a stump lying in the path.

He was holding the reins of the horse who thought better of entering the forest, with a jerky Darius sitting atop. Conall tugged gently, urging the beast to follow to no avail. Conall reached back to pet the nuzzle of the mare and jumped when his unshielded hand hit a solid wall.

I walked over, shielded my hand, reached through, and stroked the horse soothingly. "You're not scared of a few forest creatures, are you, Darius?" I asked with mock sweetness in my voice. If he wasn't tied to the horse, I imagined he'd have tried to throw himself off it. I couldn't resist the urge to taunt him. "We *probably* won't let them eat you. And I don't imagine your friends are coming in here to get you."

I heard Malik snicker behind me. I imagined if I wanted to torture the information out of his brother, he wouldn't stop me. There seemed to be no love lost between them. Tempting.

Darius tried to disguise his tremor as he shot a glare in my direction.

Slowly the mare stepped forward through the barrier, ears pricking up and nostrils flaring at the unfamiliar sounds that sprung to life inside. She paused about halfway in, the border rippling along her haunches. As I tugged her forward, I swore I saw the barrier jump a foot outward. I put a hand on her nuzzle to still her and motioned my other to halt my companions.

"What are you looking at, Nayla?" Malik asked, tracing my gaze.

"I think the dome moved. I know it sounds crazy."

They were all watching the edge of the barrier, and the horse was becoming increasingly restless. Nothing changed. I shook my head and urged the horse forward once more.

"Watch your footing. The hot pools can be hidden under layers of moss and foliage." I pointed to steam escaping a large patch of grasses. Water bubbled just underneath.

We traveled carefully for over two hours, going deeper into the forest, the entire time waiting anxiously for our promised guide to appear. Surprisingly, we had encountered no creatures yet, which only made the forest more ominous.

Suddenly, a winged creature zipped in front of Conall, halting his progress. It flew back across his path, stopping this time in front of him, beating its wings, hovering. He and Malik were both reaching for their weapons. I trudged over to them and pointed out the small patch of dense leaves Conall had been about to step in. Conall's eyes went wide as he stuck his blade deep into the hissing puddle, not finding its bottom. He looked back at the creature, who had a comically wide grin plastered across its gourd-shaped head.

This winged creature was nothing like Meethra, our godfly friend, who was beautiful and radiated light. She was somewhere between an insect and a miniature Skyborne with delicate limbs, a pair of long translucent wings, and a small but pretty face, like the images depicted in books of mythical and vanished beings. This creature was like a miniature Uden, still fleshy and well-fed. Its bat-like wings looked like they could barely hold its weight as it flapped alongside us. Its skin, which wrapped its pudgy body, was a translucent gray yellow-green and gray veins snaked under its skin.

Malik nudged Conall in the ribs, "Say thank you."

Its maw opened to an impossibly wide grin, exposing rows of jagged, sharp teeth as it hovered in front of him, waiting. Hesitantly, a visibly paled Conall obliged, "Thank you."

The creature flew with us for the next few hours, pointing out any of the dangers in our path we didn't appear to notice and steering us north until we reached a cleared footpath.

"Do you have a name?" I asked it at some point. Walking in silence was becoming boring, and curiosity about these creatures, Uden, their master, and their realm struck me. It flew over next to me and shook its head, not making a sound, excess skin wiggling as it moved.

I heard gurgling wet sounds coming from right ahead. We approached a clearing. Peering over the remaining foliage hiding it from our view, we saw the remains of a large stallion adorned with plates of leather armor dyed in the Drakestone colors. Many creatures were feasting on it.

Our mare was becoming nervous, no doubt watching these forest creatures greedily devour its kin. The three of us watched with some sick fascination.

The horse had been pulled to the base of an enormous tree trunk and was now lying broken on its side. Its exposed abdomen moved. Thump. Thump. Something inside it was trying to get out. Suddenly, there was a split in the weaker side of the abdomen, another thump, and it cleaved in two. Guts and a dog-sized creature, with a row of spines on its head, slid out. It looked at us, momentarily cocking its head as if remembering something. It blinked twice, clearing its eyes, and turned, flapping around violently, shaking the horse's blood and innards off its skin.

"Feeling a little powerless, are you?" I snipped at Darius. Goading him was the best way to keep from retching. It worked. His quivering had resumed at full strength, and he was trying to speak through his gag.

"We should keep walking while there's still light." Malik, ignoring him, walked north across the clearing toward the connecting trail's opening.

"My kin draw them past the boundary, livestock and other animals who venture too close. It's a sort of seduction common with our kind. Good idea to be on your way. Best you not linger and test them." It was Uden's voice, echoing in the clearing's space. I involuntarily shivered at its eeriness and saw my companions do the same.

It was then I noticed our guide was studying Darius uncomfortably close. I realized the smell of the horse's blood must be testing its control. It landed on his torso and climbed up, bringing its nostrils against his neck and the vein that flowed there. It made a gurgling sound and licked. Darius was now desperately trying to dislodge the creature.

Uden stepped from the shadows of the trail-head Malik was headed toward. A commanding sound echoed, and the creatures stilled, including the one tasting Darius.

Uden stepped into the clearing and sounded again. Our guide reluctantly unattached itself from Darius and flew over to Uden. They conversed through a series of unintelligent sounds, then the guide pointed at the horse and smiled at Darius before flying over to it. It pulled up a piece of the deceased horse's armor and sunk its sharp teeth into the flesh beneath.

Malik looked at his brother, who was deathly pale, and bent over, roaring in laughter.

A grin threatened to escape as I approached Uden. Conall, who was a little green, looked between Malik and I, shaking his head disapprovingly.

"Welcome," Uden said.

I glanced toward the feasting creatures, then back to Uden. He was perfectly capable of killing me. Possibly even before I could raise my shields. This was an exercise in trust. I took a deep breath. "You are familiar with my companions, Malik Dsiban, the former heir of Drakestone and Conall Tiernach, presumably the former heir of Eastdow. And, of course, our additional guest, Darius, Malik's younger brother. Darius, is it safe to assume you are now heir to the Regency of Drakestone?"

Darius was struggling to say something through his muffle. "Darius, nodding is sufficient," I said. He looked between us and obliged, wide-eyed at the paunchy creature looming casually in front of us.

"Ah, well, congratulations on your new appointment then." I paused for the theater of it. "Gentlemen, may I present to you the iniquitous and scheming, Uden." He chuckled at that last bit as I continued, "Master of the Swath."

He paused, blocking the trail entrance, thinking. "I think I like that." He surveyed the feasting creatures with unmistakable pride, then turned to study Darius for a moment. "I was hoping you were bringing this one as an offering, of good faith perhaps?" He walked up to Darius and ran a webbed finger along his thigh, tilting his head to the side in question, though I'd already told him no. His half-smile exposed his blood-stained maw and struck terror in Darius' eyes.

I couldn't help grinning, knowing full well whose benefit he'd said that for. "I'm afraid not, *cousin*. But maybe if he doesn't cooperate."

"Ah, well, I will keep my hopes up then. Follow, if you please." He turned and led the way down the path.

That evening we found a place to camp deep in the forest. There was a clearing where trees had grown, no, had been woven as they'd grown, creating little shelters at their base. I helped Conall sort out the provisions. We hadn't eaten since that morning and were all famished. Malik even removed Darius's gag and unbound his hands so he could receive a portion, though he refused to eat. Or maybe Uden's creatures had stolen his appetite.

I lit a lamp and sifted through the book from my mother. I was fatigued by everything that happened over the last few days, but my curiosity was very active. The book was old, much of it written in a language now not widely known. But new entries were made in it which I could read. Most of it was like a genealogy. I recognized many of the original family's names—Dsiban, Tiernach, old Sol Ros names. The ones carried forward to the regencies now. But there were others I didn't recognize whose lines ended abruptly, Innar, Harnak, Gashua, which began in the second half of the book. There was something there, I thought—a reason my mother wanted me to have this book.

I looked over to where Uden was sitting cross-legged, leaning against a tree watching us. "What you said earlier, about serving your time, and before about the realm of the banished." He nodded in acknowledgment. "What did you mean?"

"Do you think that we all accidentally arrived here on this realm, so difficult to thrive in? When we were sent here, I was young. I didn't know everything there is to know, but I understood it to be a judgment bestowed upon us by a higher power. A punishment intended to initiate a resetting of sorts. My kind had done things, cruel things, and it had removed us from the equation."

"What type of power—a god?" The possibility of this all being the entertainment of bored Makers briefly crossed my mind before Uden swatted the thought from my head.

"No, girl. No stories of Makers and otherworldly omnipotent beings. Yet, something with an essence very similar to the very object you carry. That is what my kind worship. I remember waking in darkness, feeling their energy, then being thrust through darkness. This forest is where I landed with the others."

I wasn't so sure of his explanation. I touched the small box at my breast and felt it hum in greeting.

"What cruel deeds did your kind commit that sent you here?" I asked him.

He was quiet for a long while. "Greed. And the terrible acts that it drives one toward. The oldest of my kind railed against the punishment. They denied everything they had done. I didn't understand then.

I believed what had happened to us was unjust, too. But now I'm not so sure. There has been much time to think."

"Seems like an awfully stiff sentence for greed. What happened to the other older creatures?" I asked since Uden obviously wasn't going to divulge more on what his kind had done.

"Some died naturally. Others were, er... See, they could not die to the old ways. The ways which I believe caused our banishment. Since they refused to change, it made it impossible to live together in this cramped forest with so many of us... so we eliminated them."

I shivered at the thought of the massacre he described. "And now you are the oldest creature here, Master of the Swath?"

He smiled. "I am."

"You haven't been to your home realm since you were a child. Why do you even want to go back there?"

Uden appeared thoughtful for a moment. "My life is nearing its end. I would like to be home when I die. And my legacy, I suppose, would be for my kind to make their way back somewhere they could flourish. Better than they'd been before we were banished."

"You aren't flourishing here?"

"As nice as this little domed hell hole is, hardly. Uden, our home, was an enchanting place comparatively. Much more suited to our kind. And things are changing in this realm, Nayla. You may not sense it yet, but the energy that set all this in motion is active again. I feel it."

"Because I took the ember?"

"It can be the only explanation."

"I saw the dome move."

"Are you certain?" he asked, observing me.

I shrugged my shoulders uncertainly, wondering what had caused the godflies' banishment, making a mental note to ask Meethra.

CHAPTER SIXTEEN

UDEN TOLD US about his realm, his home, or what he remembered of it. It sounded like a fantastical place full of creatures, cities, and landscapes my Skyborne mind could barely imagine. And he shared his perspective of the Skyborne and the histories of the skirmishes and power struggles between us from their vantage point in the Swath. He didn't have too high of an opinion of our kind.

"Until you met me," I shamelessly added to his tale.

I turned to him. "How is it you know so much of what goes on outside the Swath?" It had only just occurred to me in the last day that Uden always seemed to have a surprising amount of information that went on outside the Swath. Both Malik and Conall turned to listen.

"Voices carry on the winds, the trees speak, and I have other sources…"

"You are so cryptic, you know." He laughed at me.

"Until we meet again, *friends*."

"Thank you, Uden," I said as I raised my shield around our group so we could pass through the domed barrier. When I turned to look back, Uden was standing with his webbed hand pressed into the solid invisible wall.

❧

We deemed Seabrook to be safe enough to take shelter in a traveler's inn for our last night before we would reach the city. The inn was in a small town used as a hub for travel and small rural markets located halfway between the Swath and Seabrook proper. The building itself wasn't much to appreciate, made from unrefined stone, wood beams, and thatched roof resting tiredly over the second story. The inn had two rooms available, and considering the extra body in tow, we took both.

Conall and Malik agreed to keep Darius in one, so I had my first moments of true solitude since being stuck in prison in Eastdow. The three of us developed such an easy rhythm over the last few weeks; being in my room without either of them near was strangely off-putting, instead of welcome. I tried to enjoy the quiet, but it only led to my unraveling thoughts. I quietly stepped out into the hallway, only to find Conall doing the same.

"Malik?" I asked.

"He said he'd bring Darius down for dinner after a while. I don't know about you, but I could use a drink." Conall raised an eyebrow at me as he passed, making his way to the stairwell. We took a table in a quiet corner of the meal hall downstairs and ordered two beers from a worn-thin red-haired female who was obviously put out by our existence.

"She seems nice." Conall laughed as he drank deeply from the mug she'd slammed down in front of him.

We were keen to listen to the conversations taking place in the booths and tables around us. The inn's guests took care to speak in hushed tones and made wary glances in our direction, but listening with our enhanced senses, we caught most of their conversations.

Word had spread like wildfire about Eastdow's failure to activate the ember, their High Priest's death, and the escape of whom was responsible. Several of the tables even guessed we may be those very fugitives, but the Skyborne of Seabrook, having always held the shorter straw, didn't seem to mind having that kind of power take refuge in their land. None appeared willing to stick their neck out for our capture anyway, despite what we might be worth.

Soon, Malik appeared at the bottom of the stairwell, ushering Darius along. It occurred to me that I might have been unsure of letting the two brothers alone together and considered that they very well could conspire against me, much like I had done inside their territory not so long ago. I watched Malik's face as he walked Darius to our table in the corner and knew it wasn't true. Malik nudged Darius toward the far seat so he'd be blocked in.

"Shields were how you got out of the forest?" Darius asked, looking from me to Malik. "You *knew*." He paused a moment before he added, "Traitor."

Malik tossed a long strip of folded-up cloth I recognized as his gag onto the table. "Watch it, Darius."

"Malik and I weren't formally aligned until..." I considered exactly when that had happened. I continued, "until you showed up in Eastdow, and we ended up in prison. Ah, but how things change."

"They will change again. Wait." It was a clear threat.

Conall had enough. "Shut up, Darius. Unlike your brother, you picked the wrong side." The ember agreed reassuringly from my pocket.

Malik looked at me. "Have you heard anything worth repeating?"

"Talk travels faster than us, apparently. Morale has declined. The Skyborne are getting restless, especially now that three," I looked at Darius and corrected myself, "*four* future Regents and the ember have gone missing. Priests are trying to maintain control with new prophecies, but no one seems to buy it. There have been a few minor riots, over resources mostly."

Conall shook his head, "I feel like after all the time I spent training under my father to take the regency one day, I am only now seeing the plight of the Skyborne."

The red-haired server gruffly set another round beer down at the table. As Darius reached for one, Malik pushed it out of reach.

"In case we weren't clear, *prisoner*. You are our *prisoner*." Malik sounded the word out slowly for Darius the second time and turned to Conall with a pointed look. "You should have made a point to see their plight. That's the job of Regent. Being sheltered is no excuse. Uden is right. This is a difficult realm to survive in, much less thrive. The Skyborne are struggling, and those in power have sold them false hope. I'm honestly surprised to hear things aren't worse."

"These *poor* Skyborne that you refer to bring it on themselves with their laziness," Darius sneered, gesturing around the room. "It's a shame they play the victim. If they took responsibility for their own wellbeing, they wouldn't be in this situation, always blaming someone else for their struggles. They aren't entitled to what our family has earned, what is mine by right. Malik, what you have always failed to face, is that there are those among us who deserve more than others. That is the benefit of ruling." Darius looked smug, even sitting with his hands bound, explaining his position.

Conall countered, "Seems to me if we were better at ruling, we wouldn't be in this situation. And don't preach to me about the struggles of our forebearers. They got us this far, and we've permitted a system where a select few justify the bounty they take, for ruling, creating the systems or whatever, and let the rest of Skyborne do the work."

"They are lucky to have what we give them," Darius gloated.

Conall considered his words before he spoke. "It's our job is to keep them safe and cultivate an environment where they can *thrive*. That is the duty and burden of our responsibility. And that is precisely what will divide us now we know that the prophecy is a lie. And I see now you are the type of male who takes what he wants, even when it is not offered to him."

Darius winced, flicking eyes in my direction. Conall's remark had its desired effect, yet Darius belligerently kept on. "Conall, they are fine; look at them." Darius boasted loudly, motioning his bound hands to the Skyborne at the tables, who were now looking toward us unabashedly. I surveyed them. Dirty, tired, one Skyborne looked sick. Our server was clearly unhappy, much less well cared for. A few who overheard him were shaking their heads in disgust at Darius's pretense.

Darius continued, "Okay, I'll play. Say you're right. What are you going to do about it? Invite everyone to come live as one big happy family in the Eastdow keep? The resources will run out faster. And then what? You're young and idealistic, barely an adult. You don't know what it's like to make the difficult decisions it takes to rule—"

"Like you do either, Darius," I cut him off. I couldn't let Darius drone on, and I could tell Conall was about to lose it. "I was there, and your parents clearly run that territory while you apparently spend all your time cozying up to pretty girls." I turned to Malik and Conall, pointing at the gag, "Why exactly are we arguing over politics with our prisoner?"

I was about to throttle Darius when a tough-looking dark-skinned girl, a little beyond Jude's age, I guessed, stopped at our table as she was walking by. The girl was tall with lean muscle showing through her low-slung rust tights and orange shirt. *Shirt* wasn't exactly the right word. I had never seen clothes quite like what she wore. It was a band of fabric that wrapped closely around her chest, and many other smaller bands wrapped weaving through each other, creating a decorative pattern across her shoulders and abdomen, leaving much of her skin exposed.

She directed her attention to Malik, waiting. When he said nothing, she said, "Friend of Seeley's?"

"That's right. You?"

"Aye, may I sit?"

He motioned to a chair.

She pulled out one of the blocky chairs from the table and took place, reaching for the drink the server intended for Darius. "Thanks," she lifted it toward him mockingly. "You should send word to him you have the prisoner coming, too. They'll need to make a proper arrangement."

She obviously knew who we were as she surveyed us. The girl got the server's attention on her next pass and requested a writing utensil. When she brought it back, the girl pulled out a rolled piece of paper and began writing a note. She finished and let out a high-pitched whistle and looked toward the window, then toward Malik. "I'm Bara, one of Seeley's aids and messengers. I thought you might recognize me, Malik?"

Malik watched her for another moment before a glimmer of recognition showed on his face. "Ah yes, my apologies. I didn't know your name, though. It's my pleasure."

A small bird of prey swooped in through the window and landed on Bara's shoulder. She smiled. "This is Cleek, one of the birds I've been training. I read in one volume in the library about how they used them for communication on Idia before the crossover and how they trained them. I guess we lost the art." She tied the note to Cleek's talon and stroked the bird's chest.

"He's beautiful," I exclaimed. I'd seen the falcons soaring around the mountains but had never seen one up close. I reached a hand out to touch him. "May I?"

Bara laughed, "Yes, Cleek is friendly enough. I can't say the same for the others, unfortunately. Put this on." She pulled a glove from her belt and tossed it to me. I slipped it on, not entirely understanding. "Go ahead and reach your hand toward him." She smiled with pride.

I did as she said, and Cleek jumped from her shoulder onto my hand. As his claws dug into the glove as he got comfortable, and I saw the glove's purpose. Our server set a small plate with two small slivers of raw meat on the table. Bara must have been here often enough; she knew the bird's order.

"A snack for him," Bara explained as she took a piece and lifted it for his inspection. Cleek swallowed it down greedily and twisted his head to eye the next. As Bara gave it to him, I asked, "Is that all he gets?"

"The art is to feed them just enough, so they are nourished, but not sated, and they want to attach themselves to you and come back. It creates a symbiotic relationship."

"Interesting." I moved my hand toward Conall and Malik so they'd get a better look at the bird. Conall smiled and ran his knuckle down Cleek's chest feathers like Bara had.

Bara cleared her throat, "Seeley asked me to send word as soon as one of us found you. He's been worried. That's what I put in the note, so you're aware. And a mention of this one." She motioned to Darius.

"Ah, thank you. We unexpectedly got caught up."

Bara laughed, "I heard. We'd best be off." She got up and pushed her chair back under the table. She motioned to the window and whistled again. Cleek jumped from my hand and flew out swiftly. I handed her the glove. "Thanks for the beer," she taunted Darius again as she left.

"I like her," I announced.

⁓

A day later, we approached the city of Seabrook proper, its tall weather-washed stone walls the color of sand rose high above the mouth of the river. Girthy round buildings with steeply peaked conical roofs resembling sandcastles were built into the joints of the sectioned walls.

The message Bara sent appeared to have arrived because we were expected. A large gate was visible, where I could see sentries followed by two guards exiting on horseback riding out to meet us. When the guards approached, Malik motioned toward Darius, whom they then flanked and led to the keep.

Inside the walls, the sentries handed us off to two attendants who led us into a great hall, filled with tall tree-like columns reaching toward the sky, branching out, making a canopy of the vaulted ceiling. We stood in the open center of the space, watching the light create shadowed patterns from the intricate carvings in each window. As we waited, three Skyborne glided around the columns into the room and came to greet us.

"Be welcome and at ease, friends," the matriarch invited. She was a mid-height female who looked like she was carved of obsidian stone and radiated strength. She had the darkest skin I had ever seen; it almost glowed like the ember. Her deep eyes were kind and sympathetic; the brightness of her teeth showing through her broad smile was stark against her lips, painted with metallic rust.

All three knew Malik, so the matriarch, Femi, directed her introductions to Conall and me—herself as the Seabrook Regent, along with her husband, Alrun, and a son, and presumably the heir Seeley, who flanked her. As it was in my own territory Arborvale, whoever carried the bloodline was the Regent regardless of gender. The one other territory in our realm that followed that social structure was Monterra, the mysterious territory breeding the creatures that shared the mountain range and northern half of the continent with Drakestone.

Alrun was as breathtaking an image as his wife, the Regent. He was practically colorless. There was no other way to describe him. He shared the same ethnic features with the Skyborne I had seen so far from Seabrook, but where they had skin and hair in varying shades of deep browns and mochas, his was free of pigment, while his textured hair which grew wildly atop his skull, was a yellowish tan.

His dark eyes were inquisitive and reserved as he bowed at his introduction.

I saw Malik eyeing the Regent's son. Seeley, who bore a striking resemblance to his mother, lifted his chin in aloofness. He didn't appear as old as Malik, who was in his late thirties, but he had to be around four or five years older than me.

Femi and Alrun embraced Malik, while Seeley, with both hands, embraced my own. He stood only a few inches taller than me. His frame was narrow, with lanky limbs and a slight paunch. His round eyes met mine, and a smile escaped his control.

"I've been dying to meet you, little thief. Malik painted quite the picture about you in his letters," he crooned and winked, bubbling with welcome and excitement. Our arrival must be a welcome break from the monotony of his duties as heir obligated him to.

Alrun looked at his son disapprovingly. I didn't know what to think, though first impressions, I liked them and I hoped they felt the same about us.

As Conall and I were clearly having trouble deciding to whom we should direct our attention toward being the clear outsiders in this circle, Femi intervened, offering us shelter and protection for as long as needed. We were to be shown to our rooms, clean up and rest, then meet them for a late dinner to discuss, which I assumed meant to explain our circumstances and plans.

Conall and I thanked her and Alrun with our profuse gratitude, and with that, they bid us a pleasant afternoon and left through the side door they had entered.

Only Seeley remained with us and two attendants who were tasked with delivering us to our accommodations and seeing we were situated.

"You could have ridden out to greet us," Malik said to the Heir Seeley when his parents had left us.

The beautiful Skyborne huffed and shrugged his shoulders as he fiddled absently with one of the gold laces on his fine indigo tunic. His was playing hard to get, I realized. I looked from Malik to Seeley, with obvious surprise on my face. I don't know that I had ever met two more opposite Skyborne. Malik had this air of nefariousness, though I knew it wasn't indicative of his character, and Seeley was perhaps the most immediately warm and effervescent person I had ever met.

"What?" Malik's offense rising, "you've never seen—"

But I cut him off, "*NO*, of course it's not that. It's…" and I looked to Conall for a little help.

"It's just your personalities are so *different*," Conall bluntly answered for me.

"Well, I wasn't going to put it like *that*. But yes, Seeley, you seem so *wonderful*, and Malik, you are—"

"A bastard?" Malik finished for me. We *all* laughed at that.

Seeley gave me a sympathetic smile. "I will admit it took me years to wear through his brittle and cynical exterior," Seeley said, stroking Malik's arm gently. "But in the end, he found me to be utterly irresistible." Hand on hip now, he continued, "and furthermore—"

"Here we go," Malik huffed.

"Well, naturally, I'm pissed you stayed away so long. And you stopped sending messages," Seeley pouted. "I was worried for you."

The way he shared his warmth freely made me immediately adore him.

"Sounds like something you two need to work out *in private*," I gestured, and they clasped hands and took the opening I gave them to leave us.

Our attendants led us after them to our own quarters.

We had allies. That was good.

It was the first hot bath I'd taken in well over two months, and I planned to revel in it. Beside the tub, attendants had set out pastes, soaps, and salts. I picked a jar up and was inspecting the contents when there was a knock at the door. An older female entered the room. "Don't be alarmed. I'm here to help you, and by the Makers, you look a terrible mess."

"Oh, I'm okay. I can manage, thank you."

She responded by handing me a looking glass. I reached toward my face, running my fingertips across it. My reflection was as rough as my skin.

"My guess is you don't even know what half of what these creams do. But suit yourself." She turned toward the door.

"Okay," I called with a quiet, surrendering voice. "I will take the help, thank you."

"That's better. I'm called May." She reached to me and ran a hand across my hair. "It is so dry, honey. But don't worry, I will get you turned around." May reached for the jar in my hand, opened it, and massaged the cream into my hair. By the time she stepped out of the room, I had thoroughly been scrubbed, brushed, and left with my clean hair in a hot towel and a thick clay paste on my face with instructions to rinse it off when I was finished soaking.

When I emerged from the bathroom in my silky robe, I eyed the fluffy white bed beckoning me. I crawled in with the towel still in my hair.

I awoke to May rustling around with my things. She was unpacking and sorting through my dirty clothes, including the ones I discarded on the bathroom floor. My heart skipped a beat in panic. She must have seen it on my face when she looked at me because she pointed to a drawer in the small table beside the bed and smiled. I reached into the drawer and pulled out the pouch containing the ember. It vibrated reassuringly. I looked back at her.

"I didn't mean any offense, May. I'm sorry. It's... See, when I took it, it had been so heavily guarded, and there has been so much headache over it, and I left it just sitting there on the floor." I shook my head at my carelessness.

"No need to apologize. We understand the weight you carry. I've laid out some clothing for you. Best get ready for dinner." She smiled warmly and took a pile of my dirty clothes with her as she exited the room.

I surveyed the items she'd set out. The mustard gold skirt was a loose, gauzy fabric that set high on the waist and flowed down loosely with several open slits. The top, made of soft cream fabric, was similar to the one Bara wore but embellished with gold designs. I put them on and surveyed myself in the mirror.

Most of the clothes from home were decidedly more modest, either because of the crisp temperatures in Eastdow or the humble materials available in Arborvale. The way the skirt moved, no doubt to let air flow through to combat the stifling heat here in Seabrook, but it was also very feminine. After being in Vera's strong and lean body so long, seeing my delicate curves accentuated with this clothing only made me feel more awkward in my skin. My utilitarian traveling clothes worked so well to ease me back into my own form, I only now realized it.

I was still staring at myself when May breezed back into the room. Assessing me, she grabbed two combs from the dresser and swept the sides of my hair back from my temples, and pinned them in place. She dusted on makeup in a similar style to Femi and deemed me ready to go.

"One last thing," May pointed to the drawer.

I went and retrieved the pouch. "But where do I put it?" I was used to having tunics and blouses with pockets.

"You have a hidden pocket here sewn into the skirt." She pointed in-between one of the flowing layers. Sure enough, the pouch slipped right into the pocket. It was positioned so I could feel its presence even.

"Thank you," I nodded to her.

"I saw you when you arrived. You stood like a small but mighty statue. But you must embrace this side of you too. You are a beautiful girl, Nayla. Be proud of the gifts of your adulthood." May reached for my chin, lifting it. "Chin high, shoulders back."

I only then realized I'd been standing with my chest concave. I straightened and took her advice.

"That's better. Now you are doubly fierce." She gave me a wry smile and led me back to the great hall.

⸙

That evening I was the last to arrive in the great hall for dinner. Femi got up and came over to greet me with a light embrace and a light peck on both cheeks. She looked me up and down, "Our attire suits you well." She leaned to my ear, "Freeing, isn't it?" Seeley grabbed my hand, giving me a quick spin, and whistled loudly. I laughed and dramatically batted my charcoaled lashes for him.

We all took our seats, and Conall, after having only stared at me until then, was guided by a graceful Femi to a chair by my side. "Wow," he leaned over to me finally. "First, you're not Vera, now this? I'm not sure I can handle you."

If I didn't know any better, Conall was flirting with me. "You can't," I cooed, looking him in the eye and gave him a wry grin. His smile dropped, and he took a barely audible swallow. His warm brown eyes were so earnest in the moment, molten almost, I had to look away.

Throughout dinner that night, we shared with as much brevity as possible everything that happened over the last few months. Femi and Alrun did not press for more, satisfied with our account.

The night carried on with more wine and stories. Seeley shared how he and Malik met and eventually became lovers, a sweeter story than what I would have expected from Malik. In front of everyone, Malik gave Seeley and his family credit for showing him a better approach to the guardianship of their Skyborne than he'd learned growing up under the harsh governance of his ancestors in Drakestone.

Femi even talked with pride of the Skyborne in her territory and what they'd overcome to stay unified. Conall kept the group laughing with stories of our training together and our camping trips. Alrun was the only one quiet, thoughtfully sipping his wine, watching the rest of us carry on.

Finally, as the night ended, Conall, who'd already gotten his bearings in the keep, offered to walk me to my room. Every so often, as we walked down the hall, there would be a door leading out to an open-air veranda. As we passed one, Conall stopped short. "Listen."

I laughed, "I don't hear anything."

"Nooo," he slurred, "really listen."

I used my power to heighten my senses. Soft music wisped around my ears. He grabbed my hand and led me out onto the balcony, and the music became louder. Somewhere beyond in the courtyard, there was a deft musician smoothly sliding a bow across a set of strings. It was cheerful and soothing, and I could just make out figures of couples dancing in the courtyard under power-lit lanterns.

"Dance with me," Conall demanded.

"What, Conall?! No... you're being silly."

"No really, Nayla, I'd ask somebody else, but you're all I've got." He gave me a tipsy toothy grin, intending to sway me.

"Fine." I stood there with my hands on my hips.

He took three intentional steps toward me and had me in his strong arms. He smiled and made his move.

With the wine and the dancing, my entire soul was spinning. I had no idea what a fine dancer Conall was, and it no doubt played a role in how well he fought, I thought. It was fortunate, too, because I'd learned to be proficient enough when I was younger, but after I'd left Arborvale, dancing skills weren't my top priority.

Conall swept me effortlessly across the balcony, making circles so perfectly arranged I didn't even have to think. It was the first time I'd lost myself since those nights with Darius, though I had never left those so completely I forgot to be Vera.

I didn't know how long we'd been dancing when my sandal caught the edge of a stone, and I tripped into him, becoming instantly aware of his hard body against my own. The wine-drunk part of me appreciated the corded muscle of his chest. I was now pressed against it, and his spiced and woody scent wafted up my eager nostrils. Before he realized my appreciation, I stiffened, embarrassed, praying to the Makers he didn't perceive my thoughts.

He righted me, both of us laughing. "You were doing so well." He made a funny face as he shrugged his shoulders. We were standing face to face, his hand still on my waist from steadying me. I could see where this was going to lead if I wasn't careful, and I knew we'd both had too much wine to make the decision to cross that line between us.

"We should go to bed," I whispered.

"Okay, Nayla. If that's what you want."

He gave me a soft smile and took my hand, leading me back to my room.

CHAPTER SEVENTEEN

WHEN I WOKE up, the sun was already streaming brightly through the window. There was a plate of bread and a fresh set of clothes, more modest and casual for day wear, set out for me with a note from May, I assumed, instructing me to make myself at home in the section of the complex which was the family's home.

That afternoon I found myself wandering through the halls, then out of the building into the main square. There were carts with fabrics, bread, and fish for sale in one corner. I headed toward it to see if any of the vendors carried live plants when I noticed a small gathering around a secondary exit to the keep. As I approached, a delicious smell wafted through the air. Wooden tables lined the alley, and citizens were sitting talking merrily and eating out of stone bowls. Femi and Seeley, along with many kitchen workers, were at the door bringing out trays of soup to the awaiting crowd.

Seeley spotted me, and I waved. He walked over to me, "I was wondering when you'd emerge. Need some food or at least some bread to soak up the damage?" He was smiling mischievously at me.

"Very funny," I replied, studying the stained apron and casual ensemble he was wearing. It was a contrast from the refined picture he'd painted last evening. "How can I help?"

He must have sensed the earnestness in my voice because he handed me the tray and pointed to a far table. Once I'd delivered the food, I met him back in the kitchen for a refill.

I took the ladle from him, spooning the fish stew into bowls. "Do you guys do this every day?"

"We try to," he said, wiping the thin linen of this tunic across his forehead. "It makes it easier on them to work with full bellies. My father works with the anglers to ration the catch. Some get salted for storage, some go to markets, and the rest comes to us. We use it for us and the workers, then make soups and pies in the kitchens for the citizens. Sometimes there isn't enough, but more often there is."

Femi walked up to us. "We hear of unrest in the other territories since…" she trailed off for a moment after she caught my eye with a sympathetic frown. "My ancestors never wanted to rely on the prophecy, so we've tried to build a system in Seabrook that would be sustainable. Of course, everything has its flaws, but we make efforts to work together and manage our resources collectively, so everyone has enough. We are all glad you and Conall are here, Nayla. We will do what we can to help you when you find what that is." A tear came to my eye at her earnestly. She grabbed my wrist and squeezed it warmly before she took the tray I'd been refilling and went to deliver it.

Seeley smiled proudly at his mother as she left.

"Wow, it must have been amazing to grow up with parents like that." I shouldn't have said that, I realized, after I thought of my mother and how apparently little I understood of her. "Did Malik tell you we met my sister Jude, and he sent her to bring my mother and sisters here?"

"He told us, yes. Malik thinks they may be in danger when your father passes. To get to you—" he broke off.

I had been lurking in the quiet halls for fifteen minutes when Malik stepped out of a shadow. "What are you doing?" he asked slyly.

"Damn it, Malik! You scared me."

He raised an eyebrow at me.

"I've been searching for the library, for our meeting. Remember? This place is a maze. I should have asked for a tour. What have you been doing?"

"I went to visit our prisoner before I came looking for you." He put his hands casually in his pockets as he led the way.

"How is Darius?" I asked. "Comfortable, I hope."

Malik laughed at that. "I doubt that. But still uncooperative. We may need other methods, eventually."

"You know I'm against torture, Malik."

"You think so little of me still?" He actually looked hurt.

"No, of course not. You're right. I'm sorry."

"Well, when our godfly friend shows back up, she might be able to help us, I think."

⁂

We entered the library. Seeley, Conall, and Alrun were sitting around a large ink-stained table in the center of the room stacked with books. The Age of Sol Ros, The Makers' Promise, and The Sources of Social Power were among the titles. I added the historical genealogy my mother sent us to the stack. There was a large tapestry hanging on the far wall depicting enormous seafaring vessels hauling nets full of such a large catch the Skyborne of Seabrook proper would never have to worry about their next meal. Beneath it were a few large navy overstuffed chairs, each with their own round side tables. Malik and I pulled out the more utilitarian chairs around the main table to join the others.

"Shouldn't we have heard from Meethra by now?" Conall asked. "I'm starting to get worried."

"Me too," I replied. It was a grim thought I'd been avoiding.

"Meethra?" Alrun asked.

We told him I'd met our godfly friend and how she and Conall helped us escape the cells in Eastdow and then again with Darius and his soldiers.

Alrun was thoughtful for a moment before he turned to his son. Seeley shook his head. "That is concerning. I'll tell Bara to have the scouts keep an eye out."

"What do we do now?" Conall asked.

That was the question.

"We received a bird from Bara that your mother and another young woman were spotted and are now being escorted to the keep. They'll be here by dinner."

"I guess we'll find out where their alliances lie soon enough," I said, feeling not entirely trusting and nervous to see my mother for the first time in ten years.

"What about Sundale? Do you have any relations with them?"

"We do. I've met their Regent Ian and his sister Asha before, though rather briefly. I will have Bara send a falcon requesting a meeting. I believe Cleek has made that flight before," Seeley chimed in.

Malik looked surprised and impressed at Seeley, reaching over to squeeze his shoulder.

Alrun explained, "We do some trade with Sundale. The relationship has been amicable since Femi cultivated it when her tenure began. Ian is a young leader, but either he or Asha should come to represent the territory."

Alrun, Conall, Malik, and I continued debating a course of action as the hour dragged on.

"I believe I may have a relevant contribution," Seeley announced, having been contemplative as we talked. I raised an eyebrow at him. "Our family took the duty upon themselves to create a catalog of written histories of this realm after the crossover. Those volumes are buried in this library. The Skyborne, who crossed over, went through painstaking efforts to record as much from memory as they could. They weren't scholars, though. Just warriors and healers doing the best they could. They began taking first-hand accounts soon after they arrived. We have been the stewards of those original volumes ever since."

Alrun furrowed his brow, "that is true, son, but we've talked to the master librarian. He was unable to give us any useful information."

"Agree, father, but," Seeley turned to us, "before you three arrived, I did a little research on my own. I had a *feeling* of where to dig."

"You had a *feeling*?" I asked him, incredulous.

"That is what Seeley calls his sights. *Feelings*." Alrun obviously didn't approve.

"You have sight?" Conall asked, shocked, turning to Malik, "that would have been helpful to know."

Malik shrugged. "Not my gift to reveal."

"Anyway," Seeley cleared his throat, "I came across a single volume, called The Seventh House. It was very old, must have been one of the first catalogs. It talks about the Dar Kepler as just another association of powerful families like the six houses that make up the Sol Ros, though it seems their hierarchy was structured differently than ours. I don't understand all of it, but if what I've seen is true, then it paints another picture of who the enemy is. What we've been taught of them, anyway."

I thought of what we all had been taught of the Dar Kepler, the sect of Skyborne from the Southern lands of Idia, who harnessed forbidden power of the Void. They'd greedily tried to use it to steal what had belonged to my ancestors, their lands and prosperity. It was what the War of Two Sects was predicated on, which had led to the crossover. Besides the creatures of the Swath, they were evil Skyborne children were taught to fear.

"There is a lot here to sort through. I've read most of this stack," Seeley motioned to a large stack of dusty volumes.

"How are you able to keep track of all of this?" I asked, reaching for the genealogy and another interesting book in the unread pile.

Conall set the book he grabbed on the table with a plop, and a plume of dust whirled up into the air. "Now you know why I never wanted to become a scholar," he coughed.

I flipped through one and determined it was only an older and more brittle version of a modern copy I was familiar with. I set it in the discard pile. I became absorbed in a small book detailing the complex four-fold role of trade, military, politics, and theology that created the structure of early Sol Ros society in Idia.

"Listen to this," I announced, getting their attention. "During the preceding hundred years before the War of Two Sects, there were members from the six great houses who began a campaign to end the social stratification present in Sol Ros society. Some Lords of the lesser houses went so far as to suggest even the *Innar's* society be welcome in the Northern lands if they chose." I looked to Seeley and Alrun to see if they recognized the name, "The Innar?"

I flipped through the genealogy cross-referencing. Sure enough, it was one of the surnames in the second half that's history had ended abruptly.

"That is the surname of the ruling family of the seventh house if I remember correctly. They led the Dar Kepler," Seely confirmed.

"Wait, so what I'm hearing is there were allegedly Skyborne in Idia, from the Sol Ros sect, who wanted the Dar Kepler, led by this Innar family, integrated back into society? Based on what we know about them, that seems far-fetched," Conall stated skeptically.

I flipped a few more pages and surmised that they had used the conflict that ideology caused was used to further justify the social order of six houses of Sol Ros society. I conveyed that to the group, to their relief.

I noted the fear of the Dar Kepler was still strong, even in our unusually open-minded group.

Sentry's horns sounded from the gate. Conall and I rushed over to the window. I couldn't make out each figure, but I could tell by the style of their attire that it was Jude and my mother, Renia Kalederan. I turned to Malik and Seeley, "It's them."

Seeley was up in a second by my side, embracing me as my emotions flooded in. He pulled back, holding my shoulders, "They're finally here. I can only imagine what you must be feeling." He shook me gently with excitement, turning my smile into a laugh. "I'm going to go prepare to receive them. Meet us in the great hall." Seeley grabbed Malik's arm, leading him from the room.

When they'd left, Conall stopped me. "Are you okay?"

"I am. I'm excited and nervous. The last time I saw my mother, she wished me well as my father sold me off to Torin and Lathrais. I don't know whether to hug her or choke her."

"What about your sisters?" he asked.

"Well, funny thing about that. We thought instead of coming for me, they were taking Carina as a bride for you." I was trying to hold back my laughter. "She was so disappointed when that wasn't the case. I'm sad you won't get to meet her now."

Conall's face was red now. "Well, maybe there is still a chance for her," he said, attempting to be suave to hide his embarrassment.

"Oh, you haven't met Carina yet. If she wants you under her thumb, that is exactly where you'll find yourself."

⚓

Conall, Malik, Seeley, and I were standing in the great hall as Alrun led my mother and sister in. He was thanking them for coming and apologizing that Femi couldn't be there to greet them herself. Femi periodically paid visits and brought supplies out to small towns in the territory. She liked to do so herself because she felt it was the duty of her position to serve and be accessible to the citizens. I watched Renia, my mother, as Alrun finished his explanation. She inclined her head toward him in interest and admiration. Seemingly because the way Femi and Alrun ran the territory was a sharp contrast to my father's and even Conall's.

Renia slowly, almost hesitantly, turned her head toward me. A thousand emotions flashed through her eyes at that moment. The hesitation, I saw, was her reaching deep for composure. I was grateful she didn't embrace me, I thought as I stepped closer to Conall's side. She turned to Alrun and extended her thanks for their kind welcome.

Alrun turned to us. "It would be my pleasure to introduce you to my son, Seeley."

"It is my honor to make the introduction." Seeley bowed deeply and continued the introductions. Malik must have sensed my unease or had his own private reasons because he and Seeley cornered her, engaging my mother in conversation about the journey and her first impressions of the city. Jude hesitated but threw her arms around me once the formality dissipated. Even at my slight frame, I stood several inches above her. I stroked her chopped raven hair, appreciating this moment I believed could never happen.

Jude released me and began animatedly telling poor Alrun and me what seemed like every waking moment since we'd sent her on her mission. Conall was staring at her with a wry smile on his face. A pang of jealousy rippled through me at that. As if sensing my emotion, the ember vibrated, scolding me as I scolded myself. *He is not yours. He might as well be your brother*, I reminded myself. I shook off the thought.

I knew the drill. Attendants would soon arrive and show them to their rooms to freshen up and rest from travel. Then we would all meet for dinner. And like clockwork, the attendants came, and they led two women out.

Alrun and Seeley left us to find Bara to send word to Femi.

Malik finally reignited the conversation. "Where did you say Renia was from?"

"Arborvale, I believe. My father met her in a small trading outpost and brought her back to be his bride. She had the four of us, one after the other. Why do you ask?"

"It's her accent," he replied. "Like she masks it with the Arborvale sound, but something else is mixed in there."

"That is why you cornered her?" I asked.

"Yes. Does she have any gifts you know of?"

"No, nothing more than the common power. I assumed my gifts came from our father's line."

"I wouldn't be so sure of that. My power prickles when it reaches toward her like it did when I first met you."

"I don't see why you shouldn't ask her about it if you're concerned. Answering you is the least she could do." Conall looked at me then and put his hand on my shoulder, and squeezed.

"I will feel it out tonight at dinner, but follow my lead if I ask." Malik turned to go, waiting for my agreement. Or approval.

I nodded.

I brought Conall back to my room. I didn't want to wait for dinner alone, and he seemed to be amiable to follow. The emotional toll it took seeing my family again after all this time was exhausting. Especially having to manage the pretense of our positions.

I threw myself across the foot of the bed, face down. I felt Conall crawl onto the bed next to me. I turned my head toward him. He was lying on his back, staring at the ceiling.

We laid there for the better part of an hour. Finally, I rolled onto my side, propping my head up with my arm. "It's a lot to take in, but I feel like it is starting, after all this waiting. Something bigger than us."

The ember vibrated in agreement.

"I don't know," was Conall's response. He cocked his head toward me, eyes full of vulnerability. Longing. I knew he was as eager as I was to figure out the next step.

"Well, I can tell you the ember agrees with me." I poked him in the ribs where it's ticklish, and he squirmed an inch away.

"I still think you're imagining things." He grabbed my wrist before I could poke him again. I tried to pull away, but he gripped it tighter and brought my fist so near his face I could feel the heat of his breath on my hand.

My heart was beating wildly then. "Conall?" I asked nervously.

"Nayla, you are everything to me. My best friend in this realm and any other." He closed his eyes and brought my fist to his lips, and held it there for a long moment. His breath sent warmth up my arm to my chest. When he opened his eyes, he looked at me with a strange intensity. My hand was shaking then, my traitorous body responding to his utter maleness.

He looked at my shaking hand and placed it on his heart gently. "Do you think if we hadn't spent the last ten years as brother and sister, we ever would have—" He trailed off. He knew I knew exactly what he meant. He glanced back up to meet my eyes, his boyish lashes heavy over his chestnut eyes. I could feel his thundering heart under my hand, pressed beneath his. His thumb stroked the back of my hand hesitantly.

If there was ever a moment to make Conall, this beautiful, kind, perfect male in front of me, mine, this was it. I studied his face, truly studied it, and the tension in my body dissipated. I saw my best friend, my partner in crime; I saw my brother. Not my lover.

With that decision, I jerked my hand back and full-on assaulted his ribs with my pointer finger. "Oh, Makers, Conall, you are so nonsensical." He was batting my now two jabbing hands away as we both were bent with stitches. Finally, I let him sit up. We had been laughing so hard actual tears had to be wiped away. We were sitting on the edge of the bed, arms linked, chatting with my head on his shoulder when a knock came at the door. Conall got up to get it and visibly stiffened when it was Jude who appeared in the doorway.

"Oh, I'm sorry," she said, blushing and turned away.

"Jude," I called after her, "it's just Conall; you don't have to run. Come, join us."

She looked between us, I'm sure seeing my reddened eyes and the rumpled bedding.

"Stand aside." I pushed Conall out of the way.

"I will leave you two—" Conall said before I cut him off.

"You will do no such thing." I didn't realize how threatening or desperate my voice came across until they both didn't argue. I was a little nervous to be alone with Jude after all these years. In all reality, we had no idea who each other were now. Conall's presence would create a buffer.

"Okay, you want to see the ember?" I said, grasping for something to talk about. I reached into my hidden pocket and pulled out the box.

"I'd been wondering where in that lack of fabric you'd been keeping it," Conall commented, raising his eyebrows at me.

"It is a convenient way to keep cool, you know," I interjected. "You're just jealous you still have to wear all that cloth." The men's clothing was of a lighter woven material but still cut very much the same as the other territories I'd visited.

"Carina would love these clothes," Jude commented. "Very freeing." She brushed her hand down her fitted trousers. "It suits you, Nayla. I can't imagine seeing Balene in this, though, and I'm certainly never putting a *scrap*," she emphasized the word, "of it on."

I pulled out the box with one hand and flipped the lid open with the other. Jude went quiet and leaned over to look at the contents. She looked up at me. "That's it?"

It vibrated. "You've offended it."

"See what I mean?" Conall said.

"So, that small thing killed your High Priest? How?" she asked.

"I don't know how. We don't know how or why it works. He touched it, and darkness crept up his arm before he stiffened and slumped over dead."

"You saw it happen?" She was questioning.

Conall jumped in, "We both did. No one has touched it since. Well, besides your sister."

"Really?" she asked, looking at me with wide eyes. "How do you know what it thinks?"

"I've been paying attention to how it responds when things happen, and I don't know how to explain it, but it pulses in a way like it's communicating with me."

Jude sat contemplatively. "I believe you. I've never seen a Skyborne die before."

Conall and I raised our eyebrows at her, so she continued, defending herself, "how many Skyborne have you seen die, Nayla?"

"Do you mean in general, or ones I've killed?" I looked her in the eye then, and she drew a quick breath in. She was still so innocent.

She looked at Conall, "And you?"

"The same, I'm afraid. When your sister came to us, we trained together. Trained to fight and to kill."

"Is what they say about your ability to take on another's face true too?" She was looking at me as if she was deciding between being intrigued or frightened.

"Yes, I can take anyone's appearance. And sound like them too. Or change small things about myself. That is what Lathrais and Torin came to see. They heard I could change my features back then."

"I remember you could do your eyes, but—"

I explained Vera's death and told her about the training with her and Lathrais before she'd died. Conall helped me fill in the gaps after I was brought back to Eastdow as a healed Vera. There hadn't been time to explain at our camp weeks earlier, but I still felt guilty.

"Did you know your sister was dead like I knew Nayla was alive?" she asked Conall.

"I did, deep down, I think," he responded. "Vera and I never got along like Nayla and I, though, so I knew something was different. But after my mother took her life, I was more certain then. I still never brought up that I doubted because I didn't know how to explain it. I let my best friend endure that secret because I was too afraid to ask her. And I'm truly sorry for that."

We hadn't spoken about it since our fight over a month ago. "Oh Makers, Conall, stop, I can take it. Get out. I need to get ready for dinner."

CHAPTER EIGHTEEN

S EABROOK DIDN'T SEEM to have the assortment of ruling officials as the other territories I had been to. Or they weren't invited with the goal of keeping our presence quiet. I appreciated that either way.

A handful of attendants stood in the room waiting to serve, plus the rest of our party, and Femi, Alrun, and Seeley were gathered around one large dining table. Renia made it a point to sit across from me, and Malik sat next to me. Jude took a liking to Alrun and found a place to be near him. Seeley and Femi were on the other side of Malik, who jumped right to the chase.

"Renia, that is an interesting accent. Tell me, where are you from?"

Jude jumped to her defense, "She is from Arborvale, like the rest of us." She hadn't warmed to Malik's particular charm yet. Seeley saw that and stroked his partner's back lovingly.

Renia raised a hand to quiet both of them. "I have a story to share, and I will answer all your questions," she looked to me, then back to him, "but we should save that for tomorrow, if that's agreeable to you, Malik?"

Everyone was watching him now. Reluctantly, he nodded in agreement.

Femi raised her glass, diffusing the situation, and toasted her honored guests and the new alliances we were making. We all clinked glasses, and little pockets of cheerful conversation sprouted.

⁓

When I got back to my room, I laid down on the bed, thinking I'd get undressed in a moment, but fell asleep mildly wine drunk. I forgot how strong the dreams were when I carried the ember in my pocket. That night the dreams started the same, falling through what I now understood as a portal into another realm. But instead of hitting the hard ground, I landed on a soft bed of feathers. It was the same Skyborne sitting cross-legged, but this time the glowing orb was in his outstretched hand, displaying it to me.

I got a better look at him for the first time. He was only a little older than me, with smooth skin kissed lightly by the sun. The planes of his face were hard and angled, but his pale blue eyes were soft and inviting. Not intense like the dreams before. I had thought he'd been wearing a cloth on his head before, but it was his hair I could see now. It hung straight down to his shoulders and was pale like the lightest sand, unlike any I'd seen in this realm.

I tried to sit up, tried to follow the wrenching in my core that drew me toward him. Something was fixing me in place, but I felt no fear this time. He never broke my gaze as he moved onto his knees, and crawled toward me, lean muscles rippling with every movement. I looked down at myself. Instead of my normal attire, I was wearing the Seabrook clothes, and the way I was lying exposed much of my legs. The male let his eyes rove over me freely as if it was his right. Kneeling at my feet, he reached a structured hand out, his long fingers grazing my foot curiously. I could feel light callouses tracing their way up my shin, over my knee. He held his fingers there as he toyed with the hem of my garment, obviously wanting to do more but cautious.

Warm liquid energy flowed through my body. I couldn't move, trapped between fear and anticipation. I eased my thigh toward his reluctant hand, urging, and he jerked back, startled. I woke, panting. Traces of heat laced up my leg, a remnant from a recent touch. I reached between my legs, warm, wet and swollen with excitement. I guess it was better than the terror the dreams had caused before. *Much better,* I thought, the wine still making my head swim, as I moved my fingers with more intent.

I thought of the male, briefly hoping I'd never have to meet him face to face, but welcoming more dreams as sleep took me again.

୶

The next day I woke up and took the box out of the skirt's hidden pocket and set it on a table in the bathroom as I walked over to warm the water for my bath with my power. "Dirty thing," I said aloud, half blushing to it about the fantasy. It vibrated cheerfully in response.

୶

The clothes May had laid out for me were more somber colors of deeper rust and burgundies, the utilitarian version of their clothes here I knew. The prospect of interrogating Renia was not something I was looking forward to. As I finished getting ready, there was a knock at my door. I expected to see Conall or Jude, but it was Malik.

"How are you holding up?" he asked.

"I've been better." But I couldn't necessarily think of when.

"Why are your cheeks flushed?" he pointed to the mirror. I saw myself, and he was right, which only made me flush further.

"Hot bath," I said.

He looked at me incredulously, tapping his fingers across the desk.

"Okay, but you can't say anything to the others." He nodded in agreement. I continued, "I had another dream. I fell asleep with the ember in my pocket. But it wasn't a scary dream."

"I see," he said before bursting into laughter.

"Jerk," I said, turning away inflamed.

"Maybe I can borrow it sometime? Sounds pleasant."

"Ha. Ha. Laugh all you want. I don't even know why I told you. Definitely not making that mistake again."

"Besides the sex, was there anything different that you noticed? Anything helpful?" he asked.

"First, it wasn't even sex, he just touched my leg, but I did get a better look at his face. And this time, it wasn't in that courtyard, but in a room, I couldn't see, and the pale orb was hovering in his hand like it did in mine."

"And his other hand was occupied, you said?" He used his hands to gesture that he was taking notes.

I exaggeratedly sighed, rolling my eyes.

"It sounds like this object he carries is the twin or opposite to the ember. Do you think this male is in Idia?" I pondered the thought. That meant I wouldn't be running into him anytime soon.

"It's possible."

"Thank you for taking me seriously. I feel like I'm going crazy, and I know Conall thinks I imagine it, but I don't think it is just an object."

"You aren't remotely crazy. You are strong and brave. This is good because we have to go have a difficult conversation with your mother. Are you ready?" Malik reached out and squeezed my arm reassuringly.

"Ready as I'll ever be."

And one more thing. He had opened the connection in our minds to speak to me as we walked down the hall.

What's that? I thought back.

Never be ashamed of enjoying yourself.

I looked over at him, and he was grinning, clearly enjoying himself.

Oh, Makers, I whined, and he shrugged, laughing it off. *Do you ever use that skill for anything useful, or is it especially reserved for our little side conversations?*

I can only do it with a few who have a high enough level of power. Seeley was the first. Then you. I could feel it when you were in Drakestone. It was a part of the reason I could sense you weren't Vera and also aid you without your knowing. Sounds like your sister Carina might be able to do it too. It would explain how she has been so influential with your father and others. It comes with a little nudging influence. I haven't tried it with Conall yet. I fear it would startle him.

You haven't nudged me, have you?

No, I would never do that to you, Nayla. He looked hurt.

So, you and Seeley are having secret conversations all the time, aren't you? I thought incredulously back to him.

All the time. Malik's deep laugh filled the hallway. We got to the room we'd agreed to meet in, having continued our conversation, appearing to walk in silence.

❦

Femi agreed to take Jude around the city while Alrun and Seeley would sit in on this conversation. Conall walked in, escorting my mother.

An uncomfortable quiet formed after we'd arranged ourselves around the table. Seeley gave us each a very annoyed look before he broke it. "Good grief, you all are so severe, I can hardly take it. Let's hear your tale, Renia. We wait with bated breath."

Renia looked amused by us all. Slowly she made eye contact with each person in the room before she sat tall and stated, "My father is Regius Kymar Shal, Regent of the sixth territory, Monterra."

You could have heard a pin drop then. My mother had always appeared settled in her position as my father's wife, demure even. I now saw where the stately way she carried herself as the wife of the Regent came from. She was a female who should have been a Regent herself one day.

Her resolve faltered, and her voice quavered as she continued, "I was pregnant when I met Carina, Balene, and Jude's father." None of us spoke. She took a deep breath in, and as she exhaled, the depth of her olive skin tone lightened slightly. The dimension and texture of her hair shifted too. Her lips became fuller, and her eyes more almond and just noticeably turned up at the corners. Her traits were mirrors of my own. Looking at her and thinking of my sisters, it was clear they were her daughters, but they now more strongly resembled *their* father. I leaned back in my chair, keeping my face carefully blank.

"I was this powerful when I was young. This is where you get it." She sheepishly smiled at me. She continued after we'd adjusted to the shock. "All of my girls know the truth, now."

But it was Malik who interrupted, "If Ephram isn't Nayla's father, then who is?"

She looked at him and shrugged her shoulders, resigning herself. "Yours."

Malik adjusted in his chair and stared at Renia for a long moment before he said, "Makers." His hand drug down his face and dropped to the table with a thud. We all jumped.

Renia surveyed Malik's clenched jaw, reading his anger then, and straightened her shoulders. "Your father was powerful, and I was young. I was so taken with him I didn't care that he had a wife and children. I knew it was wrong. When I realized I'd become pregnant, I knew they'd make me get rid of the baby, so I fled. Ephram found me in a small town, and I took on a new appearance and pretended to be lost. He saw I was in the early months of pregnancy, and since his first wife hadn't been unable to conceive, he gambled that I'd carry you to term, and at least he would seem to produce an heir. It was our secret. But then we had three more girls."

My head was spinning now, and I needed air. I got up but stumbled. Conall and Malik were there to catch me instantly.

"This is too much," I said to no one in particular. I couldn't breathe.

Malik took my face in his hands then and opened our connection. Everyone except for Seeley would have thought he was just staring, but he thought, *Hey— look at me—Focus. You are strong and brave, remember? No, you are more than that. You are steel. And you are apparently my sister.* His normally sharp eyes softened. *You're not alone, okay?* I nodded. *Now stand tall and take your seat and say whatever you need to say.*

I steadied myself, allowing myself to be bolstered by him. *Thanks,* I thought.

And like that, I'd gained an older brother. It kind of made sense with Malik. Our easy banter back and forth, how I got his dark humor. I'd sort out what that meant about what had happened with Darius later, I thought and shivered instinctively, horrified.

I looked at my mother. A strange clarity struck me. I didn't know if I could ever forgive her for letting Ephrem, the Skyborne who I'd thought was my father, send me to Eastdow, though she likely had no choice. I knew I was grateful for fleeing and for what she was doing now. I could at least tell her that.

I squared my shoulders and faced her. "I am grateful for what you did. That was an incredibly brave act." My voice felt stiff and hollow.

Renia fought back tears. She looked at me with a grim smile. "I don't expect you to forgive me, Nayla. I've made many wrong choices in my life. Maybe one day you and I can get to know each other better, and I can ask for your forgiveness."

I stared at her in disbelief.

"Shal?" I breathed.

"What?" Conall said, leaning toward me.

"I was just thinking about my name. The family name in Monterra follows the line through power like the other territories where females still can hold the regency, not strictly the male lines." I looked at Seeley. "You have your mother's family name, Temmar, which was her mother's, right?"

Seeley nodded, following me.

I turned toward Renia, "So if you were a Shal, that would mean my name is Nayla Shal, not Kalederan or Dsiban."

Renia smiled. "You can still be a Kalederan if that is what you wish."

"No," I said firmly, startling her. "I've spent too long pretending to be someone I'm not. "Nayla Shal. That is who I am. Go on, Renia," I told her.

She shook her head, tossing her rolling inky hair as she regained her composure. "Since I was to be heir, Regius Kymar, my father, educated me on the history of our kind. Carina and I have pieced together a little on Idian society and the War of the Two Sects. The six Sol Ros houses united to defend against the encroachment of their lands by the Dar Kepler, who'd started chipping away at the borders of the civilized Northern lands and even attempted to infiltrate their society."

"That makes sense with what you'd read yesterday, Nayla, about some Sol Ros even being proponents of that," Conall commented.

"The Shal Regius, at the time, united the leaders of the six houses to extinguish the Dar Kepler before they could be integrated. There were many battles during the war. The day came for the final conflict. The Sol Ros forces were prevailing, and Shal Regius and representatives of each house were strategically positioned above the assembled armies to command and step in with their power, if and when they needed. But before it began, one witness, a foot soldier, saw a sudden darkness enveloping her and every other soldier in her unit. She described them suddenly falling and falling until they hit the earth. They had landed here, in this realm. It appears there was mass confusion for days, but eventually, leaders from the six houses who'd crossed over congregated. Among the commanders, warriors, and healers who were swept through in the crossover, there were matriarchs who were positioned to lead the battlefield healing. They realized the Shal Regius was not among them."

"What happened to the Regius and the Sol Ros who were left behind?" I asked.

"No one knows."

"That is when the matriarchs, many in their decline, found themselves in this unknown land." I'd heard this part of the story before. My mother continued. "They sent out sentries to explore the continent and tried to create order. With most of their power they'd experience on Idia cut off to them, survival was hard, and many died in the first hundred years. Eventually, they designated the six Territories for each of the six houses, established new Regents from the surviving members of each house, and drafted the Covenant.

Renia continued. "My great-great-grandmother was the last of the matriarchs who made the crossover to die. She reached over three hundred years. When she died, her son took over, and things in Monterra changed. He believed his mother had been too gracious by not demanding our family's right to rule, as we had done in Idia. He took the title Regius, instead of Regent like the other territory heads, and taught that to his children and grandchildren. Among them, my father, Kymar. He would have passed this claim to me as well had I not fled. Since the ember has been active, I believe he will work tirelessly to find it and return to Idia to take what he believes is his birthright."

"That seems insane. Monterra didn't even have the ember in the first place," Conall interjected.

"When I left nearly thirty years ago, Regius Kymar and Karish were scheming about raising an army of hybrid beasts from this realm to use against the Dar Kepler in Idia," Renia replied.

"What type of beasts? Like the creatures from the forest?" Conall asked, looking at Malik, no doubt thinking of what he'd described of Emerson's experiments.

"I don't know, I didn't think they had made any substantive progress when I left, but I knew they were working deep in the mountain. In a few of the books Carina found, they suggested this realm had been more diverse before we got here. Maybe it has something to do with those creatures they're creating."

"Possibly," Malik whispered.

"Uden talked about this realm as a realm of the banished, almost as a place species were sent as a punishment by the Makers. If the six houses were only protecting themselves, why were they sent here?" I asked.

Alrun cleared his throat. "Non-biased histories are rarely told."

"Do you think the ember sent them back and took their power? I always thought of it as a force of power, like what Malik has. But, you know, *stronger*." Seeley elbowed Malik in the ribs, goading him. A valiant attempt at lightening the mood.

"I find it hard to believe that both *my father* and *my grandfather*," I said, choking on the words, "have been magically breeding species to take over a realm we don't even know if we can get to. If we can find some way to get rid of this thing," I said, patting my pocket, "or hide it at the bottom of the sea, I think that would solve—"

"Nayla, hold on," Conall cut me off as the ember vibrated its discordance. "Renia, I assume your family held the seat of the Regency because they had the strongest access to the energy that surrounds us?"

She nodded, "Yes, our power was stronger, from what I understand."

Conall continued, "Then that means Nayla has some from Karish and Regius Kymar. It would explain the depth and diversity of what she can do. And maybe even why it took so long to fill in. And with the ember, if you truly have its favor." He was looking at me now, but he didn't continue.

"Go on," Alrun urged.

He did. "That's the thing. I still don't know what it means, but if that thing can send thousands through realms, we need to figure something out quickly. There isn't enough space in this realm to hide it here forever."

"I need to go to Monterra and find out what they are up to," I decided.

"That is not a good idea." Malik was firm on this one.

"I need to see these creatures with my own eyes. To know what they are capable of." Before he could protest again, I steeled myself. "I've done it before, and you were the only one who knew. I can do it again."

"I agree with Malik, Nayla. It's too dangerous," Conall pleaded.

Alrun, Seeley, and my *mother* weren't saying anything, but I could tell they agreed.

I looked at them all, glaring. "I'm going."

Malik shook his head, accurately reading my determination. "Fine, but I'm going with you, then."

I wanted to argue, but one pointed look from him halted my planned resistance.

"Good," he said, grinning at my silence. "Time to make a plan."

CHAPTER NINETEEN

D O YOU THINK *Darius is lonely?*

I grinned, looking around for Malik. *I hope so,* I responded.

He slipped from around a corner and grabbed my shoulder, "Come on," he said aloud.

Malik and I made our way through the winding sandstone staircases to the lower levels of the keep where the prisons were. Femi informed us they were generally vacant, as Seabrook had, through great diplomatic efforts, not made any political enemies. *Until now,* I thought after she'd told me. And when the Skyborne here committed crimes, fair punishments were mostly willingly carried out by the offender. It held only the worst of the worst.

We passed a line of empty cells and the occasional inhabited one, where I saw prisoners of both genders in neatly ordered rooms, sitting, reading, or reclining in thought on comfortable enough looking pallets. They looked well-kept enough. Nothing like the prison I'd experienced in Eastdow. And less dank, too. A few prisoners got up and pressed their faces through the bars, curiosity drawing them out to watch the two olive-skinned strangers led by a stable-looking guard down the hallway.

We came to the end of the line, where there was a corner cell that was a little darker than the others. Darius was sitting on a low pallet inside, facing opposite the doors. He made no acknowledgment of our approach.

"We haven't heard him speak. He sits there during the day and lies flat on the cot to sleep. We offer him food, but he doesn't move. We slide it in there through that little slot." The guard pointed to a little opening in the bars with a ledge attached to it. "Usually gone when we come back, but we never see him eat it. I'll be right down the hall when you're ready to leave." He pivoted and walked away.

"Hello, Darius." Disdain was dripping from my voice. "Aren't you going to turn around to greet your brother and I?"

Nothing.

"Okay. I have an idea. I share one juicy piece of information with you, then you answer a question for me. Deal?"

Nothing.

"Trust me, you *will not* want to know this. So, I'll go first. Did you know that you and I share something in common? A family bond. Your father was apparently quite the charmer, according to my mother." It repulsed me saying it, but it would serve its purpose.

I paused, waiting for him to put the pieces together—still nothing.

Malik put a hand on my shoulder as I continued, "So, tell us what type of creatures your family is helping Kymar create?"

Only my heightened senses could have detected the slight flinch and change in his breathing. *He knows about them*, I thought to Malik.

"I suppose your confirmation is enough of an answer. How do you feel about incest, Darius? Did you know that you have a half-sister?" Malik continued following my line of persuasion.

Nothing. Though I swore I heard his heartbeat quicken.

"So, Drakestone and Monterra have been breeding creatures deep in the mountains for at least thirty years or longer, so they must be about ready to have a trial force, if not a full army of wickedness. Tell me, why is Torin involved? How can you trust an ally who orchestrated the theft of the most precious object from you? How do you know he won't betray you? He is only out for himself, you know, not the Skyborne in his care, not even his son. Unless he is an only expendable pawn?" Darius, though as hard as he tried, answered us through the slight shifts in his posture. I pressed on planting seeds, "Kymar used Torin to get the object out of Karish's hands while still keeping him as an ally, knowing eventually he'd be able to force Torin to hand it over. Smart. Too bad it went missing. And Regius Kymar—you know, he believes he's the sole heir to the seat of power for the entire realm of Idia. Are you and your father so willing to fall under his command? If he succeeds, I wouldn't be surprised if he names himself king or some other ridiculous title. And after he finds out what your father did with his first-born daughter, I can't imagine that alliance will hold."

Still nothing.

Malik and I waited for long minutes before Malik finally said, "You aren't enjoying your sister and I's company?"

He visibly stiffened. After several deep breaths, he slowly turned toward us.

"Ah, nice to see you, Darius. You look well." I sneered, repressing the bile rising in my throat.

Finally, our prisoner spoke. "You are both liars and traitors. It is only a matter of time before they come for me. And I know you won't torture me, so I just have to wait."

"Well, I imagine they don't know exactly where you went off to, and you won't be missing for much longer." I gave him my most wicked grin as I worked a shift over my appearance, perfectly matching his visage. His eyes widened in horror as I raised my hand to my face, "Oh, my, *this* is going to be fun."

Malik let out a menacing laugh under his breath.

"You know you chose the wrong side, Darius." Malik's voice was scolding in the way only an older brother could be.

"They know you can change, Nayla. When you go to Drakestone, they'll know you aren't me. But you'll find that out. And you'll also find out they don't have a ridiculous moral dilemma when it comes to coaxing information out of their prisoners," Darius hissed.

"We just need to know one more thing. The creatures. Are they in the mines deeper in the mountains," I paused, "or the ones around the keep?"

I'm sure he regretted being baited to turn around when his eyes flared ever so slightly at the word *keep*.

"Thanks. You've been particularly helpful." He was apparently done responding. "Later, *brother*," I replied with mocking sweetness, and we turned.

As Malik and I went to find the guard to guide us out of prison, I thought to him, *do you think it was a mistake revealing my lineage to him?*

It puts your mother at risk, true, but I believe it will make them hesitate before killing you outright if they ever have the chance. And that is if Darius was ever to escape. So, it's a calculated decision. He paused for a second. *When exactly did you put that elaborate theory together?*

I laughed. *I told you I was multi-talented, didn't I?*

I'm proud of you. That took guts.

⋆

When Malik and I entered the library to an awaiting group, Conall took one look at us and shook his head. "What are you two having such a good time about?"

"Oh, you know, just the joys of tormenting Darius. You should have seen his face, Conall. It was a scene I'll be re-living for weeks." I looked at Renia. Before I'd told Darius, she'd given me her blessing to use the information she told us with him.

Malik and I relayed the story of the encounter and my theory. The group seemed to absorb the information, marinating on the ramifications. While we were gone, Renia and Alrun had come up with a plan to send Malik and I north by sea. She showed Malik, Alrun, and I a little-used entrance on the map through the mountains leading to the backside of the keep from the North Coast. Within the hour, we had a solid plan.

Before we dispersed, Renia pulled me to the side. "I have something for you, from your sister." She unrolled her fist, revealing what was in her palm.

My eyes flared. "If I get caught, they'll find it. It's not worth them knowing we have it."

"Come, I can help you hide it." She ushered me into a small side room in the library, away from the others. She gave me a conspiratorial grin as she pulled a knife from her skirts. "Give me your arm."

⋆

The next morning, we all met at the marina at the base of Seabrook Proper. They arranged to send my mother and Jude back south to Arborvale by sea as well. Bara, not willing to give up Cleek, would send the second most Skyborne friendly falcon with them to have an efficient way to communicate. I hugged Jude tightly.

Renia leaned forward, but restrained herself. "Goodbye, Mother," I said experimentally, scratching my itching forearm. She put her hand over her mouth. It was the first time I hadn't called her by her first name, and that meant something to her. I wasn't sure if it had for me yet, though. After everything, I didn't know if it ever would.

"Please be safe," she responded.

I smiled and turned. Conall had me wrapped in his arms in a blink. I took a deep breath of him in. He smelled like home. He'd put on a more amiable front amongst the group earlier, but I spent forever last night trying to convince him not to try to stop us. But he was keeping his word and holding his tongue today.

"I need you to do something for me," I whispered, shoving the new pouch I carried the ember in into his hands. He looked up at me, shocked.

"You need this. It will protect you," he said.

I was glad I hadn't brought it up last night. "They can't get it. No matter what happens to me. The risk is too great."

Conall relented, placing it in the hidden pocket in his tunic. "I will protect it with my life if it comes to it. I don't plan to fail you, Nayla, so don't let it distract you."

"Good," was all I said.

"Don't get caught, *again*," Seeley mumbled, oddly somber.

I laughed, attempting to lighten the mood, "We'll try not to. And don't you dare lose our prisoner."

Seeley forced a laugh. "We'll try not to."

Or anything else was what was unnecessary to say as I glanced one last time at Conall. Malik and I turned to a sailor who'd introduced herself as the first mate of the vessel, which would take us to the mysterious northern territory of Monterra.

I took a deep breath and said, "Lead the way."

Chapter Twenty

I NSIDE THE FISSURE, the walls opened, but only slightly wider than my arm span. I could smell the moisture in the air and hear faint trickling water from snow melting in the daytime sun running through cracks in the stone. My mother's instructions had been to follow the right side of the tunnel. In the past, from what she remembered, they rarely used the path through the mountain. It was probably safe to use light, but we decided not to chance it. I placed my hand on the gritty wall and followed it, occasionally running my fingers through a dribbling stream.

We walked for long hours. My body ached.

Nightfall must be approaching. Should we stop soon? I asked Malik.

Let's find the next alcove. You need to tell your stomach to keep it down. You're going to draw attention, Malik teased. My stomach had indeed been grumbling for the last hour.

Renia told us it was about three days' travel before we'd reach the place where we'd need to exit the tunnel and make the short trek to the gate. It was another few hours before we found the next natural alcove large enough to tuck into.

Here seems good, I said, setting down my pack against the wall. I took out the small pack and pulled out some flatbread and hard, salty cheese, cutting off a section and handing it to Malik.

Is it bad that I'm already missing Femi's fish stew? I complained.

Malik chuckled under his breath.

When Darius and I were younger, our father made us go through these insane practice scenarios. Did Darius tell you about them?

I shook my head, biting off a piece of the tasteless dried wafer.

Once, our father's men ambushed us in the middle of the night in our beds. They tied our hands, gagged and blindfolded us, then transported us all the way to the Bare Lands. They took off on horseback, leaving us still tied, with nothing more than our sleeping clothes.

Wow, that seems a little extreme.

He had this idea that when we got to Idia, we wouldn't know what to expect, and he wanted us to be skilled enough to survive until we could take back our lands.

What happened in the Bare Lands?

We helped each other untie our wrists and gags. We wandered around for a day and a half before we became worried. You would have loved watching Darius choke down those little stingers. I could barely make out a melancholy smile with my enhanced vision.

You ate those?

Yep, cut off the tail with the stinging barb, and they taste like... chicken?

Gross. I guess I won't complain about my flatbread and cheese. I was thoughtful for a moment. *What happened between you two?* I asked.

I don't know. I think things slowly eroded. Changed the way I saw him. Or he changed. Still, I would have never thought he was capable of what he did to you. I winced a little when he said it, but he continued. *There were things that happened. He was oddly eager when it was time to make a kill, for example. And his entitlement. You saw a little of that. He and my father bonded over their matched desire for power. I think the Regent was a little disappointed that Darius wasn't his firstborn.*

Did you want to be Regent?

I would have done it, but no. Did you?

No. Being sent away by my family was not okay, but I think I enjoyed the training with Conall and the life I've had for the last ten years. Despite everything. I got so good at being Vera. Even my inner dialogue became hers. There were times, I think I forgot who I was the eighteen years leading up to that. On one hand, that depth of belief was necessary to keep up the ruse, but on the other, it feels like I lost a piece of me.

৵

I woke with a start, my power pricking me awake. I turned my focus deeper down the tunnel for what might have alerted it. I sensed nothing, just pitch black and dead quiet.

Malik, I called out to our mental channel.

I felt it too.

I felt a sweep of his energy move past me, deep into the shaft.

Six Skyborne. A patrol, probably.

Not ideal.

If we have to kill them, it could create an issue for us later.

Then let's hope they don't come this far.

We waited, crouched into the alcove. If they didn't have a torch, they would probably pass us undetected. We weren't that lucky, though. A warm glow came into view.

Shit.

Don't hold your breath, Malik urged.

I exhaled softly, motioning to the direction we'd come. *Look.*

Looking in the other direction, I saw another faint light coming into view quicker than the other. This light didn't have footsteps accompanying it. A few moments more, I should have picked up a scent or breathing. It was within a few hundred paces when I realized the source of the light.

Meethra? I whispered.

Nayla, you're safe. Relief rang in her voice. *Oh, but you didn't bring it, did you?* Her small godfly's eyes were wide.

No, Conall has it, I thought.

Good. He will keep it safe.

I nodded to the rapidly approaching torchlight. *Can you help us with them?*

How many?

Six, I replied.

The godfly zipped out of sight.

"Look!" a Skyborne shouted in the distance.

"What was that?"

Thump. One down.

"Damn, godfly! One must have escaped," another gruff voice sounded.

Thump. Thump. Three more.

"Get back here, you little gnat!" he yelled.

Thump. Thump. Thump.

That was six, right? I cautiously asked Malik.

We approached Meethra's light. "Your timing was incredibly convenient," I said as we stepped over the collapsed bodies of the six guards surveying them.

She zipped around excitedly. "They'll be out about half a day. You should probably tie them up."

We did. And we snatched their weapons too, for good measure. The little godfly looked exhausted. I opened my pocket, "Care for a ride?" I said aloud, thinking there wouldn't be another patrol for a while. Meethra positioned herself in my pocket, relaxing immediately.

"So, you were supposed to meet us in Seabrook," I said. "What happened?"

"I felt them. The draw here was too strong to resist." She sheepishly wrung her tiny hands.

"How did you find us?" Malik asked.

"I felt the vessel and flew over to see. I sensed you'd been there. I searched the lands around the shore where they dropped you to no avail, so I determined that you'd found a tunnel in the cliffside. That's when I saw the crack in the rock big enough for your kind. Why are you here?"

"She had to see them," Malik answered for me, giving me a pointed look I could see in Meethra's light. "Emerson's creations. We think they're at the mine under this mountain. It was either here or in one of the mines further east."

"We need to know what we are up against. It's prudent," I defended.

Malik shook his head and huffed.

"My kind are here. And there's something like a foul odor to my senses. I think you've found your creatures."

꙳

We came to the sliver of light filtering in through a crack in the interior side of the mountain overhead two days later. I peeked my head out the small opening. I could see the keep below, in a U-shaped valley between the mountain peaks. From my vantage point, I could see the gate to the city, the first obstacle I'd have to overcome. Outside the city's wall, I could see movement. I enhanced my vision. Four Skyborne on horseback were leaving the city, heading across the valley. There was a smooth place on the jagged rock jutting up at the edge of the flat expanse.

I stepped outside of the shelter of the crack and immediately got hit with the brisk air whipping through the rugged terrain. I looked back to the men, who one by one appeared to be entering a large opening in the rock face. That was the access point to the seat of the territory from the south, and therefore all the other territories. It was how they secluded themselves so well.

The sections of the wall near the mountain appeared new. The openings Renia told us about were no longer there. Our original plan wouldn't work as well as I hoped now that I had seen the layout of the keep with my own eyes, not to mention the logistical issue of the tunnel.

I made note of the different entrances of the major buildings in the city's complex and saw a section of it that butted up into the side of the mountain to my left and not too far below me. That must be the area underground my mother talked about. I couldn't see how I could get to it directly without being noticed or becoming injured traversing the treacherous terrain. I'd have to walk right through the front door, as I suspected. Alone.

To do that, I'd have to come through that tunnel to be believable. That might have been a problem, but now that Meethra was here. I looked at her hunkered down out of the cold in my pocket. *I need your help.*

⤐

"Nayla, be safe. In and out, quick. See what you need to see, then disappear. I'll be here waiting on you."

He crushed me into his hard chest. "You have nothing to worry about, Malik. Trust me. It's not like this is the first time I've snuck into the lion's den. And Darius isn't going to show up anytime soon."

"I still don't like this. And I'm not there to help you this time."

"You and Meethra are going to make sure those guards under the mountain aren't able to alert anyone to our presence. I'll be fine." I said, giving him one last reassuring squeeze. I turned and scampered across the craggy terrain, not giving him a chance to argue.

I looked back. Malik had retreated into the little cave we'd found not too far from the entrance to the tunnel where we agreed to meet.

⌁

Meethra and I were like snakes, coiled, ready to strike when we heard the expected hooves clopping up the south tunnel heading toward us on their way back to the city. I already shifted into Darius's image. I wore my own clothes in the style of the men of Drakestone, which would make playing his role easier. I pulled my cloak over my head to cast Darius's features in shadow. Meethra perched atop a dead torch we'd found as I walked down the tunnel. As our targets got nearer, she glowed brighter, giving the appearance of glowing torchlight.

Based on our watch, the men had been gone at least two days, long enough to reach the area outside the Swath and make our story plausible.

"Halt," the leader called in a commanding voice. "I don't recognize you, stranger."

I lifted my head so he could make out the image of the Skyborne standing before him.

"Darius, sir?" The Skyborne furrowed his brow in confusion. I grinned, relieved he'd recognized Darius. "I didn't know you were in the city. You weren't on any of the lists when we left."

"I wasn't in the city."

Meethra unfolded herself and darted quicker than my Skyborne eyes could follow around the heads of the men. She rained down her transparent dust on them. I saw the effect of what she'd done with it before, but it always lured them into sleep. She explained that instead of lowering their level of consciousness, we'd offer them different memories. Memories she'd woven in the hypnotizing dust. And it would be up to me to convince the men to accept them as truth. She said some godflies used this talent in darker ways to rule over and exploit other beings in their

| 185 |

realm. Sounded like the exact type of sinister antics that could've landed them in this realm.

When she finished, the Skyborne blankly stared at me, holding my bright torch. The guard who had spoken blinked before he looked to the guard in the rear, who was obviously the lowest ranking of the four and grunted.

"Oh, I think you should take my horse, Darius, sir," the Skyborne muttered awkwardly as he dismounted and handed his reins to Darius.

I mounted and moved up beside the leader. "You must forgive me, *Captain*? Your name has slipped my memory."

"Captain, yes. Name is Murray, sir."

"Ah yes, that's right," I nudged my new mount, and it paced forward. The rest of the men, including the Captain, followed suit. "As I was saying, I don't know what I would have done if your fine men hadn't found me. It was a gift from the Makers I could escape the Swath. The boundary must be weakening, which is a chilling thought, don't you agree?"

He nodded.

I continued, "Because the creatures inside are even more terrifying than the rumors, I can assure you."

"You were very dehydrated and starved," the captain said, but in a questioning tone which was still trying to accept the memories.

"That's right, I was dehydrated and starved. You and your men found me and shared your food and drink. And I know my father Regent Karish and your Regius Kymar will be indebted to you for saving my life." I looked at Captain Murray, then to each of the soldiers, reinforcing the belief with Darius's charming smile. The warm, open smile I knew Darius used to convince others to trust him. I thought of poor misunderstood Malik and almost laughed at the contradiction.

"Yes. It is our duty and honor, sir." Murray still looked a little confused but led us out of the tunnel. The light was blinding at first upon exiting the darkness. Meethra sped off. I glanced around for a sign of her once my eyes adjusted, but she disappeared to safety as planned.

It took about an hour to go through the gates and make our way to the great hall. I alone stood waiting, no doubt being watched. I studied the design of the building's interior. It was so different from the light-filled great halls of the other territories I'd been to. There were no windows and numerous interwoven serpent-like columns creeping up to the ceiling, giving the space a delicate but unsettling feel. A dark reddish-brown stone I wasn't familiar with made up the columns, walls, and ceiling which were polished so smooth light from the many torches reflected eerily around the space. I could hear the echo of water dripping, though I could not locate its source.

Footsteps echoed from deep in one of the dark hallways off of each side of the dais. *Breathe*, I thought, chastising myself for shifting from foot to foot. There were many steps leading up to the main landing. A high-backed chair, which appeared to be ornately carved from the stone itself, sat atop it.

A *throne*.

More footsteps joined the others. Before long, men were filing out of the hallway to the left of the dais. They walked habitually and positioned themselves on either side of the cascading staircase, standing at attention. If their goal was intimidation, it was definitely working. Finally, the Skyborne I presumed was Kymar, appeared from the same hallway and walked up the stairs and ceremoniously placed himself on the throne.

Regius Kymar, *my grandfather*, it struck me, was older than I expected. He was a wiry Skyborne, starting to become bent with age, but with an overtly fiery disposition none-the-less. I expected him to look similar to my mother and I, but he looked more similar to Conall and his father than anything with his light beige skin, which would likely tan if he were in a southern climate. His muted sable brown hair fell at his shoulder. The hair at the top of his head was pulled loosely back and tied in a knot at the base of his skull. A thin black metal band with a single embedded fuchsia crystal at its center encircled his head, mimicking a crown.

Malik prepared me enough to know to keep quiet and only speak when asked. Kymar was not one for friendly conversation. He shifted in his seat, observing me.

Finally, he spoke. "What type of trouble did you get yourself into this time, Darius? It seems Karish is having trouble with his sons these days. One turns a traitor, and the other goes missing only to be found by my men claiming to have escaped from the Swath." He huffed in disbelief. "Tell me, Darius, how is it you came to be in that Makers-forsaken place?"

I was unsure if he planned to continue lecturing or if I was being prompted to speak. After long seconds, I cleared my throat. Best to stick to mostly the truth.

"I was leading a hunting party tracking my brother and the girl Nayla. Torin's son helped them escape, and they were running. We followed them as they traveled along the Swath's boundary. The girl communicates with the creatures in the forest. The creatures must have told them my men and I were coming. It shames me to admit this, but they ambushed us. Killed all my soldiers and took me prisoner. They took me into the forest with them."

Kymar raised an eyebrow. I continued.

"We traveled for days before they exited the forest. The girl has some sort of power over the creatures in the forest. She bade them keep me as her prisoner, so they did. Until I could escape." It couldn't hurt to make the Regius think I could control them. Might make him hesitate.

"No one has ever escaped the forest perimeter. Your story is suspect, Darius. You're not a traitor like your brother, are you Darius?" Kymar sneered in obvious disgust. I realized I was on trial again.

"I beg your pardon, Regius, but I saw the girl who'd shifted herself as Torin's dead child Vera get pushed into the forest. I saw it with my own eyes. The next time I saw her was at Torin's sham of a ceremony that killed that priest of theirs. The boundary is changing. Nayla even claimed to see it move, as if it is expanding."

The Regius cocked his head to the side, considering.

"I see. If you were a child of mine, you'd be getting lashes for your failures. I am not a Skyborne to take another's responsibilities, though. When I send you back to your father, I must be fine with whatever punishment he'll bestow upon you." He leaned forward in his seat, "Darius, did the girl have the ember?"

"Yes, Regius." Here was the gamble, I thought as I answered him truthfully.

"Did you see it?"

"No, Regius."

"Then how did you know she carried it?"

"I could feel its presence. Like the way it felt when it had been in Drakestone. And she would occasionally place her hand over a hidden pocket in her tunic."

I could feel his next question before he asked it. I had to gain his trust as Darius, so I had to answer truthfully.

"And where did they exit the forest, *Darius*?"

I swallowed. Even Kymar would have realistically made Darius nervous. "It was near the river. Seabrook or Drakestone's territory, I think."

"Was Malik bringing the ember back to Karish, Darius?"

"No, Regius."

"Seabrook then." He nodded to his guards, of which several moved in my direction. "You don't mind if we search you, do you, Darius?"

"No, Regius." I raised my arms from my sides, welcoming the men to do their jobs.

The men were no doubt looking for the box I no longer carried. They frisked me thoroughly but turned up nothing. Surprisingly, they'd let me keep the few weapons lent to me by the soldiers who'd found me. That was a good sign. A guard signaled the all-clear to Kymar and returned to his position. Two other guards remained by my side.

"Very well," he said, sounding disappointed.

"Regius, if I may?" I asked. He inclined his head for me to continue. "Before I return to Drakestone, I could gather a report on our progress to bring to my father. If it would please you, of course."

Regius Kymar cocked his head to the side, "the guards will escort you to a room where you can freshen up. You will join my family for dinner. In the morning, I will make sure you get a full tour."

CHAPTER TWENTY-ONE

A YOUNG WOMAN THREW her arms around my neck, going in for a kiss I narrowly dodged. I looked at the dark, deep-set eyes staring up at me. *Emerson.*

I didn't expect her to be so striking—this evil little creature in front of me. The evil little creature seemed to be on more than a first-name basis with Darius.

I honestly thought I must be going insane, as a pang of jealousy hit me. This man had meant nothing to me. I hadn't even been myself with him. He'd assaulted me for the love of the Makers. And he was my half-brother. At this point, I wasn't sure which salacious fact was making my blood chill.

Therapy. I was going to need years of therapy to sort all of this out if I survived.

It was messed up, but betrayal still stung as I took her in. We had to be about the same age. She was tall with long, lithe limbs and svelte curves. Her deep brown hair, which had threads of bordeaux running through it, was sheared off well beneath her shoulder blades. I reached up to run my fingers through its straight, silky length, not missing a beat.

Delicate fingers tipped with sinfully pointed wine-colored nails matching her lips teased down my chest. "Didn't you miss me?" she purred at me before running her tongue across her pillowy cupid's bow.

Shit.

I looked around the dining room as the rest of the family filtered in. Leaning down to her ear, I whispered, "There'll be enough time for that later." I nudged her toward the table, hoping she'd let it rest.

"We could skip dinner?" she taunted, turning back. Her eyes were dripping with desire. This was a woman used to getting exactly what she wanted. I grabbed her wrist before she could grope me and brought her hand up to my lips.

"You know I would love nothing more than that, but I am under the mercy of your father at the moment."

Wickedness flashed across her eyes. "Just one little kiss?"

Seeing no other option, I gripped her delicately curved jaw and pulled her toward me, covering her lips with mine. She moaned as she deepened the kiss. Before I knew what was happening, she'd pressed me into a wall, and her devious tongue was sweeping across mine. I was breathless when she pulled away.

She blinked twice and let out a breathy exhale, beaming.

Emerson threaded her fingers through mine as she pulled me to the table. She seated herself next to the Regius and me next to her.

I repeated the story I'd told the Regius to the rest of his family.

Emerson seemed genuinely impressed, reaching over and warmly squeezing my hand. "I believe you, Darius. You poor thing. What were the creatures like?"

"How many were there?"

"Did you notice anything different about the boundary?"

"Do you think you could escape it again? If you had to?"

She peppered me with a million questions. Ominous questions. I answered each one of them patiently and as honestly as I could. *As Darius.*

"Varying sizes, winged, molted, gray-green translucent skin. Fat."

"Dozens."

"I thought I saw it shift."

"That's not something I'd really like to try again."

For the rest of the dinner, she was almost gleeful as she chirped about her work that day. The boundary she explained did seem to be moving. Expanding. She'd visited it herself to observe it after she'd heard the rumors.

"All the more reason we need to get the ember back and make our return to Idia." Kymar clapped Emerson on the shoulder and turned to me, "I hear your carelessness was to blame."

Emerson rotated toward me, raising her eyebrows in question.

"My father invited the girl in. It was only my job to keep her distracted until she left. I did my part." I shrugged, hoping they'd drop it.

"You and I will talk about how you kept her distracted later," Emerson smirked.

Berith, the younger brother who had been quietly talking to their mother during Emerson's inquisition, turned to me. "We also heard you were at the ceremony in Eastdow, Darius. I would love to hear about that from a firsthand account. I hear it was really quite the spectacle."

Again, I obliged.

"What was the girl like?" Emerson crooned.

"What? Vera?" I asked.

"No, the real one. What was she like?" she repeated.

"Well," I thought, thinking of how I would describe myself from Darius's perspective. "She's petite but fit. Light olive skin, long narrow nose, high cheekbones, dark almond eyes. Umm... dark hair down to about here." I motioned below my shoulders.

"Was she attractive?" Emerson blinked sweetly.

"I guess so. I wasn't really paying that close attention." I was really ready for dinner to be over.

"It seems like you were paying *very* close attention. What about her body? Did you find it attractive?" she teased, sliding her hand up my thigh.

"Emerson, that's enough." Anya, Kymar's wife, finally spoke.

She was nothing like I expected. Kymar, yes. He seemed like an evil mastermind. Emerson? Not in a million years. She was endlessly curious. And intelligent. Playful. I had a hard time reconciling how such grotesqueness could be produced by such a disarming woman. She mesmerized me. I caught myself teasing her back and waiting to hear what she'd say next. She listened so attentively, too. Hanging on every word, even.

I did my best to focus on studying the Regius's family, despite

Emerson's roaming hand. Anya had features that were exaggerated, making her more abrupt than beautiful. And unlike Emerson, their son Berith was a mirror image of his father. Anya was the only one who seems to have a gentle nature. She barely spoke the rest of the dinner, but that did not stop her from eyeing me suspiciously all night. My mother had told me hers had died in childbirth along with her baby, and Anya was Kymar's second wife, which made Emerson, the oldest and heir. It also meant she and Berith were my half-cousins.

This was the family who would have forced my mother to either end her pregnancy or, if it was too late for the herbs to take effect, to destroy the baby once it was born. Once *I* was born. I was all for a female's choice, but not by force.

After dinner, Kymar promised the update in the morning and suggested I stay in my usual room. That gave me a brief panic. If I wandered the halls all night, at least I'd be able to steer clear of Emerson. I shuddered at the thought of what would have to take place if she cornered me in my room as I watched her prowl over to me.

"I'm going to go freshen up. I'll see you soon." Emerson stood on her toes and pecked me with a chaste kiss before slipping away.

I walked into the hallway, turning in the opposite direction the Regius and his wife had taken. I figured it was a safe assumption that my rooms were in the opposite direction of theirs.

I'd been roaming the halls for a while, mapping out the layout of the keep using a servant's form, when I heard the Regius' voice. I must have woven almost a full lap around the oval-shaped building. I needed to find the door to the tunnel that led to the mines quickly, see what I came here to see and get out of here. The longer I stayed, the riskier the situation got.

I couldn't turn away.

"Anya, your daughter never fails to amaze me. She is worth your weight in gold and then some. It is going to kill me when I have to tell her Berith will be the next Regius, not her." I heard a female's woeful sigh. "After she has served us so faithfully. As have you, my Queen."

"Emerson would make such a better Regius than Berith."

Kymar cut her off, voice becoming muffled. "That's enough, Anya. You knew she would never…" Kymar's voice trailed off before I heard a heavy door shut.

I didn't get to hear what else he said. I stood there for a moment, dumbstruck.

That meant Emerson was not a relation. If she was only Anya's daughter and not Kymar's. I sighed louder than I should have, thinking about the kiss we'd shared. I'd done it to stay alive, more or less. But I'd enjoyed it, I thought as my cheeks flamed.

I needed to regroup. I shifted from the servant's visage back to Darius when I came to an area of rooms that reminded me of the guest suites at the other keeps I'd been to.

As soon as I saw her, I tried to spin around before she noticed me.

"Oh, there you are," she exclaimed, holding the door she'd been exiting ajar. "I came for you as I promised."

Shit. Shit. Shit.

I'd have to knock her out. There was a very limited window to accomplish what I'd come here for. I stalked forward, thinking of the way Darius moved. Thinking of what Darius would say.

"I'm glad you waited."

"I was actually just leaving." She crossed her arms. "It seems you've tired of me."

Another out presented itself. Darius would be tired after his alleged adventure. But what man would ever be so tired he'd reject Emerson after seeing her in that nightgown ready to go. She'd know that too.

"Why don't you come in and give me another chance," I pleaded, leaning over her and pushing the door open. I smiled as I brought my lips near hers, teasing before I pulled away, stepping into the room.

She followed me in and shut the door, bolting it.

"You don't seem like yourself, Darius." She was practically glaring at me.

"I've not exactly had the easiest last few days, Emerson. I just escaped the Swath for Maker's sake."

"That doesn't sound like you," she held firm, eyeing me squarely.

I sat down on the settee in the sitting area of the suite and ran my hand through the loose shoulder-length dark locks atop my head like I'd done in the weeks Darius had been my lover.

"What does sound like me, Emerson?"

The corner of her mouth turned up.

"Mmm... well, that one time, after your father abandoned you and Malik on that sinking boat in North Sound for one of your training exercises and you both finally made it here, you hadn't slept, *really slept*, in how many days?"

"I don't know, three?" I answered, calculating.

"Four."

I sighed. She was exhausting.

"You were so tired, I could tell. I remember I tried to get you to rest, but you couldn't keep your hands off me. And that night, you drank my body like you were the thirstiest Skyborne alive. *Then* you slept. Remember?"

He would have wanted her. Any male would, I thought as I looked her over. Her nightgown was a sheer emerald green material, with a velvet trim and velvet strips strategically placed to cover certain areas and hold the flowing panels together. It revealed just the right amount of skin.

I was going to have to kill her. I didn't want to do it before I'd seen them, before I knew she deserved it, but I was this close to getting caught.

She watched her delicate middle finger circle the lip of a water glass she'd picked up, making it sing. It became louder, peaking the already tense energy in the room.

"For the love of the Makers, Emerson." I eyed the glass and that sensual finger.

She cocked her head at me as I approached her.

Suddenly she launched the glass across the room. It shattered against the wall with a crash.

"Is there another female, Darius?" she demanded.

Oh Makers, that's what this was about. I tried not to look too relieved as I chuckled, shaking my head.

"Look at you, Emerson. What woman could ever compare to you? To everything that you are. You know there is no other." I appealed to her vanity.

"You mean that? You really do?" Her voice had a mocking edge to it.

I watched Emerson circle me like a cat rubbing against me. My only choice was to respond to her in like. I reached toward her.

She was playing with me, like at dinner.

I went stiff.

I realized she *knew.*

I knew it, and she knew that now too. Damn my reaction.

The others I wasn't so sure about, though I didn't know what motivation she would have not to tell them. It was worth the gamble. We stared at each other, sizing each other up. She seductively slid her arms around my neck and nipped at my bottom lip, licking and teasing it. I grabbed her by the waist and carried her to the nearest wall, deepening the kiss. I was anatomically correct in my shifts, and it showed as I ground my hips into her, sending a foreign sensation through my body.

Two could play at this game.

I wasn't sure how far she'd take it, hoping I didn't have to find out, like a game of chicken. "Nayla, is that your name?" she asked tentatively, sliding her tongue over my inner lip. Makers, she was a good kisser. I might have enjoyed it if she weren't supposedly evil. I *was* enjoying it. The way her supple body felt against mine.

"Don't you think Darius would be jealous if he knew you were making out with me?" I taunted her.

"I think he'd want to watch."

I carried her over to the bed and tossed her onto it before looking back to confirm she'd bolted the door.

She was baiting me. I knew it but couldn't resist the urge to best her. She thought she could play with me wearing a Darius shift. She'd been with him before, so easy to pretend. What about when I was me? She knew. What did it matter now?

I dropped the shift of Darius.

Emerson gasped as *I* smiled down at her from between her legs.

"What?" I asked her as I clenched the upper hand.

"I didn't expect you to be *beautiful,*" she said, eyes becoming heavy-lidded.

I felt in control as I ran my calloused fingers up her shin and thigh, moving her dress to the side the way the pale-haired Skyborne had done to me in my dream. Heat thrummed between my thighs as I stared at her bare skin and the barely hidden promise higher up. *Makers, what are you thinking?* I scolded myself.

"All the questions at dinner. You knew then?"

She grinned broadly up at me, eyes twinkling. She'd been playing with her food. *Me.*

"You told me about the Swath growing. That was confident."

My fingertips hadn't moved from her upper thigh as we'd assessed each other. Abruptly, she seized my wrist. I jerked it away, but she held firm.

"Aren't you afraid of me?" I asked her.

"Should I be?" she whispered. Emerson pulled my wrist forward, pressing my hand into the apex of her thighs, making sure I felt the wetness underneath her undergarments.

I kept my hand there as I leaned over her, resting on my other arm. We both grinned, like two children caught doing something very naughty.

"This is a terrible idea," I murmured as I nudged her undergarments to the side.

"Aren't those always the best ones?" she asked breathlessly, arching into my hand.

I could no longer fault Darius. *There was something about her*, I thought as she deftly unlaced my tunic and pulled it over my head.

We weren't playing anymore. And neither of us could resist this appalling chemistry between us. I was such a fool.

I don't know who moved first, but our lips crushed into each other. Her hand was in my messy black waves as I worked the bundle of nerves between her thighs.

She yanked my undershirt down and took my full breast in her hand, nibbling the hardened nipple between her teeth. I had both of the velvet straps to her dress pulled down, so it revealed her small, firm breasts. We toyed with each other, exploring with our hands and mouths. She easily uncinched the waistband of my trousers, the Drakestone style, and wiggling her fingers inside to find the warm pool of desire for her beneath.

I claimed her mouth again as we laid on our sides, pleasuring each other.

"Makers," I cried as the first wave hit me. Emerson worked her fingers until I was shuddering against her. She giggled as she bit my earlobe and neck, bringing me over the edge a second time. She seemed very pleased with herself for a moment before her gaze turned lusty again. I sucked on her lower lip as I curled my fingers forward. She jerked, clenching around them instantly, and I increased the rhythm. It didn't take long before she broke apart in my arms, digging those claws into my forearms.

"Nayla," she gasped as I felt a wave peak, her forehead pressing into mine.

We didn't waste our feminine ability to have multiple orgasms. And we didn't stop until we both glistened and were blissfully sated.

She was the enemy—the too decadent treat. And I'd gorged myself on it.

⚬

"So, who won?" she asked. So soft and feline. Innocent, even.

"Call it a draw?" I asked her, smiling despite myself.

She ran a pointed nail down my bicep, eliciting chills. "You ready to switch sides yet?" she asked as we laid in the afterglow.

I ran my fingers through her hair. This woman was doing terrible things, from what I'd been told. Now that I'd met her, I had an even harder time imagining it.

"Is that why you slept with me?" I asked her.

"I could ask you the same thing."

"You could undo everything you've done. I could help you," I pleaded to her, leaning up on an elbow. I leaned over and slowly savored a kiss.

"You'd want me to kill my creations?" She looked honestly hurt.

"From what I've been told, they are abominations."

Emerson jerked away from my hand, her dark eyes narrowing.

"You haven't even seen them. You know nothing of what I've created. They are my life's work. My children." She had sat up and drew a blanket to cover herself.

I raised my hands defensively. "Emerson, Kymar is using you. I overheard him. He plans to make Berith the heir, not you."

She looked truly shocked. And I didn't know why I was telling her this. Sex always clouded my judgment, apparently.

"You're lying."

"I'm not. I overheard him talking to Anya when I was sneaking through the halls earlier. I know you aren't my cousin."

"Well, that's reassuring. I was kind of wondering what type of weird stuff you were into." She gave a tentative laugh.

"You could come with me," I pleaded one last time.

She let out a low husky laugh, looking away. "No. I couldn't," she said with finality.

Then she struck.

Her fist shot out, intending for... my windpipe. Makers. The little viper.

Her delicate fist grazed off my chin instead. Her other hand went for my hair; wrenching my head back, she sunk her teeth into my neck.

"You bitch," I cried out, tossing her off me onto the floor. She had the audacity to look offended.

I jumped down, straddling her, and grabbed her head.

She latched on to my arms, digging her nails in with a desperate intensity. I could feel my pulse slowing. I was becoming light-headed. She was doing this with her ability to heal. My eyes went wide as she sneered. I was seeing *very* clearly now who was inside the pretty package.

We made eye contact briefly. The one look was a lifetime of conversations. Whatever might have become of this weird chemistry between us was dying as soon as it started. I took a deep breath, yanking my arm free from her grip, and cracked my elbow across her temple, knocking her out. I should have killed her, I knew, but I couldn't. I'd add that to the list of things to regret later.

I got dressed. Tied her to the bedpost and gagged her.

Taking her appearance, I unlocked the door and left the room.

CHAPTER TWENTY-TWO

I MADE MY WAY through the corridors, taking the shape of others as
needed. The hallways were as dark as the great hall, so it was easier
to slip by unnoticed than it had been in Drakestone.

The keep's hallways were almost as busy at night as they'd been during
the day, so it didn't seem out of place for an individual guard to be roaming the halls. I followed several corridors that went deeper into the keep
toward the mountain, but all led to dead ends or turned in the wrong
direction. I went to the second level and did the same, slipping through
more darkly lit passages.

I came to a hallway that had a thick metal door at its end. It was
unlocked. I put my ear to the door and, even using my heightened senses,
heard nothing more than wind beyond it. I lifted the latch and pushed.
The door gave, smoothly opening on its hinges. I stuck my head out
enough to catch a glimpse of what was beyond it.

Jackpot.

My arm hairs were at attention.

In front of me was a long narrow pathway atop some type of a wall
that rose from deep in the earth. The walk wall led to the stone face of the
mountain where another metal door stood. I surveyed the enclosed space
on either side of the path. Enormous walls rose a distance away on either

side of the elevated path. The ceiling angled up to a point where a long, braced opening in the ceiling ran parallel with the path.

I must be inside the structure built into the face of the mountain I'd seen from above.

I inhaled deeply, trying to sense any other presence. There were Skyborne beyond the far door, but I didn't pick up the scent of Kymar or Berith. If only I had Malik's talent, so I could sweep the interior to be sure. Emerson would have unfettered access to what lay beyond. And with her apparent mood swing tendency, I imagined anyone beyond the door would suspect nothing, regardless of how I acted.

Pulling my shoulders back and adjusting her long multicolored strands, I would have to cross the expanse and open and enter the other door with her presumed authority. It was a risk, but there was no other way to sneak inside.

I took one last breath before I strode out the door. As I slinked across the pathway in Emerson's lithe form, I glanced down to what I could make out by torchlight were mining pits in the two open areas deep below. As fire danced atop the torches placed evenly down the walls, I could make out glints of magenta, similar in color to the crystal in the metal band Kymar wore and the stone Malik has revealed to us at the cottage.

My skin prickled with energy as I reached the door, making me wish I had the reassuring presence of the ember with me.

I reached for the latch. It moved up and opened out toward me. Two older females draped in loose black frocks walked out, sneering at me as they passed.

"Emerson?"

I raised my eyebrows at the pair.

"Do you require our assistance?"

"Don't you think I would let you know if I needed your help," I replied brusquely, reminding myself I didn't need to feel guilty.

The Skyborne nodded as they let me pass.

I slipped through the metal door, closing it behind me. The first room appeared to be a meeting area, with a few tables and chairs inside. The room had two doorways. I checked the left first. It was a large kitchen, perhaps meant to supply meals for the Skyborne who worked under the mountain and maybe even feed the creatures they were creating. A frail Skyborne in tattered clothes was standing at a sink. He looked up at me from the dishes he was washing, eyes going wide. Trying to embody Emerson, I glared at him and turned and shut the door.

The next door opened to a short hallway. I followed it until it led to a set of stairs that wound up into the mountain. I climbed until I reached the first landing. There was an open hall and two more doors. I listened. I could hear two men arguing in the door to the right. One sounded like he wanted to proceed with an experiment, and the other was saying something about the cost. He wanted Emerson's approval to use resources. They both feared her.

The left door was quiet. I tested the door to see if it would make noise. I pushed it open and slid in, closing it behind me. There were no torches in the room burning. I focused my eyes and found a small extinguished one. My palm shook as I brought a small flame to life atop it.

Makers, I swore under my breath. I almost dropped the torch.

My stomach turned as I surveyed the grotesqueness. There was a large jar with a small rat-like creature with long fangs and deformed appendages preserved in liquid. I turned the jar so I could see the back of the creature. Little stubs of broken wings grew from its shoulder blades.

There were several jars in that area with variations on the dead rat creature. The next table looked like they'd experimented with a type of small humanoid creature similar to the escort we'd had in the Swath. Meethra told me she thought godflies landed elsewhere in this realm, and Malik confirmed it.

Of all the experiments I'd surveyed, these looked to be the most successful. They progressively got larger and more horrifying, with fangs and leathery wings. Insects covered the next table. Their wings stabbed to a board—specimens with long pairs of wings like Meethra's and others: flies and butterflies. There were boards with birds and bats. She had studied flight. Emerson was breeding an aerial grotesquerie.

There was a room off to the side; I only had to peek my head in to know the contents were horrendous. I had to force myself to enter. I needed to see this; I reminded myself. I came here to see this.

The jars were even larger in this room. What I saw was beyond comprehension. Skyborne children. Babies and children of about three or four were in the jars. Many of them had deformities, similar to those of the rats, and some of them even had gross fleshy wings or nodes at their shoulders. These experiments didn't seem to have gone as well.

I should have killed her.

My stomach lurched. I shifted the torch between clammy hands, wiping the sweat beading on my brow. The room was getting smaller. I turned, gripping the edge of the table, and vomited my panic into the corner. It didn't matter if someone found it later. I would be gone soon.

Get it together, Nayla, I chastised myself.

I had to get out of this room. I wasn't stupid enough to think it was a good omen. I'd seen no godflies. These experiments looked old. It was like a museum of sorts. I hurriedly went back to the landing and made my way down the hall.

It ended in another set of stairs, which I followed up to the next landing. More doors and hallways. I got to a room filled with dozens and dozens of smaller cages. This room was well lit. *Godflies*, I thought before I even reached one to peer inside. A small being, so similar to Meethra, crouched, pressing herself into the back corner of her cage. She quivered with fear.

What were they doing to these poor innocent beings?

I moved closer. She stopped shaking and moved toward the front of her cage. Her head tilted to the side curiously. I look across at the other cages. Other godflies were doing the same.

"You are not what you seem," she addressed me faintly. "Are you here to free us?"

There was such hope in her voice. Guilt flooded in. "Do you know a godfly called Meethra?" I asked, dodging her question.

"Yes, how... she survived?" she asked. Another godfly chimed in, "she and many others landed in the Swath. We believed they all perished. We thought it was too late."

I looked around to see who had joined the conversation. It was a godfly who appeared to be older than the others if that was possible. She waved me over to her.

Come, she thought, *How did she escape? Did you help her?*

I did, and if I can, I will help you. No—I will help you, I said, deter-mined. *I fear even I am in grave danger here.* I looked around, surveying the room, trying to come up with a plan.

"I just need time," I said aloud, more to myself than them.

What can you tell me? I asked her. *I don't have long.*

She told me as quickly as possible about how Emerson was using her healing abilities and the dust godflies produced to manipulate the essence of creatures while in utero. With each generation, she would make subtle changes. Heal and grow them in the womb without seeing them even, injecting the dust and the ground-up crystals into the embryos to encour-age her changes to take root.

The crystals, the cherry-colored ones the Regius wears in the metal band around his brow. Do you know what they are? I asked them.

It's what they mine all around these mountains. They call it Cerisium. They appear to be unstable and disintegrate within a few months. But they release energy when they do.

That explained where she was getting the energy from. *Hurry*, I thought. The longer I was here, the more likely they would catch me. *Where are the creatures kept?* I asked.

The next landing, take the hallway that leads back down. These two floors hold their creations and breading areas. Most of the current work is done here. There is a room where they collect a powder from the creatures that can block your kind's ability to feel their power. You should not go there.

I nodded.

Be careful, the older godfly dismissed me.

Now I knew how they created the powder. This was proving fruitful, after all.

Thank you, I thought and turned to go.

Don't forget us, a godfly I'd seen called after me meekly. I looked around for the voice and saw a godfly squatted down at the front of her cage, holding her knees to her chest.

I caught her eye, *I won't.*

❧

I hurried, following the godfly's directions to the series of rooms where they held the creatures. I could hear the sounds of commotion inside the first room. Steeling myself, I pushed open the door and stepped through.

Pale peach creatures had scooted to the front of their cages and stared at me, blinking large anticipatory eyes. Their stout little bodies were nothing like the delicate form of Meethra or the other godflies. And they were three times their size. They weren't fat either, like the creatures of the swath. They were almost like muscular babies with insect wings and overly large heads. They were practically identical to each other and horrifying.

I saw the dark-colored dust at the bottom of the cages and was careful to stay back.

Mother, one cheeped. Others followed until a chorus of monsters bleating *mother* echoed in the room. I instinctively stepped back, knocking into a table. A glass jar tipped off the edge and crashed to the floor.

I jumped.

Fortunately, the creatures hadn't gained the godflies ability to access my essence and appeared to think I was Emerson.

"Quiet," I commanded, making my voice sound like hers.

They obeyed, gripping the wires of their cages, tracking me. The one who'd called out to me had a little taloned hand pressed through the grates reaching out for me. I watched it break into a grin, revealing sharp incisors. There was a tag on his cage labeled A1. The others had number and letter combinations too.

I looked around the room and saw a pair of leather gloves and a thick cape. Understanding what they were for, I put them on. There were metal shelves on one wall with varying baskets and jars. I found one with preserved reptiles and picked it up.

"Mother," their apparent leader whined.

I shook the jar at it. "You want?"

"Mother, mother," it insisted. Maybe they could only speak that one word. Before the others chimed in again, I gave it an authoritative glare hushing it.

I picked up a scale and set it on the table next to the jar of food.

"I need to weigh you," I told it. "Be good." I had no idea if that made any sense to it, so I had my hood up and knife at the ready, just in case. A1 moved back from the cage door as I unlatched it. When I swung the little door open, it hopped out into the air and hovered in front of me, harmlessly flapping its sets of waxy wings. I pointed to the scale with my knife.

A1 flew over and perched on the little weight tray. As it did, it glanced at the jar expectantly. My skin crawled as I tossed it a small preserved lizard which it swiped out of the air, instantly tearing the head off popping it into its mouth. I approached it. "I'm going to inspect your wings," I told it tentatively.

A1 extended them for me like a good subject. Scales traveled from the back of its hairless head down the length of its spine. A pair of large salamander-colored forewings protruded above where its shoulder blades would be, followed by a smaller hindwing beneath. Venation snaked across the translucent membrane, which glinted iridescent in the torch-light. I ran my gloved finger down a section that looked like it had healed over imperfectly, leaving scaring.

Emerson could heal better than that. This work wasn't hers. It was probably another healer. Unless she'd bred the ability to heal themselves into them. It would be a convenient trait to give them. And make them harder to kill.

It had no apparent sex organs and thin humanoid arm and leg appendages but with an extra set of joints. Two razor-sharp elongated fingers and a thumb grew from the final joint, or pincers, really. I spun A1 around, studying the rest of it. It really was fascinating if you could forget how it was created. Emerson had obviously taken different characteristics from her experiments and blended them into the creature before me. And it looked capable of violence, but it sat still, waiting. Docile, really. Like Darius had described them.

There was a movement out of the corner of my eye. Suddenly A1 flashed across my vision and impaled a rat into the corner, using the points on the end of its pincers as a spear. The rat twitched, going limp. A1 looked back to me almost sheepishly as metal bowls it knocked over clanged on the ground.

It took the creature maybe half a second. Or less. My vision barely registered it.

"A1, drop it. Up."

Emerson's commanding voice came from behind me. Startled, I spun around, but she was quicker. A long blade was at my throat, just piercing it. I felt a warm trickle of blood trail down my neck.

There was a dark purple bruise around her eye and temple from where I'd struck her. She hadn't taken the time to heal it. It didn't make her any less alluring. The experiments I'd seen did, however.

"Dose her," she commanded.

A1 flew up and hovered in the air, wings moving imperceptibly fast, looking back and forth between us, trying to decide which of us was its actual mother. It slowly turned to me, narrowing large pupil-less eyes which but now had pulsing magenta centers.

I threw my body back quicker than Emerson could shoot her sword arm forward. My knife slashed through the air knocking her weapon aside. She only stood there as I swung a wide arc toward the creature.

A1 zipped out of the way easily. I swung with one arm and jabbed with the other. I was fast. Faster than most, I knew. I couldn't match A1's speed. Like the creatures in the Swath, it moved with a preternatural speed the Skyborne weren't blessed with. I felt a stinging on my right bicep.

Warm blood trickled down my arm. A1 was circling me, landing glancing gashes on my back and thighs.

Mother, I thought, sickened.

I threw my weight at Emerson. She jumped back before my knife got too close, dragging the table away from the wall flipping it between us. It only increased A1's fervor to protect her. He took that out on me.

Searing cuts were oozing on all over my body.

"Are you done?" Emerson asked, leaning on the table across from me. She seemed bored. I glared at her, panting. "If you had selected another, perhaps you would be fast enough, but A1," she said proudly, "none are faster or more deadly."

A1 was her pet. Her favorite monster.

It flew above me, emitting a fine dark dust, like when Meethra had dispersed her dust onto the soldiers in the tunnel.

I tried to hold my breath. It kept a constant shower on me until I had no choice except to breathe it in.

I could feel as soon as it took effect, and Emerson was now staring at *me*.

"How did he know?" I asked her.

"They have an incredible sense of smell. Of course, you smelled like me from," she hesitated, smiling sinfully, "*earlier*. Your blood, though."

I reached up to the small cut on my neck Emerson had made with her sword.

"Have you experienced this, Emerson? To be cut off completely from the fields of energy surrounding us?"

"Of course. It's a terrible feeling. Very unnatural. Don't you think?"

I didn't answer.

"You try *anything*, you die. Understand?"

"Yes," I muttered, dripping blood.

Emerson motioned to the creature. I felt A1's weight land on my shoulder. His sharp little pincer gently poked the side of my throat.

"Drop your knife and the rest of what you're carrying."

I knew A1 would be faster. I dropped what I had.

"Follow," she commanded and turned, walking out the door. I followed behind her, half admiring her confidence in her creature's ability to keep me in check. She seemed to have excellent control over this one, anyway. Probably the rest of them, too. Which would be fine if she wasn't completely unpredictable—as I was learning the hard way.

I followed her through more passageways and up another set of stairs that went further back into the mountain. Finally, we came to a larger area with cells lining one side. There was only one torch at the entrance. The further we walked back, the dimmer it became. I caught my boot on an uneven stone and lost my footing.

A1 jabbed his pointer deeper into my neck. "Easy," I told it as I regained my balance. Emerson didn't flinch. She stopped at a cell, pulling a key from her robe. The door swung open, and she gestured for me to enter.

When she had me safely enclosed in the cell, she released A1. It flew to her shoulder as she and I regarded each other.

"I should have killed you," I said.

I could see her upper lip curl up in the dim light.

"Well, you didn't." She turned without another word and left me bleeding in the cell.

CHAPTER TWENTY-THREE

ALL I COULD think of was how worried Malik must be. I hoped he wouldn't do anything stupid and risk himself.

And I thought about if I'd ever see Conall again or my mother. I figured it's been almost a week since Emerson deposited me here. She'd sent healers in for my cuts. The other prisoners and I were fed once a day. And every few days, A1 would come, dose me, then leave. That was the only sign of life I'd seen.

No interrogation, no torture. Nothing.

I paced my damp cell for hours on end—for days on end. There was only a bucket in the corner for waste. And a round metal plate I'd get to keep until an attendant came to collect it and replace the waste bucket the next morning—nothing else in the cramped square cell.

Anxiety was getting the best of me. I couldn't handle not taking action. There was nothing I could do, though. And each time they dosed me, it felt worse, like a terrible hangover.

This was how Skyborne went crazy in isolation. I wanted to tear at my skin just to feel something. My mind raced through memories and waking dreams. I gathered my self-control and sat on the ground in the center of the cell, counting my breaths.

᷁

Days later, I heard footsteps nearing the entrance. Torchlight illuminated the passageway as they approached, stopping in front of my cell. I stood facing Emerson.

"You are a much better kisser than Darius. I thought you should know that."

I regarded Emerson. *That's how she knew.*

"Come," she called behind her. A1 appeared at her side as she let herself into my cell. "Have you missed me?" she asked, blinking as if I might answer yes.

"You are insane."

"No," she laughed under her breath. "I'm not the one who thought it was a good idea to come to Monterra, a place you hardly know anything about, disguised as our mutual friend Darius, of all Skyborne."

Decent point.

"Did you find what you were looking for, though?" She was inches from my face. I looked at A1, refusing to cower. She jerked forward, snapping at the air between us. I jumped back.

"So how *do* you know Darius?" she asked, running her thumb across my bottom lip.

"Same way as you, apparently."

She went white.

"I'm so hurt, Emerson. I thought I was your thing now."

"How long?"

"Around the last half-light. Karish invited us to their ceremony. We'd been waiting, preparing, for the invite all year. It was the opening I needed to steal the ember. Darius is charming and handsome. One thing led to another. You understand." I smiled nonchalantly. "We had a few weeks' fling. Well, it was a fling for me. He, it seems, caught the love bug."

"What do you mean it seems?"

"He told me as much." A vein popped out of her forehead. "What, you don't like other Skyborne playing with your toys?"

"You are kind of a slut, you know."

"Likewise. Granted, I think females have as much of a right to explore their sexuality as males. You're from a territory that still permits females like yourself to be Regents. I thought that shouldn't be a foreign concept to you. Oops, I mean females who are blood heirs. So *not you*."

"The Regius said you're lying. He never said that."

"Don't be so naïve, Emerson. Or try asking your mother. I could tell she disagreed with his decision. He does really appreciate you, though. Like, a lot." I paused, goading her as she glared daggers at me. "I've been thinking about this. I think I have more rights to your Territory's Regency than you do. Did you know my mother is Kymar's lost daughter? I don't mean to make you jealous. *Again*."

"I will kill you," she seethed.

"I think you like me too much to do that. In fact, I know you do. You showed me. I enjoyed what we shared, too. It was *special* to me." I had liked it, which sickened me now. The truth I'd sprinkled in with my jab. I knew she felt what I did in that moment. If we'd been born in another realm in another lifetime, maybe things would have been different. We could have explored this static chemistry between us to see if it was something more than just sex, this reverberation between pleasure and pain.

She leaned forward and brushed her lips against mine. This time I didn't kiss her back. It only infuriated her more.

"Fine." she crossed her arms. "I can see that you're upset with me. I supposed if I am trying to woo you, I ought to bring you presents. I think you'll love the surprise my creatures found in a cave not too far from here."

My heart stopped as Emerson turned and sauntered away.

CHAPTER TWENTY-FOUR

"WHAT HAVE YOU done with him?" I screamed after her.

"Don't worry," she called back over her shoulder. "I'll deliver him to you soon. I'll expect you to thank me properly for my gift."

᷎

Worry consumed me. They had Malik and I. Conall and Seeley would soon figure it out and come for us. This was really, really bad. And it put the ember at risk of falling into their or Karish's hands. The creatures were all but ready. And if they had me, the ember, and the creatures, they could use Conall and Malik to compel me to use the ember.

Makers, I was so stupid coming here.

"That was a twisted conversation."

I whipped around to the cell next to mine. "Who's there?"

"You're the girl who stole the ember," she responded from the shadowed corner.

"Yes, Nayla, is my name. Yours?"

"I'm not telling my name to someone who seems to be on a *very* friendly basis with *that female.*"

"It's not like that. It was a one-time thing. And it was a complicated situation. You don't know how she can be."

"Apparently."

"Look, it's not something I'm really proud of."

She laughed. "I suppose we've all done things we're not proud of."

"Thank you," I said.

"I mean, I've never done *Emerson*." She snickered.

"Do you want to help me escape here or what?"

"There's no escape from here. Especially with them dosing us."

"How long have you been here?"

"I don't know. Two months. Three?" The female speaking came into view. She ran her hand through her flame-colored locks, getting snagged toward the ends. "I was here when the news came about the ember. I'm from Sundale. They became suspicious of anyone from another territory. Technically, I'm in this shithole because of you."

She wrapped her hands around the bars between our cells, moving her wan face near. Her glassy eyes were a muddy hazel. She watched me.

"I'm sorry."

She retreated to her corner. "I'm Asha."

᷅

Footsteps got my attention. It had to be Emerson bringing Malik in.

I pressed my face between the bars, trying to get a better look.

Emerson was following a large guard who dragged Malik by the shoulders. She walked around them and opened the cell next to mine. I looked at the path of blood that trailed where his boots were dragged across the ground. This too was my fault, I thought, sinking down to my knees. I crawled over to where the guard unceremoniously dropped him. His head cracked, bouncing off the stones.

He looked awful. *Makers*, Seeley had known this was going to happen. He'd seen it. It was the reason for his melancholy when we left. But he'd let us go, which meant Malik would survive. He had to. That's all I cared about, Malik surviving.

The blood, though. It was coming from the cuts all over his body. His clothes were in shreds. The creatures must have slashed him until he passed out from blood loss.

"I stopped the bleeding," Emerson said flatly. "He won't die. Probably"

I looked around his cell at the filthy ground. All it would take was a little infection to start and spread. And the nasty head would he just got.

"Emerson, will you heal him?" I begged. I looked over at my brother. "Please," I said, voice quavering as tears spilled over my eyelids.

She turned to me, wrinkling her brow. Genuine concerned showed in her eyes.

"I thought you'd be happy to see him alive." She cocked her head to the side, studying me.

"Please, Emerson. For me?" I pleaded.

"He shouldn't have been lurking around the tunnel. If he wasn't yours, he'd be dead already."

"Heal him," I implored.

"What will you give me in return?" she asked sweetly.

I sobbed, folding over my knees, rocking. I'd made bad choices before, but none had ever hurt those I cared about. I was gutted.

She'd opened my cell and moved over to where I was. She kneeled down, and I felt her graceful fingers lift my chin. Emerson furrowed her brow as she wiped my tears away with her thumbs.

"Shhhh…" she whispered. "Don't cry."

"My brother will die if you don't heal him, Emerson."

I looked over at him. More blood pooled around his skull from the impact.

I wanted to kill her, but I couldn't heal him. I needed her to do it.

"What do you want, Emerson?"

"Your consideration." She narrowed her eyes.

Mine flew in the opposite direction. "What?" I stammered.

"I want you to consider a partnership. With me."

She had to be out of her mind.

"I know you don't approve of my methods, but I want you to imagine all the things you and I could do together." She smiled slyly. "Not just the sex. We could take Idia back. You and I could rule it together. Just think of it. Two united female rulers. Utopia."

Dystopia if it involved her, I scoffed inwardly. I was careful not to let my disgust show.

"His heart is slowing. All I ask is for your consideration," she implored.

"I'll consider it," I muttered.

"What was that?" She cocked her ear toward me.

"I'll consider it," I said louder.

"I could help you forget what you've seen here. Wash those ugly images away. We could replace them…" she kissed a tear away, "with good ones. We could treat our citizens well. Better than we do here."

She was tempting me. She wasn't, but she was trying.

"Heal him, Emerson."

She frowned. Before she got up, she leaned forward and gently pressed a lingering kiss to my lips. My skin prickled and crawled. I was repulsed, but I didn't pull away.

"Just think about it."

⥼

"Nayla, you're alive!" Malik woke me from my sleep. Emerson healed him completely. Watching her work was fascinating. She moved with such care and reverence for her craft. Before she left us, she explained that he would probably sleep for a long while after. I'd fallen asleep too.

He sounded so relieved. I hurried over to him, and he reached his arms through the bars, pulling me toward him, embracing me as much as he could.

When he finally released his death grip on me, I scanned him nervously. "You feel okay?" I asked him.

"I do." He surveyed his body. "How did you heal me? The creatures did a number on me. I thought that was it."

"I didn't heal you." I turned away from him, hiding my shame.

"Who did?" he tentatively asked.

"Emerson," I told him.

"Nayla, what did you promise her?"

I shook my head. "Nothing. Nothing real anyway. Only the consideration to join her."

Asha had stood up and was watching us. She eyed me. "You're not going to tell him, are you?"

I gave her a death glare.

"Tell me what?" he asked.

"Nothing, I'll tell you later."

"She slept with Emerson. There, bandage ripped off."

"I'm not helping you escape," I murmured at her. She shrugged indifferently, crossing her arms.

"Tell me I didn't hear that correctly? You slept with Emerson so she'd heal me?" he demanded.

"Before that. She slept with her before that. Now Emerson wants her to consider teaming up to create a female-run Utopia in Idia," Asha blurted.

I held my palms toward him in supplication. "Please don't be mad at me."

"You've got to be kidding me. How could I not? How could you be so stupid? I thought they killed you, and you were fondling Emerson?"

"I'm sorry," I said

"I told you what she was doing. Did you not believe me? Your own brother? Darius and now Emerson? You are a horrible judge of character." He paused, pivoting toward me abruptly. "No, Nayla, maybe I am the poor judge of character. I was willing to fight by your side after all."

I felt like someone had struck me. His words knocked the wind out of me. "Malik, I'll fix this. I promise."

"Damn it, Nayla, how are you going to fix this?" He'd never raised his voice at me. Malik was always dark, yes, but good-humored.

Tears streamed down my face. Again.

"You knew we'd get out of Eastdow. This is no different. We'll get out of here too."

"This is not remotely the same." Condemnation soaked his voice. "These Skyborne are not Torin. You do not understand what they are capable of."

"Please don't yell at me," I pleaded.

"I don't suppose now would be a good time to mention she had an opportunity to kill her and didn't, would it?"

I spun around to Asha, "Seriously?"

"Nayla, don't talk to me right now. I need to think." It cut deep when Malik turned away.

⇜

I tried to get Malik to open back up to me several times throughout the day, but he still wouldn't even look at me. I sat against the wall, alone with my thoughts. Anger stirred within me. It's not like Malik was perfect. I'd been careless. I could admit when I was wrong. When I'd done wrong. Been self-ish or impulsive. I'd fix this. I would. And free the godflies. And figure out what to do with the ember. The thoughts kept repeating as I scratched the discreet lump on my forearm. I needed the building irritation. I needed the fuel it gave me. I stewed, devising a plan.

⋙

I looked around. I wasn't in the cell any longer. I was on the wide-open grey stone terrace again. I was dreaming.

I followed a path until I came to the now-familiar stone basin. My boots felt harsh as they stepped over the smooth stones. My reflection on the water's surface caught me off guard. Makers, I looked awful. The clothes I'd had on when Emerson had imprisoned me were sullied, and rust from the metal bars was smudged across my face. I reached my fingertips up to rub it off.

The Skyborne must have approached while I was looking at myself. I stepped away, embarrassed to have him see me like this. *This was a dream*, I reminded myself. *Lucid, but definitely a dream.*

"Let me help you." His voice was deep and smooth. Comforting. We'd never spoken.

"How?" I whispered, stunned. He stepped around me, walking over to a pedestal. The top was hollowed out, and a small bowl of water was there. In the center, there was a hole about an inch in diameter that appeared to have no bottom.

"Touch the water." He'd come up behind me.

I obeyed. As soon as I did, I felt the energy surge around me.

"Close your eyes," he whispered into my ear. I did. "Can you feel that? The energy humming in the spaces in between?"

His hand came down over mine in the pool, but he didn't touch me. He hovered right above. I focused on what I could feel, what I could sense around me.

I could feel his breath on the nape of my neck. I felt the heat of his body, a hair's breadth away from mine—the energy sparking between us. I could have spent an eternity in the comfort of that moment. It felt like honey and cheese tasted—like a warm bath or standing before a roaring fire. Reluctantly, I followed that energy with my awareness outward, away from my body, to my fingertips, and into the water.

I gasped. There was so much power there. My senses were hyper-aware. It was like when I'd used the ember by accident against Darius in the Bare Lands. There was the water, the particles that made it up, like the swords and lock. But it was a conduit.

Helping me feel.

Helping me see.

I could hear Rhijn's blood moving through his veins. Feel his hairs standing, reaching towards me.

"Open them," he breathed. I did.

I stumbled back, barely keeping my hand in the water. He moved as I did, so we never touched. I saw everything. And everything in between that. And the thrumming energy there.

"You don't need the Void stone to see this. To use it. The power is there, in the in-between. It is always there."

Void stone? I thought. He meant the ember. Rhijn knew I had the ember.

"But be careful when you are relying on your own energy as your connection. It has a limit you don't want to cross."

"How will I know when I'm near it?" I asked him.

"You will feel like you are losing yourself."

He pulled away. I turned toward him. I didn't understand. I didn't understand any of this. I was losing him. Concern flashed across his refined features. "Thank you, Rhijn," I uttered as I awoke.

The last thing I saw was the shock in his ice-blue stare.

⛬

I woke, panting. *Rhijn*, his name is Rhijn. How did I know that? I didn't think he'd told me his name. And he'd helped me. A Skyborne in another realm, Idia presumably, had helped me. I looked around at Malik sleeping and the annoying girl next to me.

I knew what I had to do.

CHAPTER TWENTY-FIVE

I GRABBED THE METAL plate I'd discarded in the corner. Placing it on the ground in a groove between the stones, I stepped on it. I had to move all my weight to it, but it bent. I repeated it until it bent the other way. Eventually, I cleaved the metal plate into two, creating a sufficient blade.

I held in a silent gasp as I dug the jagged edge of the plate into my forearm over the itching lump. Blood welled up. I wiped it on my pants before making another pass. I dug in my forearm until I neared the glass vial my mother and I had buried there.

Tears from the pain sprung into my eyes. *Don't pass out*, I willed myself.

My mother had done an excellent job healing the flesh back over the vial. My tissue clung to it.

"What are you doing?" Asha whispered. She watched me dig at my arm. "I think it's the other side," she suggested.

"Funny," I frowned at her. "I have a neutralizer in here. How are you with blood?"

She shrugged. "Here, let me see."

I pushed my arm through the bars as she crawled over.

She leaned over my dripping arm and pushed down on either side of the vial. It rose to the surface. Extending her hand, she said, "Plate."

I handed it to her.

"What are you going to do once we get this vial out of you? With this," she gestured to the deep cut and all the blood as she pressed the jagged edge into the last bit of flesh covering the vial.

An acute, searing pain shot up my arm. I clenched my teeth, leaning my head against bars. My arm throbbed incessantly. Sweat beaded on my lip from bearing Asha's carving.

"The wound, I'll heal. The powder," *gasp*, "you'll see. You ready to get out of here?"

"A girl cuts an elixir out of your arm, and we're friends now?" she asked. "You *are* easy." She looked up at me with a toothy grin. Her giddiness no doubt a result of the prospect of us getting out of here. I rolled my eyes. "Okay, one more slight cut… Okay, I think I can pull it out. I'll be quick. Don't pass out."

"Got it." I was not hyperventilating, but I was close. I took deep, regulated breaths. *It's just pain*, I told myself. *Just pain.* It had been easier with the sharp knife my mother had wielded when she'd healed the vial into a cut on my forearm the morning we left Seabrook. A stabbing sensation took my breath away, then it was over. "Tell me you got it?"

"Got it," she said, rolling the vial in her fingers.

I pulled my arm back through the bar, cradling it. I'd have to consume the powder before I could heal myself. I looked at her. I hadn't considered that she might not give the vial back to me after she'd dug it out of my arm.

"There's only enough for two," I said, extending my hand.

"I'm okay. I think I've built up a little resistance, anyway. I'm not full strength, but I'll keep up." I could see she was deciding whether she could trust me. I tried to be patient as she made up her mind.

Asha put the vial in my hand.

There was no hesitation. I jerked the cork out, building spit in my mouth. I measured about half of the contents into my palm and poured it into my mouth, swishing the metallic tasting powder before swallowing.

Asha watched me curiously as I waited.

There it was. Awareness crept back into my senses. I tossed my head back, closing my eyes to savor the feeling. I thought of what the mysterious Skyborne Rhijn had shown me. I focused my attention on my body first. I could hear my heart. I could hear my blood coursing in my veins. Feel the ache from the wound in my arm.

Come on. I willed myself.

I thought of how it felt in the dream. How easily it had come. I relaxed. Thought of the warmth I'd felt with Rhijn standing behind me. How I could sense the individual hairs on his corded arms. Of the static between us, the power in the well. I searched for the particles and the space in between.

I sensed it.

Slowly at first. I relaxed my focus, letting my senses work naturally. All at once, a flood of information came rushing at me. I fell back onto my damaged arm and winced. Opening my eyes was incredible. So complex and beautiful. The fabric that connected everything—I saw it without the ember.

My throbbing arm drew my attention. I moved my finger to the cut. It differed from before when I'd healed. There was no need to touch it. I hovered my hand over the wound and willed the particles to rearrange themselves, stitching the hole back together. When I no longer felt pain, I moved my hand away. There wasn't even a scar.

I shook out my arm, getting to my feet, and turned to the lock on my cell door. This was like before. The lock crumbled as I pressed outward. That was satisfying. The door creaked as I swung it open and stepped out.

Malik had been watching me. I sensed that too. "But you don't have the ember," he said, astonished.

"I don't need it. Not anymore."

I turned to him, focusing on his lock. It broke apart.

"Here." I handed him the vial, and his eyes widened in recognition. He knew what to do. After I took care of Asha's lock, I turned back to Malik, who shook off the effects of the creature's dampening powder.

"I'm still mad at how careless you were."

"That's fine." I stared at him. I'd apologized for my stupidity. I didn't have time for this. "I'm going to go distract Emerson and the Regius if they're here. I need you guys to do something for me."

I explained to them the plan I'd devised as I'd been stewing.

"Be careful, Nayla. No distractions." Malik's large hand crushed my shoulder in emphasis.

"I'll be fine. We'll all be fine."

"You know where to meet us?" Asha confirmed.

"See you there."

⤺

Malik and I swiftly took out the two guards at the exit of the prison, taking their weapons before we headed in different directions.

I ran through the hallway, knowing very well Emerson could be in the workshops this morning. I needed to lure her away so she couldn't release the creatures. Frantically, I looked in every room for her. She wasn't here. Only a few healers turned monster creators. The look in their eyes as I collapsed their airways, standing six feet away from them, kept appearing in my mind. This power I was using wasn't natural. They looked at me like *I* was the abomination.

Stumbling, I reached out for the wall, disoriented. I shook it off and kept going. Each time I got to a door with the creatures in it, I fused the metal into the stone. I could feel the creatures hissing and spitting inside. Briefly, I felt bad for the keeper I'd sealed in with them. By the time I got to the bottom floor, I was panting.

The first godfly zipped past me and circled the room. Then another. Minutes later, Malik and Asha appeared on the landing.

I surveyed the hovering beings. "This is all of them?" I asked, turning to Malik, assuming they found all the cages.

"It is."

"Ready?" I asked them. He nodded. I cracked the door. Malik swept his power past me out the doors.

A moment later, he said, "It's clear."

I looked at the godflies. There were only about thirty or forty of them. A pang of sadness struck me for them. Meethra had said there had been more.

"Fly to the top of the mine. There are openings in the structure. Be discreet. Go north, toward the mountains. You can't let them see you." I cautioned.

The one I assumed was their leader stopped hovering near my face. "Thank you," she said solemnly. I had to choke back my emotion. I did something right.

I pushed the door open. They streamed out and upward. We watched. After a moment, they were out of sight. Simple as that. Now the real challenge came. The three of us had to get out through the only entrance into this labyrinth of a keep.

Malik suggested we ask for the godflies help, but they'd been through so much. I couldn't.

"Come on." I raced across the top of the long walk-wall that spanned the chasm of the mine with Malik and Asha on my heels. I tugged the metal door, cracking it. Malik's power swept in again.

"Three, no four Skyborne."

"Please tell me you can fight?" I asked Asha, eyeing the sword she'd found.

"Gladly."

"Some idiot left this door open." The man's voice was near enough to come through the crack intelligibly. He opened the door further. Malik spun around from behind the door, driving a long blade into the man's chest before he could register our presence. He collapsed to his knees.

The men behind him shouted in alarm.

"Drive them back. I need to take care of that." I pointed at the walk-way and the structure built into the mountain behind us.

Asha and Malik clanged swords with the remaining two men, pushing them into the building behind me. I stepped into the doorway and turned to survey the dark stone that made up the structure. I closed my eyes, feeling its material makeup. I sent pulses of energy into the stone, changing it bit by bit. I could feel the humming vibration of the energy around me shifting and bending. The rock gave a loud groan before the face of the building collapsed in on itself. The boom was deafening. Everyone in the keep would run toward us now.

It probably only destroyed the outer facing rooms, but it was enough to slow them down. I focused on the walk-wall. I needed to hurry.

"Nayla, that's good enough," Malik pleaded.

"Not until I take the walk-wall down. You and Asha go." I pointed to the hall toward the right. "I'll finish this, then distract them. I'll meet you at the tunnel and try to steal horses if I can."

He hesitated.

"Go!" I pressed.

He turned and fled, and I went back to work on the stone. Another few minutes and I had it crumbling. It wasn't as loud as the building, but the large rocks that comprised it crashed and exploded as they fell, reverberating in the domed space.

I was staring at the destruction I created when I heard Kymar's voice. "Take her."

I whirled, bringing up my weapons. I knew I needed to heed Rhijn's warning and not overextend myself. My head was already reeling from collapsing the stone.

I launched myself at the nearest soldier, disarming him. Another swung a careless arc toward me. I kicked the disarmed man into its path. It caught him in the side of the neck, and blood sprayed everywhere.

I stepped over the fallen Skyborne on the offensive. Their speed or skill was no match for mine. Both soldiers came at me. I parried one's blow, tripping the other and sending him off balance. I helped him catch it, steadying him with the end of my sword. I left him pinned to a wooden door as I disarmed the other, making a last pass against his throat with my dagger.

He collapsed against the wall and slid down it.

"I sure hope those weren't your personal guard," I said to the man who believed he inherited the right to rule over all the other Skyborne, "*Regius*."

He laughed nervously. "I think there's been a misunderstanding. Had I known you were my guest, I would have been much more welcoming. I had no idea Emerson had you. She's always up to something." He edged away from me.

"You take another step, and I will embed this dagger into your throat."

He held his palms up toward me. "No need for that."

Footsteps sounded down the hall. I plucked the sword from the man and door, aiming it at Kymar's chest. I jabbed it deep enough for a thimble of blood to well up under his tunic. His eyes and hands instinctively went for the minor wound. I took the opportunity to step behind him and raise the dagger to his throat.

Grabbing his greasy tie of hair, I guided Kymar toward the footsteps.

Emerson came into view.

"I see you got to her first, father," she sneered, surveying the dead men. "You didn't think you'd need more than three men to stop her? That was very foolish," she chastised the Regius.

"I'm sure there's something Nayla wants. Isn't that right, Nayla?"

"When it comes to me, Nayla can have whatever she likes. Again. And again," she said coyly.

Emerson approached, twirling the dagger in her hand. She took several calculated steps forward. The whole keep had to hear the commotion. But curiously, she brought no one with her.

I edged back toward the open door to the mines, driving the dagger a little deeper into the Regius's neck.

"I will kill him, Emerson."

"Please don't, Nayla. I'll do anything. Whatever you ask. Tell me what you want." Emerson had a mischievous look in her eye. This wasn't good.

"Emerson, don't, we need you alive," Kymar scolded.

I was amazed by Emerson's mocking tone. Did the Regius not hear it? Or was she like that so often he just expected it? I subconsciously eased the pressure on the dagger.

"That's it, just lower the dagger." Kymar pleaded.

Emerson had the tip of the dagger pinched between her fingers, and a breath later, it flew.

Instinctively, I dodged behind Kymar.

His breath caught and gurgled. I peered out from behind him. Her dagger was buried deep in the precise center of his throat.

"Why?" he bubbled out, blood now running from the corner of his mouth.

I released him, stepping aside.

"I throw knives. For fun." She looked at me and winked. "Sorry, *Dad*. Looks like I'll get to be Regent after all." Utter disbelief shown in his bulging eyes.

Emerson raised a delicate boot and smashed it into his stomach, propelling him backward. My grandfather lost his footing on the threshold of the door, plummeting backward to where the walk-wall once stood, into the chasm of the mines.

"I can't believe you just did that," Emerson said to me, smiling curtly. She walked over to the open doorway, staring out at the destruction I'd caused.

"Oh, Nayla, what have you done. Do you have any idea what a setback this is? What am I going to do with you?" She ran her hands through her hair in distress. "If you killed any of my babies…"

I launched myself at her, cutting her off. She dodged easily. Every attack she slipped away from. And she never struck at me.

"This is getting boring," she stated, ducking and coming up behind me, sinking her teeth into my neck.

"What is wrong with you?" I cried out. This stupid bitch was a biter. I touched my neck. It was bleeding. Great. I probably had some disease now.

I changed my tactic and grabbed her wrist, pulling her toward me. I didn't know what I was going to do with the dagger I was pulling her toward. Kill her? Really kill Emerson? There was something wrong with my brain. I didn't have the chance to finish my thought. Her boot caught me in the stomach like it had Kymar.

It sent me back toward the doorway and the awaiting darkness below. I threw my arms out, grabbing the edges of the doorway. My arms were barely wide enough to catch. My foot slipped, and the sweat on my palms caused me to slide down. I dug my nails in for purchase. I could still feel the surrounding power, but I couldn't see what I could do to keep myself from falling. Panic crept up my throat. The more I struggled, the more my hands slid closer to the edge.

I felt around and found a crevasse in the rock face I was hanging against. I jammed the toe of my boot into it. If I could just push up enough to grab the threshold, maybe I could climb up.

Emerson stood over me, watching me struggle with her arms crossed. "From what I heard, you escaped the Swath, the Eastdow prisons, and *my* prison. How are you going to get yourself out of this one?" She squatted down to look at me. The panels on her dress split to reveal the smooth skin of her thighs beneath.

"You *could* help me if you wanted," I suggested, eyeing her.

"True. But what would I get? Did you consider, like you promised?"

"I did."

"And?"

"Still considering."

"Doesn't appear that way."

"Okay, I'd be alive. I won't be any fun to taunt if I'm dead."

She wasn't going to help me. I was the enemy, after all. I pushed down on the crevasse to test it. It would hold. If my fingers slipped anymore, I'd fall. And I had one chance to catch the lip of the threshold.

I pressed my foot down, thrusting myself upward, shooting out a hand to grab the lip right in front of me. I caught it. But my other hand gave. I was dangling by a fingerhold over certain death. My life was not supposed to end like this. No one would ever know what happened to me. Or even that I was really dead. And they'd endanger themselves trying to find out.

I swung my flailing arm up to the edge in desperation.

A hand grabbed mine.

Claws dug into my arm as Emerson, and I gripped each other's forearms.

"Use your feet to climb," she insisted.

I dug into every bump and nook in the rock face. Emerson was pulling on my arm with both hands now, with her foot braced against the door frame.

My heart was hammering when I got my chest up over the edge. I laid there with my face resting on the cold stone, legs still dangling behind me.

"All the way out," she said, pulling me into the hallway.

I collapsed beside her, and she rolled onto her back. Side by side, we laid there staring at the ceiling.

"Why didn't you let me fall?" I struggled to catch my breath. To slow my heartbeat. I was feeling thin. Overexerted.

"I need you alive. And I think you and I are just getting to know each other. It would be a shame if our story ended so soon. And I will rebuild this." Emerson waved a lazy hand in the direction of my destruction, sighing. "And then we will find you in possession of the ember, and you will take us to Idia. Either willingly or by force. Your decision."

"How are you so confident?"

"This realm is small, and I am powerful. And I have all the resources I need at my disposal." Her brow furrowed as if she were confused as to why I did not understand this.

"I could kill you right now, Emerson," I said as I rolled over her, putting my knife to her throat.

"A life for a life, Nayla."

I lowered my weapon—bad choice. But I couldn't do it. She *just* saved me.

"You need to get out of here. I'll give you a minute head start. GO." Emerson yelled, grinning playfully.

I sat up abruptly. This was fun for her. "You are legitimately insane."

"Timer's ticking," she said, tapping her temple.

⁓

I jumped up and ran. And ran. I flew through hallways, blowing by attendants. Guards spun, uncertain of what to do as I sped past them. I was at the front of the keep when I finally heard alarm bells ringing and the distant echo of Emerson's voice screaming for the soldiers to seize me.

I got to the front entrance. Six soldiers guarded it. I halted as they unsheathed their swords. *Shit.* Too many to fight realistically.

I closed my eyes, breathing, sifting through their anatomy, landing on their hearts. I forced my energy across the invisible fabric between us, disrupting the very makeup of their beating tissue. Like puppets, all six reached for their chests, going wide-eyed before collapsing to the ground.

I was becoming good at this, I thought, right before I joined them on the floor. Too much, I was using too much. It's what Rhijn had said.

I recognized the footsteps coming toward me from across the room. I pushed myself up on my forearms. No. I'd not let her take me again.

I staggered to my feet, running toward the cleared path out the large doorway dragging the sword I carried. I felt like my soul was parched. This was more than any training I'd experienced. Emerson was steadily making her way towards me.

Running, I took the first street I came to. At the end, men on horseback were coming my way. I dodged into an alley, running to the next street over. Turning in the exterior gate's direction, I ran. I made it as far as the open market which the city gates opened into. I slipped into the crowd. I moved south as discreetly as I could. The crowd to my left parted. Skyborne at my right scattered.

Within a few moments, soldiers on horseback surrounded me.

Emerson was ominously walking down a street toward me.

"I thought you'd be harder to catch a second time," she called from the distance. "Or maybe it was my fault. Two minutes might have been better."

"You know I don't have the ember," I yelled, heaving.

"But you know where it is, and you will help me find it. I can be very convincing." Emerson shook a little bottle she held in her hands I could just make out. I didn't know what would happen if she dosed me again. I wasn't prepared to find out.

I lifted my sword to the Skyborne, who was approaching with chains.

"The destruction in the mines and what you did to the men back there. I saw A1 dose you," she said. "How is it you are unaffected by it now?" Emerson was studying me.

I swung the sword at the man. "Stay back."

Another approached me from behind. I was at the edge. Maybe I was over the edge. I didn't know. I reached deep within myself.

A flash of light darted before my eyes. Then another.

Run, Nayla, run.

It was Meethra. And the other godflies.

The soldier with the chains slumped down unconscious.

The surrounding ones followed suit. The only one the godflies dust didn't seem to affect was Emerson. I hesitated, assessing her.

Run!

A riderless horse moved in my periphery. I spun, launching myself onto it, nudging it into a gallop. I grabbed the reins of another horse as we went, urging it to follow. Malik and Asha had to have made it to the tunnel. I didn't see any sign of them.

"Close the gate," Emerson cried.

I'll make it, I thought, nudging the horse to go faster.

Snow had fallen and covered the unplowed ground of the valley. I followed the worn path toward the tunnel.

"Fire," I heard a man call. An arrow whizzed by my head. *Damn it.* I took that thread of energy I'd found and threw a shield up around the horses and me. The effort was dizzying. I slumped forward in the saddle, dropping the reins of the horse I was towing. I was almost out of range.

Replacement soldiers had mounted horses and were leaving the gate, I saw as I looked back. I had a solid head start on them. Finally, out of range, I dropped the shield. The cost. What was the cost? I felt drunk; I was so disoriented.

Movement from around a boulder caught my eye. *Makers, I can't catch a break.* I slowed the horse to a walk, expecting an ambush.

"Malik," I cried as my horse hit a low spot, and I slid out of the saddle.

"Easy," he said, catching me before I hit the ground.

"You look like shit," Asha said. Her pale face was spattered with blood, and she had more than a few scrapes and cuts on her.

I smiled, happy to see her. But where was the other girl who was with us? The one with the pretty red streaks in her hair.

Malik caught the second horse's reins and brought it over to us. "You and Nayla can ride together."

I stood there.

"Hurry up. We have a good lead on them." He tried to put the reins in my hands.

"Nayla, come back to me!" Emerson wailed in the distance. The anguish in her voice was jarring. That's who we were missing. We should have saved her too. What was happening? Why were we leaving her?

"We have to save her," I demanded to Malik.

"Nayla, you are lucky you escaped her. Come on."

I turned back. Emerson stood atop the parapet wall surrounding the city. The panels of her green gown flapped in the wind, making a striking contrast with the red through her hair. The image she posed was so forlorn as she reached out to me. And poetic.

"Nayla, what are you doing?" Malik asked, but I didn't really hear him.

"Come to me," she called again.

I felt the tug, the draw. I stepped forward.

"You don't understand," I told them. "She saved my life," I

remembered. She had. I'd almost fallen into the mines. And she hauled me up over the edge. And she healed me before.

"It's the power. It's doing something to her." I heard Asha caution Malik, but I didn't care. This wasn't the power. I didn't know what she was talking about. I owed that female something.

I felt Malik's arm reach around my waist to haul me back. I pulled away from him, spinning as red-hot anger flashed through me. "What are you doing?" I demanded. "You have no right."

His mouth gaped open. I tilted my head to the side. Horror replaced his usual smirk. He wasn't looking at me. I followed his gaze. He was looking at the sword I'd pressed into his gut. *Makers.* From the corner of my eye, I saw a glint of steel swing toward my head.

CHAPTER TWENTY-SIX

WATER SPLASHED OVER my face. A woman with bright red hair squatted over me, smacking my cheeks. Memories came flooding back in. All my blood felt like it rushed to my stomach at once.

"Malik," I cried. "Where's Malik?"

Asha helped reached a hand down to help me up and pointed over to a pallet in the forest where Malik lay unconscious.

"He's alive?" I asked desperately.

"He's sleeping. He needs to be healed, but he's fine. I saw you stir. What the hell happened?"

I rushed over to Malik, but Asha grabbed my hair and yanked me back to her. "Not so fast. He needs to rest, and *you* need to tell me what the fuck?"

"Where are we?" I asked her.

"In the Swath. Malik promised you could get us out of here. He was in no condition to do any more fighting."

I surveyed the area, remembering the hushed eeriness under the canopy.

Asha snapped her fingers in front of my face. "What the hell, Nayla? I know I don't know you that well, and you seem to occasionally make questionable decisions, but that was messed up."

"I don't know what happened. Rhijn warned me not to use too much. But I woke up before he could finish."

"Umm, who's Rhijn?"

I told her about the dreams—specifically, the one where Rhijn had helped me see.

"So, you're telling me you have a sexy lover in another realm who helped you spring us out of prison?"

"It sounds crazy, but yes. Kind of. I guess that's what I'm telling you. He's not my lover, though. He probably isn't even real."

"If you say so."

I reached up, rubbing the ache at the base of my skull. "You knocked me out?"

"You stabbed your brother because you were power crazy. It was only prudent. He said you could heal him."

I rushed forward, but Asha jumped in my path. "No, off the rails, I'm going to join the bad guys nonsense this time, right? If you can only use a little power without losing your shit, then just do what you need to heal him and cut it off." She drew a dagger and aimed it at my chest.

I'd shown restraint when I'd killed Kymar's personal guards. And with Emerson. I cringed internally. "I didn't use too much on purpose. I only did what I had to do to survive."

"I'm not kidding," Asha said and followed me over to Malik with her dagger in hand.

They had torn a piece of Malik's tunic and made a compress for the wound I made in his stomach. Malik stirred as I removed it. The angry gash festered. I would need to heal the growing infection too. I shuddered, assessing how deep it was. It was shallow. I must have pulled back at the last moment, thank the Makers.

"I didn't hit anything vital," I said, hovering my hands over the wound. I didn't think I'd be able to live with myself if I had. I shut my eyes, trying to connect to the energy around us. My awareness lit up like a new flame. I studied Malik's injury. "I'll start with your blood, the move to the wound itself. It shouldn't hurt too much."

Malik blinked, looking up at me, sneering. "I don't need your commentary. Just get on with it."

It didn't take me as long as I expected to heal Malik's wound. After I discarded the bloodied rags and rinsed my hand in a nearby warm pool, I sat next to him on the pallet. He jerked away when I reached for his hand.

A steady stream of tears ran down my face as we stared at each other.

"Malik, I'm so sorry."

"I forgive you," he replied, smirking.

"Really?" I asked, leaning forward, eyes wide.

"No, Nayla. If your choices weren't already questionable enough, you stabbed me." His features strained as he wrestled for composure.

"Malik, you don't understand."

"You're right. I don't understand." He grimaced as he pressed his palm into his freshly healed stomach, testing it. "Your work is better. How do you feel?"

He wasn't asking because he cared. He wanted to know if I was going to lose control again.

"I'm fine," I said, looking away. "If I could try to explain myself."

He got up, turning his back to me. "We need to go." Malik swept his power out into the forest.

A few minutes later, Uden joined us, leading us toward Seabrook. Malik didn't speak to me again.

CHAPTER TWENTY-SEVEN

I STARED AT THE ground as we walked, occasionally glancing at my brother. Fortunately, Asha had an uncanny ability to diffuse the tension, or the hours we'd walk would have been torture. She seemed to be easier to forgive than Malik. I hadn't stabbed her, though.

"What are you thinking?" she implored. "Or can you not say in front of this guy?" She jerked her head toward Uden, who'd been quiet this whole time listening to us. She was teasing him, and he let a slight smile pass over his flaking face.

"Oh, I'm sure he knows way more than anything we can tell him. You, on the other hand. Can I assume if you are not with them, that means you are with us?"

She gave me a side-long glance that suggested she was not the one whose loyalty should be in question. "I'd be dead, eventually, if it wasn't for you. My loyalty is the least I can offer. I can also offer any aid Sundale can provide. You said Arborvale and Seabrook are allied. You can count Sundale in too. My little brother is Regent."

Sundale was between Seabrook and Arborvale, so gaining their alliance made a united south-western section of the continent. I hadn't saved her for that, but I was still glad for it.

"Okay then, I thank you. And there will be much more to do before this is all over." I reached over and squeezed her wrist. I was grateful when she didn't pull away. Asha was only an inch or two taller than me, but even as worn down as we all were, she had a presence of a much taller female.

As we walked, I told her everything I knew, and that had happened over the last six months. I told her what happened after she and Malik left me in the tunnel. How Emerson had killed Kymar, then saved me. And about what I thought had gone wrong with the power. I hoped Malik was listening.

✄

Night was setting in. We decided it'd be best to get a little sleep and wake up early to make the rest of the journey out of the forest and to the inn tomorrow. Uden started a fire. I was a little warm and sticky under the canopy where we were. We were near Seabrook now. I understood what he was doing when an insignificant creature crawled into our campsite, dragging a rabbit behind him, dropping it at Asha's feet. I heard her stomach growl in response. I didn't know what to say.

"Thank you, you wonderful little creature," Asha said warmly. It was her way. She was like Seeley in that, warm and kind, someone who put others at ease. It was amazing to me she still had that in her after what she'd been through.

I didn't. Malik never did. He was watching me, but I ignored him. I was starting to resent his judgment.

The creature grinned broadly and seemed to blush if that was something they could do.

"They wanted to reciprocate, in their own way. I've told them you will help send us home," Uden explained.

No pressure, I thought. Asha was grateful but appeared to have no idea what to do with a whole animal.

"Give the rabbit here," I said and took out a knife and began cleaning the hare.

"What will you do next?" Uden asked as I turned the rabbit turned over the fire.

"Find Conall and Seeley. And I guess figure out how to use the ember. I need you to do something for me."

He cocked his head.

"Before, when I told you I thought I saw the barrier of the Swath move, you reacted. Subtly, but I saw it."

"I have sensed a change. I only suspected it then."

"And now?"

"It seems to be growing. Though I can't say how much, it doesn't seem to be insignificant."

"What do you think caused it," Asha asked.

Both Uden and Malik looked at me.

"The ember," she understood.

"Anyway," I continued, "Emerson also believes the Swath is expanding. I need you to measure it. I want to know how much each day." I needed to know how long we had until the Skyborne and the creatures under the canopy were living in this realm as one big unhappy family.

⁂

The next morning it was only a short distance of a few hours as I'd suspected to the edge of the forest. We said our goodbyes once again to Uden. I told him I thought about it and could probably use the shield to bring him with us as I was doing with the other, but he gave me an *are you serious* glance.

It was Asha's turn to say goodbye. He turned to her and held out his hand as she had done before, "Asha, you are safe if you ever need a refuge in this forest, *my friend*."

"How come she doesn't require a deal?" I raised an eyebrow at him.

"I've never met Skyborne I liked before. Most of you are so unsavory."

"And it's still a mystery how we've ended up here, Uden," I laughed under my breath. I turned, shielding Asha and Malik, and we passed through the barrier of the Swath.

CHAPTER TWENTY-EIGHT

I T WAS LATE afternoon when we arrived at the traveler's inn. There was no point disguising myself now traveling with Asha and Malik. I swung the door open and walked over to the bar to ask for rooms. Seeley told us that we could mention that we were guests of the Regent, and Remi would take care of the expense. I was grateful because we had no other way to pay.

I took the two keys handing one to Malik, debating between ordering lunch and a beer or heading straight up for a nap.

"What's a nice girl like you doing in a shoddy place like this?" a familiar voice purred.

Shrieking, I spun and threw myself into Conall's arms.

"Oh, Conall, I'm so glad to see you." When I finally pulled myself away from him, I turned to see Malik and Seeley in a similar embrace. Asha was standing between us awkwardly.

We had only been away a month, but I felt butterflies seeing Conall.

Asha introduced herself when they looked at her questioning.

Seeley brought us over to a table they'd been occupying.

"How did you know we'd be here?" I asked, astonished.

"Meethra. She came directly here after you escaped," Conall grinned. He rubbed between his eyes, flexing and stretching the muscles of his face. "I think that was worse than when you left for Drakestone as Vera."

"Hold on, what's going on between you guys?" Seeley interrupted, looking back and forth between Malik and I. Makers, he could read others well.

I took a long drink from a beer Conall had procured for us. "Nothing, it's fine."

"It's not fine, not really," Malik countered, recounting our misadventure. I was grateful he left out the part about what happened between Emerson and I. When he got to the part about me stabbing him, I winced, wrenching my hands under the table. I had to force myself to look at him.

"Malik," Seeley scolded, "don't you think you're being a little hard on Nayla?"

"Sounds like she didn't have a choice. It wasn't her fault you were captured or stabbed. Not really." Conall shivered. "If she hadn't used that much power, do you think you'd all be sitting here now? Is that what you would have wanted?"

I looked at Malik apologetically. He ran his hand down his face, shaking his head. I was grateful for his continued omission.

"I said it's fine. Malik needs time to process what happened and forgive me. I don't fault him for that. And you both shouldn't either." We hadn't known each other that long, really. I didn't want to rely on the fact that he was my half-brother, to assume that it would be fine. What happened would have made him question things. That was expected. Especially after how supportive and trusting he'd been.

Seeley and Conall looked like they were ready to keep after Malik.

I eyed them sternly. "I'm serious. Leave it."

⁂

Asha and I had to share a room with two small beds and an even smaller wash chamber. When I got up, she had already cleaned herself up and changed into an extra set of clothes Conall and Seeley brought for me. "I assumed you wouldn't mind," she said, gesturing to the outfit she wore, which was like the more utilitarian one Bara, Seeley's sentry, had once worn.

"No," I smiled. It was a little fitted on her, but it worked.

"I got fresh water for you."

I could smell myself, so I accepted gratefully.

Asha was sitting in a robe at the desk, staring at a piece of paper holding a writing utensil when I came back into the room. Her hair was still a damp mess, and I saw the discarded brush laying, flung apparently, across the room.

I showed her the brush and a vial of hair oil. "May I?" I asked her.

She laughed. "If you're brave enough."

I took the basin and brought it over to the desk, moving the paper aside and heated the water, and mixed in the oil. I dipped the brush and moved it through her hair. It was still so dirty from her time in prison, I had to discard the water and pour a fresh bowl, but by the time I finished, her hair was stick straight, silky and bright again.

I handed her a little hand mirror for her to look. "Thank you," she said. She stood up and walked over to sit on the edge of the bed. She placed her hands neatly on her knees. She was trying to keep her composure, but the pulsing vein in her forehead gave her away. "What is it?" I asked her.

"I need to write a letter to my brother, but how can I put what happened to me in words?" She sucked in a breath, bursting into sobs. Asha hadn't spoken about how she'd been imprisoned or what they did to her. I didn't ask. I went over to her and sat, putting my arms around her. She wept until I didn't think she could continue. Finally, she looked up, "I'm sorry, I haven't cried since it happened. I didn't want them to see me as weak. That's terrible, I know."

"Asha, you have nothing to be sorry about. You are so strong, and you have been through so much. You're not alone now. Let us help you write the letter."

She smiled. "Thank you, but no, I will write it. I want to send it tonight. I'll do it now. Do you mind if I have some privacy?" She rubbed her red-rimmed eyes.

"You're sure you're okay?" I asked her as I stood up and walked to the door.

"I am," she replied. "And thank you, Nayla."

∽

I left Asha and went to Conall's room.

"Asha needed some privacy," I told him as he opened the door to let me in.

We sat in two soft chairs by the open window.

"I almost forgot," he said, reaching into an inner pocket and pulling the familiar box out. My stomach jumped when I saw it. He set it on the table between us wordlessly and pushed it over to me. I picked it up and put it in a concealed pocket of my own without opening the box to confirm its contents. Feeling its presence back on my person was more reassuring than I expected. I could see relief flash across Conall's face. Whether it was from relinquishing the heavy burden or the fact that I had shown that I unquestionably trusted him, I didn't know.

"So, did you see what you needed to?"

"I did. It's probably worse than I imagined. I didn't destroy it all; I tried. It will take time for Emerson to recover. I bought us time." She was Regent—no, Regius, now, I thought, shivering. "I hate to admit it, but Torin is right. Things are building to a breaking point in this realm. The Swath is expanding. Don't get me started on Emerson."

"The powder Malik said you cut out of your arm was the same as what you gave us when Darius had drugged us?"

"Yes," my mother brought it when they came to Seabrook.

He watched me, waiting for an explanation. "How did your sister know we'd need it? Or how to make the exact antidote? She had to have had some of the creature's powder."

"My mother was a little cryptic when I asked her about. She said something about my sister Balene having a connection to the healers in Monterra. I was so grateful to have it; I didn't push."

"Hopefully, they have more of it. Sounds like we'll need it."

It was so good to be back in Conall's presence. So comforting, I thought, yawning.

"Do you think she's had enough time?"

A faint knock sounded on the door.

I opened it. Color returned to Asha's face.

"I'm done," she said. "I gave it to the innkeeper to send. I'll see if Seeley will lend me a horse so I can travel home in the morning to tell Ian the rest of the story in person."

She looked as weary as I felt. I looked back to Conall.

"Go to bed, Nayla. I release you," he said, putting his arm around me, dropping a kiss onto the top of my head.

❧

That night with the ember back on my person, the dreams I hadn't had for weeks flooded in more vividly than they ever had before. I felt as though I had awoken every hour from a different version of the dream. What was always the same, though, was Rhijn. He haunted and tantalized me, coaxing both fear and desire from me. I wanted to know who this Skyborne was and what he had to do with me. I wanted to feel the way I felt when he had touched me, but I didn't want him to touch me. He helped me. But he terrified me.

I saw him closer now in these dreams. Sometimes I'd be standing beside him in front of crowds of Skyborne. Others were with us, but I couldn't see them. Only him. And he didn't speak again. In the last dream, he raised his hand toward the crowd looking at me with his piercing pale blue eyes. The power in his eyes was so intense, I woke up in a cold sweat. After about the fourth version, I wasn't getting any rest, and I was becoming increasingly frustrated. So frustrated, in fact, that I angrily said aloud to no one in particular, "Stop it, I've had enough. No more dreams."

The no one, in particular, I had been speaking to only hummed soothingly. Asha didn't stir, and I fell back into a deep sleep once again.

This time it was a black abyss for a long while. My dream began softly that time. I was standing in the darkness, but I could see even deeper darkness ahead of me calling toward me. I obeyed its call and followed.

This time, instead of falling as I stepped over the edge, I floated down slowly. The contrast in the light was so bright it took me long moments to see where I landed. The space was similar to the holy site I'd seen before, but instead of the sandstone floor, there was turquoise blue water all around me. I was lying on the edge of the stone well reclined back, dipping my feet in the cool water. As my vision cleared further, I saw him. He was chest-deep in the basin staring at me. His shoulder-length hair was wet and pushed back from the sides of his hard yet handsome face. My breath quickened. The Skyborne moved toward me, each step excruciatingly slow. I couldn't move this time either.

As he neared me, the water must have gotten shallower because more of his torso became exposed. Water trickled down his slim but toned physique. I was trembling again in his presence. Not from fear this time. From anticipation. He was standing at my feet, still half in the pool. In a low voice, he asked, *Can I show you something*, as he reached his fingers toward my foot as he'd done before. *Yes*, I thought. I must have said it aloud in the dream because he stopped short. The hunger I was feeling at that moment was almost overpowering. *Please*, I said.

Standing over me, he grinned for the first time. Warmth flooded through my body, followed by an almost violent pleasure when his fingers contacted my skin. I stopped seeing anything in my dream as I arched back, letting the wave of sensation take full control of my body. As it ebbed, I could feel whatever power the Skyborne possessed humming through me. But I could tell there was something more he wanted to show me. I fought for control, not allowing myself to succumb to the undulating current just below the surface of my consciousness.

Easy, he cautioned, noting my struggle. *Close your eyes.* I obeyed. I could not feel the sunlight through my eyelids. The vision I saw was absolute darkness. It was moving. An invisible grid like he'd shown me before stretched out as far as I could sense. And I could see what looked like spinning disks of stars and cosmic debris dotting the grid of nothingness. He drew my vision in closer to one of the disks. It was beautiful. Arms of dust and glowing orbs reached out from a dark center. I'd never seen anything like it. The vision focused on a single star and the debris circling it. I reached out to touch the largest piece instinctively. The Skyborne drew me out of the vision, and I was staring up at him again.

That, what you showed me, what is it? I asked him.

Home. Idia, he said.

I woke with a start.

❧

Sunlight was streaming in through the closed window, and the day's heat was beginning to warm the room. As I sat up, a bead of sweat trickled down between my breasts, and I felt dampness on my neck at my hairline.

I got up and walked over to open the window. I tapped my pocket with my first finger, "I thought I said no more dreams." It was silent. "Though I suppose if I do have to have them, the last one is preferable." It buzzed. "I'm glad you're amused, but I'd really like to know who this Skyborne in my dreams is and why I keep seeing him." Silence again. It occurred to me that maybe it didn't actually know what I was dreaming about, only my reactions to them.

Asha sighed deeply.

I looked at her. She sat up and stretched her arms wide. She stared at me incredulously.

"What?" I asked.

"You're talking to yourself. You losing it again?" Asha asked.

I gave her a sarcastic smile and tapped the box I carried.

"I see," she said. "You look like hell. More dreams?"

I was trying not to turn bright red.

"All night. Probably since I've been away from it for so long, it's making up for lost time."

I got dressed and went to see if Conall was going to go for breakfast. He wasn't ready, so I told him I'd wait for him while he finished. I slumped onto the bed and went to work on the dirt under my nails.

Loud thumping sounded on Conall's door. Whoever was outside was still banging when a shirtless Conall cracked it open. I tried to find something else to look at. I'd had enough inappropriate thoughts lately. I needed a break from sexually attractive Skyborne.

Malik pushed into the room, followed by Seeley. He held a small piece of paper in his hand. "Bara sent a bird. Darius escaped. He's leading soldiers from Drakestone and Monterra here now."

"He knew we'd come through here," I said, shaking my head. "How long do we have?"

"Half an hour, maybe," Malik replied.

"Damn it, that's it? I said.

"We can head toward Sundale. Asha's brother will give us sanctuary," Seeley suggested.

"Torin's men approach from the south," Malik explained.

"How?" Seeley asked.

"The creatures," I guessed. It was confirmed that at least some of them had survived. "They've probably been staked out waiting on Seabrook's borders. Asha's brother wouldn't know the threat they posed if he was even aware of them."

"Then we'll go to Seabrook Proper. They won't attack the city," Seeley suggested.

"We can't run; it'd be too risky." Malik rubbed his jaw.

"We could try," Seeley said, shrugging hopefully.

"The horses we have aren't built for speed. They'll catch us before we get to Seabrook," said Malik. He was in his element, cold calculation.

Conall wrinkled his brow. "What about the Covenant?"

"I don't think there is a Covenant anymore," Malik hastily replied.

My blood, I could feel it in my fingertips. I became aware of the individual beads of sweat forming on my upper lip.

My friends were rapidly debating how to get us out of this doomed scenario. Malik was pacing back and forth in front of the window.

I walked over to it, enhancing my vision. Off in the distance, I could make out the movement of approaching horses.

Anticipation pulsed through my body. I knew what I had to do.

Slowly, I turned toward them. Even Seeley's usually calm voice was booming now.

"Quiet." They didn't respond.

"Quiet," I yelled.

They stopped, silently facing me. I looked at each one of them. Waiting. They'd been waiting on me. I smiled.

"It's time to go to Idia."

CHAPTER TWENTY-NINE

T HE FIVE OF us had gathered into my room.

"Wow," I said, "so this is happening." My voice broke with my nerves. My heart was thudding in my chest.

We dashed around the inn, collecting as many of our things, food, and weapons to prepare for anything we might encounter. I surveyed us. We had packs slung around our bodies and weapons discreetly sheathed all over us in case we weren't welcome. It wasn't bad for twenty minutes. Malik had suggested that any larger displayed weapons might come across as too aggressive, so we'd opted to forgo those.

"You guys look like mercenaries," Asha said. She hadn't hesitated when I told her the change of plan.

"Thanks," Malik said, winking at her.

My stomach was doing flips, and I knew their nervous joking was in reaction to theirs doing the same. I saw Seeley reach out and take Malik's hand.

We are all in this together, I thought. That, at least, was reassuring.

"You guys ready?" I asked them.

"I'm not doing anything else today," Conall replied and held out his large hand palm up. I placed the box on it and flipped the lid open.

Asha walked nearer and stared down at it. "I don't know what I was expecting," she said finally. "This thing killed that priest?"

"It hadn't welcomed his touch," Seeley whispered.

I took a moment to make eye contact with each person in our little party; Asha, Seeley, Malik, and finally Conall.

Conall nodded. I turned to the ember. "You know what we need you to do," I told it. I glanced up at Conall, who was smiling, shaking his head.

When the tip of my trembling finger made contact, it began making a slow, comforting pulse. It was matching my heartbeat. I looked at the others, whose eyes were as wide as mine. I could feel something creeping up my arm, darkness that slowly enveloped as it climbed. Panic rose as I fought to not jerk my arm away. The blackness stopped below my elbow. It was an exercise in trust. The times I'd used it before had been automatic. They had just happened. I had to make myself trust it, and this trace of ancient power was trusting me. The gravity of that did not escape me.

We all were acutely aware that we had no idea what would be waiting on the other side of the portal.

"You ready for this?" I asked the ancient power now merged with my very essence. I felt a vibration. Conall looked up at me, surprised. "I felt it answer you."

"I would refrain from saying *I told you so*, but it is just too tempting," I laughed.

The whinnying of horses being halted abruptly echoed in through the window. Soon I could hear a flood of boots stamping across the dining area's wooden planks.

We formed a circle, standing back-to-back, leaving a small space for me to fit in.

"Try thinking *portal*," Conall said.

I *was* thinking portal. I closed my eyes, concentrating on this place, *Idia*, and imagined doorways, gates, realms, anything I could come up with related to the opening a passageway to this mysterious place. I closed my eyes, ignoring the banging I heard coming from down the hall now.

Concentrate. I closed my eyes and thought of the spiral of stars Rhijn showed me. *A disk.*

I opened my eyes, running on instinct now as the door being kicked in *down* the hall crashed. I bent down to drag my finger across the ground. A dark quivering line followed in its path. I passed each one of my friends, being careful to stay inside the circle I was drawing. I hesitated right before I connected the circle, "See you there."

I connected it and moved to stand in my place, not knowing what to expect. We all clasped hands. Conall took my left in his clammy palm, and a fearless Malik embraced my ember shrouded right. Thank the Makers, I thought, squeezing Malik's in return.

We were in the last room. And they had reached it. *Come on. Come on.*

We had barricaded the door. They hammered on it relentlessly. It was holding.

Come on, I begged as the door groaned.

The same pulsing black began growing inward from the circle I'd drawn until it connected and covered the entire space where we stood. The door gave, splintering inward. A1 followed my Darius burst into the room. Suddenly, I had a weightless feeling and heard a few gasps from my companions as the sensation of falling hit us. I brazenly caught Darius's gaping stare.

Then darkness.

Epilogue

S OMEWHERE, IN ANOTHER realm, a light-haired Skyborne camped in the desert. Waiting.

Waiting, the same as he'd done months earlier, as the small piece of golden ribbon floated through the hole between realms that had opened in a flash before him.

DEARLY BELOVED,

I mean dearest reader. I love you. Ahhh, I'm messing this up. What I'm really trying to say is, THANK YOU for reading my book! Did you like it? A little even? What would be amazing is if you popped over to Amazon or goodreads and left Realm of the Banished a review. I know leaving a review can be time consuming, but it helps us indie authors more than you know. AND every time a review gets left a bunny gets a hug. It's true!

(Disclaimer: no guarantees of bunny hugs can be made.)

If you share REALM OF THE BANISHED on the socials that would be cool too. No pressure. But like REALLY cool.

Find me on Instagram @j.m.waldrop

and my website www.jennifermwaldrop.com for:
Character Mood Reels
Name Pronunciation Guide
Giveaways
Newsletter
and More

ACKNOWLEDGEMENTS

I want to say thank you to a few very special people whose support, insight and feedback was invaluable to me in the writing and publishing process.

My husband, Max, and sister, Kristen, spent countless hours listening to me talk about characters, working through plot holes with me, and just generally supporting my path to becoming a published author, and ultimately bringing this story to life. One couldn't ask for a more supportive and amazing family.

I will be forever grateful to the following beta readers who helped me understand how my work was being received from a reader's perspective with chapter notes, inline feedback, and thorough reader reports and impressions. Thank you to: Marissa Gallmeyer (@mari.read.books), Virag Viszus (@nerdy.bookdragon), Bernie Nestler (@geckoreads), Taylor Wilson (@drbookworm_), Stephanie (@the_abundant_word), Srishti Rathour, and Jacob Flowers-Olnowich.

A particularly big thanks goes to my beta reader and friend who helped me also with ideas and feedback for the cover design and gave me encouragement throughout the process. I am beyond appreciative for Anakha Ashok (@iawkwardturtle).

Finally, I am grateful to have worked with two outstanding editors, Alison Rolf for the hybrid line/copy edit and Chersti Nieveen for the developmental edit.

ABOUT THE AUTHOR

Jennifer is an artist, small business owner and author of the new novel Realm of the Banished. She holds a Bachelor of Fine Arts with a minor in Art History from the University of Central Oklahoma. Jennifer enjoys creating and paints with that same imaginative stroke throughout her writing.

When she's not writing, you might find her whipping together her favorite dark chocolate mousse, power walking a beach in a tropical destination, or lost in the minutia of one of her excel spreadsheets. Jennifer lives with her husband and two dog children in Oklahoma City.

Made in the USA
Las Vegas, NV
27 June 2021

25516359R00157